Battle Under the Many Colored Moons

Richard Stephen Kram

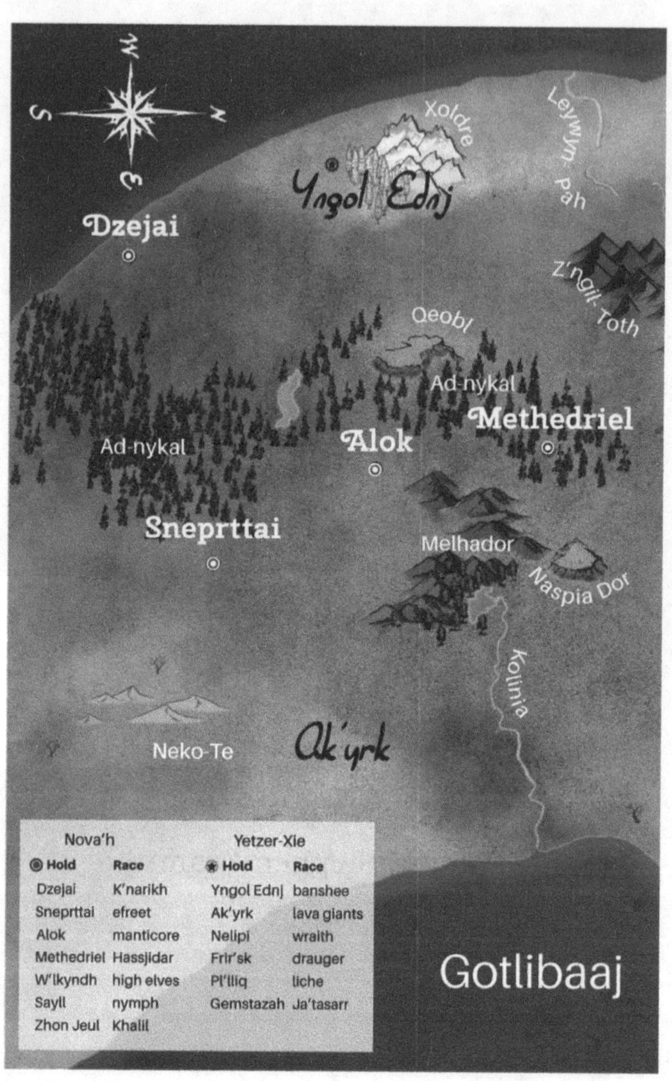

Dzejai
Yngol Ednj
Xoldre
Leywyn-pah
Z'ngit-Toth
Qeobl
Ad-nykal
Methedriel
Ad-nykal
Alok
Sneprttai
Melhador
Naspia Dor
Kolinia
Neko-Te
Ak'yrk
Gotlibaaj
Nova'h
Hold   Race
Dzejai   K'narikh
Sneprttai   efreet
Alok   manticore
Methedriel   Hassjidar
W'lkyndh   high elves
Sayll   nymph
Zhon Jeul   Khalil
Yetzer-Xie
Hold   Race
Yngol Ednj   banshee
Ak'yrk   lava giants
Nelipi   wraith
Frir'sk   drauger
Pl'lliq   liche
Gemstazah   Ja'tasarr

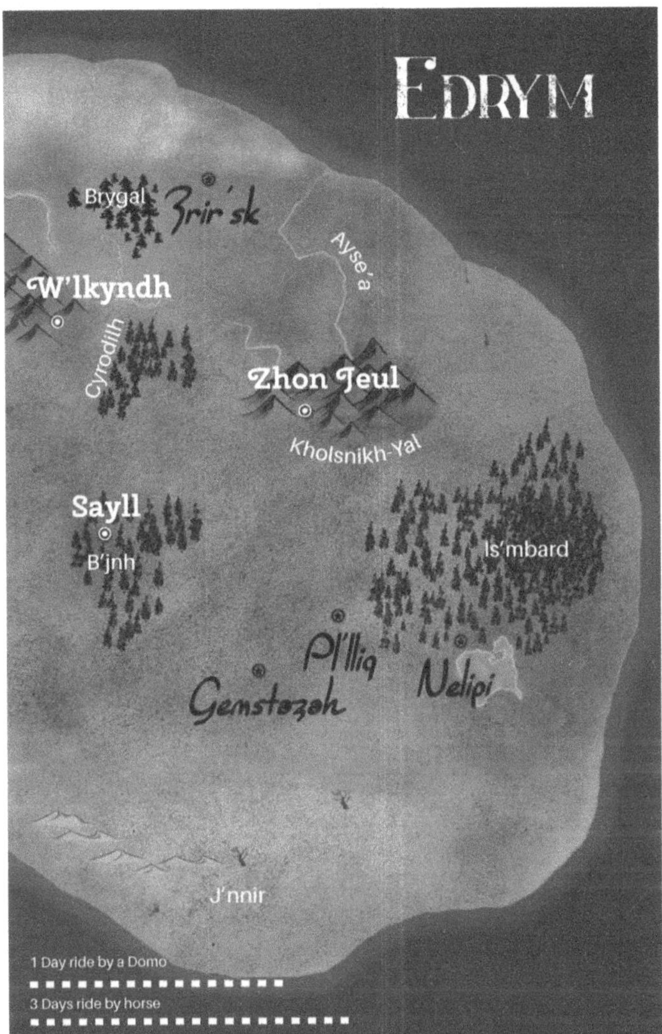

EDRYM
Brygal
Zrir'sk
Ayse'a
W'lkyndh
Cyrodiih
Zhon Jeul
Kholsnikh-Yal
Sayll
B'jnh
Is'mbard
Pl'lliq
Gemstazah
Nelipi
J'nnir
1 Day ride by a Domo
3 Days ride by horse

Also by Richard Stephen Kram

Novel

Aiyanna, Time Witch

Poetry

My Heart is Full

This is a work of fiction. The events and characters described herein are imaginary and are not intended refer to actual events or persons. Any resemblance to actual persons, living or dead, events, or locales is entirely coincidental, contrived, or fabricated. The opinions expressed in this manuscript are solely the opinion of the author.

Battle Under the Many Colored Moons © 2021
Richard Stephen Kram

ISBN: 979-8-9850291-0-9

Published by Random Brand
Cover design by Sheryl Rhoades

e-mail: kramrs311@yahoo.com

Web: richardstephenkram.com

Facebook: Richard Stephen Kram

Tumblr: aiyannatimewitch.tumber.com

To family and friends, and let's add readers, who, in different ways, make this journey poignant, fun, and totally worthwhile.

Battle Under the Many Colored Moons

Table of Contents

JULIAN

INIQUI

DOR'OSSOSS

ZHOKUL

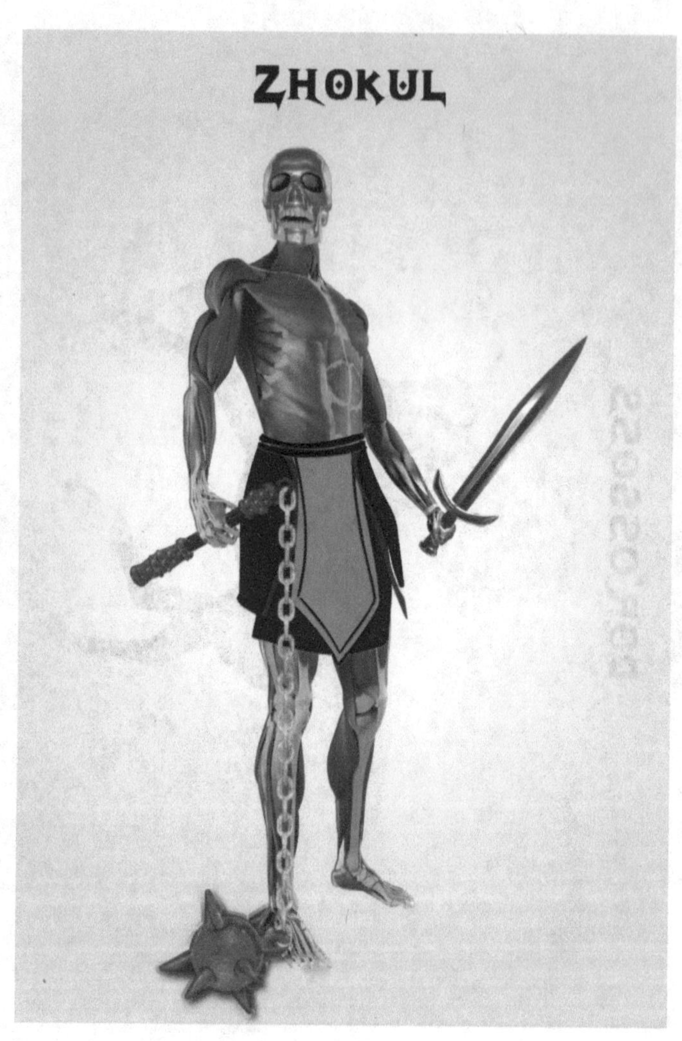

Chapter 1
The-Key-that-is-Lost

The tundra snapped with an audible *crack* under young Gjallimé's feet as he ran northeast, parallel to the shimmer storm. The powder-blue, flickering curtain skirted the ground and rose high into the sky, two hundred paces to his right.

Four shrieking banshees kept pace, gliding tirelessly on the opposite side of the river, whose deep, bubbling, warm waters constrained them from reaching their target. With long, flowing, scarlet hair, the strikingly beautiful women, with angelic faces, looked anything but deadly. But it was death shining from their blood-shot eyes, it was death pulsing in their black hearts, and it was death ringing out in their dreadful wails.

The storm blocked out the sun, making the normally cobalt sky darken to deep indigo. The green moon, Weeqq, and the blue moon, Calixto, provided ample light for the blue teenager to see the desolate landscape over which he must travel. And more than ample light to keep watch on his pursuers.

Hugging the edge of the shimmer storm, immune to its mystical forces, Kanh-apal-apli remained hidden as he followed and monitored the running boy and the four banshees. For now, the river kept Gjallimé safe.

Kanh-apal-apli watched the teenager, *he is so young.* Tattoos sparingly covered the lad's blue skin. If that wasn't enough to indicate his youth, he could not have been more than one or two inches taller than five feet. Yet he ran well, swift and tirelessly as a Rider should. *His steed would not have handled the tundra or the shimmer storm. It would be on its way back to his Hold.*

Kanh-apal-apli knew Gjallimé carried the bronze circle that was a piece of The-Key-that-is-Lost, taking it to W'lkyndh. With this discovery, the scholars among the high elves might be able to figure out a means to find the missing part of the pendant. *The tremendous power The-Key-that-is-Lost confers is sorely needed in these times.* The sooner the better.

It was almost unheard for him to get directly involved. But the river keeping the young Rider from the enemy would soon dive underground again to the source of its heat. Gjallimé would then have to face the four creatures. That outcome was not in doubt. Kanh-apal-apli directed his mount toward the running teenager. When he came into view, the young Rider stopped in his tracks.

The boy saw an imposing figure on a massive steed the color of the chocolate earth. The individual wore a hooded coat of the same chocolate color. Only his hands and part of his face could be seen. They were as cut from ice. This could only be the legendary Wanderer, last of his race and older than recorded time. He was the demi-god of lore and had not been seen in many generations. Gjallimé couldn't find any words. They were trapped in his constricted throat.

Kanh-apal-apli threw back his hood. His voice was a thunderous baritone, "It seems, Gjallimé, that we have a problem."

The young Rider with curly fern-green hair still could not make his mouth work so the Wanderer continued. "I know what you carry is of great consequence, and it would be for the best if your journey was successful. But the banshees watching from the other side will be able to reach you downstream. I do not mean to insult you by implying you could not dispatch them yourself. I only wish to lend a hand. What sayest you, young Rider?"

In awe of the booming voice, the sculpted countenance. In awe of the very presence of this legend, the teenager merely nodded.

The Wanderer dismounted, knelt, rolled up his sleeve, and placed his massive ice-like palm on the surface of the bubbling azure river. Immediately, the water around his hand began to freeze. The banshee force gathered on the bank opposite the kneeling Snow-Jarl. They watched silently as the frozen water spread, inching across the river. When the ice reached them, its width allowed the creatures to cross two abreast. They drew their blades. Each hauntingly beautiful creature wielded a long slim sword curved at the tip in one hand, and a shorter, wider blade in the other. They stepped onto the frozen surface gingerly, but Khan-apal-apli had not created a trap with thin ice. That would not be honorable.

To give himself space to operate, the Wanderer pushed Gjallimé, firmly, a full step to his right and slightly behind. His broad shoulders faced the ice bridge squarely in the middle. His bejeweled two-handed claymore confronted the enemy with the point forward, at shoulder height. If either knew about the Earth book, *The Art of War*, this fighting stance was middle attitude.

Gjallimé held two short blades, arms wide, his feet planted firmly, the right ahead of the left. The fight would be one with no sorcerers, no extra power, just inherent abilities. Weapons glinted in the light of the silver and green moons. Gjallimé's breath became mist in the cold air. The shimmer storm edged closer, blocking any retreat.

The front two banshees attacked simultaneously. Kanh-apal-apli's sword swung hard right and dashed both the thrusting straight blade and slashing curved weapon of the banshee on the left. The force of the claymore drove downward one sword of the creature in front of Gjallimé. The blue teenager stepped forward and parried the fourth blade.

Kanh-apal-apli's heavy claymore broke the first sword then sliced upward causing the banshee in front of him to lean backward. The creature had only her arm to deflect the follow-up downward cut. Her severed limb fell to the tundra.

Gjallimé gritted his teeth as he felt the onslaught of *Fear* projected by the two banshees in the rear. A copper taste pervaded his mouth. He was not surprised that he was their target since he was by far the weaker of the two. They also directed their wails toward him, and threw ice-balls, nearly knocking him backward.

He concentrated hard to keep control of his mind as he fought a defensive strategy.

Kanh-apal-apli dispatched the first creature and parried the next. He managed to slash the back of the leg of the banshee Gjallimé engaged. Her stumble enabled Gjallimé to duck and thrust his short sword deep into her belly. When he removed the blade, sticky fluid the color of eggplant spilled onto his hand, smelling like wet animal fur.

Pressing forward, the Wanderer forced the third banshee to step back. Clangs and grunts, wails, and metal-scraping-metal and filled the air. The final banshee threw a dagger that found Kanh-apal-apli's left shoulder and buried to the hilt. Ignoring the blade in his flesh, he followed a feint with a cut that landed, crippling the third creature who went down with a shriek. He leapt over the howling body and with a mighty lunge killed the fourth monster. At the same time Gjallimé, using his innate quickness, jumped in and slew the fallen banshee with a plunge to its throat.

Looking at the dead and ravaged bodies in disbelief, Gjallimé's heart still raced. He knew he would not be alive if it were not for the Wanderer. *Could I have bested even one of them?* Then bolstered by pride he assured himself that he could have taken down two. He looked up at the Snow-Jarl with both awe and gratitude.

"Gjallimé. Take my horse and ride on to W'lkyndh. My steed will find me after your safe arrival. Godspeed." Khan-apal-apli was not asking.

The lad mounted and rode on without a word. He looked back over his shoulder to see the Snow-Jarl standing tall and still, dagger protruding from his shoulder. *I was saved by the Wanderer. What does that portend?*

Chapter 2
Beyond the Known Universe

"Hey, asswipe." Eric muttered as he brushed by Julian's desk on his way to the back of the class.

Julian let a small, wry grin cross his face even as he continued to stare directly ahead. He was especially glad he already had *one of his nasties,* as he thought of them, prepared and waiting for Eric after class.

"Everyone be seated. Put everything under your desks." The booklets today were bright purple in Mr. Granderson's hands. "The sooner I can hand these out, the longer you will have to work on them."

The noise of backpacks being stuffed under the seats quickly resolved into silence. The teacher passed out the test and said, "Begin."

Julian opened the booklet and scanned the contents. *As usual, more problems than there is time for.* He had a strategy for taking these tests. He identified the three hardest, longest problems and left them for last, starting on what he thought were the easiest.

+++

"Time."

Julian put his pencil down and handed the booklet forward. *I aced it.* The next to last problem was unfinished, but he could get partial credit if the work was on the right track. *No sweat.*

He shuffled along the aisle, the last student to get up from his desk, when Mr. Granderson called him over. "Julian, your homework since your mediocre midterm has been excellent. You need to do well on today's test and the final to make it into Honors Calculus."

Geeezz I already know that, but he was polite and responded, "I've been studying hard." He was royally pissed with himself for slumping and doing so poorly during the middle of the semester. Nothing would keep him from Honors Calculus. With a 94 on this test and similar score on the final he would pull himself up to an A. *Virginia Tech, Columbia, Stanford, or Duke await. I will find friendship with those people.*

Mr. Granderson flashed an affable smile. "Calculus AB is challenging, but I think you can do it."

"Thanks." And the teenager abruptly headed off to the hall. Mr. Granderson was one of his favorite teachers, but this was his next-to-last class, on the final day before Spring Break, and he wanted to get off campus quickly. *No '99 yearbook committee meeting. Spring Break. Stupid extracurricular activities for college applications. Full of foolish kids. Foolish activities.* He had arranged with his next teacher to miss the final class of the day by completing his work ahead of time, with the excuse that he needed to see his parents before they headed out of town. It was almost the truth; his parents left earlier this morning. They went over the rules for being alone *for the zillionth time* before they left.

+++

Julian did not stick around to wait for the bus. He rode his bike today and now hustled toward Cheeseboy Games. *I don't want to be in school when the shit hits the fan.*

As the smallest kid in his class, and a grade ahead in school, Julian had gone through this crap last year when he transferred in as a sophomore. His funky haircut didn't help. The straw-blonde hair was buzz cut up the right side, while the top and left side spilled over his head, falling to his shoulder.

The kids who messed with him as a sophomore later found themselves in the principal's office for things they didn't do. He was not hassled after the first few incidents. That was how he liked it. *Just leave me alone.*

+++

Eric transferred in a couple weeks back. Either the other kids didn't warn him or they wanted to see him get the business. After Precalc, the bully headed to his locker.

"Shit!" Eric's face showed an ugly shade of red. "That punk. I'll spread his body parts across the football field." Eric harbored no doubt this was Julian's work. Bus tokens wedged around the locker's edge, jammed it shut. The other kids snickered or flashed a you-got-it smile or held their hands over their mouths. Eric glanced around at his friends, his anger and embarrassment growing.

Vernon wheezed. "Take it easy. You're lucky. At least you're not in trouble with the principal." Vernon took out his bike lock key and began to remove the bus tokens, one-by-one.

"I'll get him."

"Better you don't. Next time, you'll find yourself suspended."

"Not if he's dead."

+++

Julian smirked while visualizing the bully at his jammed locker. Eric was Junior ROTC but that didn't stop him from being an asshole. He'd hassled Julian for weeks and yesterday Eric *accidentally* bumped into him as they passed in the hall. The big oaf almost knocked Julian on his butt. It may not seem like much, but it was enough for Julian. By now, the other kids were explaining to Eric that he got off easy. Spring Break would give the bully enough time to cool down and realize the consequences of messing with him. Julian wouldn't hesitate to orchestrate an event that would get Eric kicked out of JROTC. *Heck, I might do it just for fun.*

The teenager pulled into the strip mall confident he wouldn't be bothered again when he returned after the break. *They risk peril. I am the cat that walks by himself and all places are alike to me.* Julian's personal litany. A phrase from a book somewhere in his childhood that he took to be his own. It defined him. *I don't need anyone.*

+++

"Hey," Paul said from behind the counter. "How'd you get out early?"

Julian stuffed his hands in his pockets. "Hey man, are you ready to game?"

"Sure. Gimme a minute."

Julian walked over to the big gaming table at the back of Cheeseboy Games, one of his hangouts. He and the manager, Paul, had an ongoing duel of Gattica, a futuristic war game played with miniature military units. Two long hex grid game boards lay side by side on the table. Scaled-down pieces of different types were scattered across the boards. Julian pulled his commander from his pocket and placed it on the space where they left the game two days before.

Paul came over and placed his commander where it belonged. The commanders were by far the most powerful units in the game. Killing them was one of the ways to win.

Paul gave Julian a sardonic smile, "Your move."

They battled for almost three hours. Move, attack, countermove, feint, defend. Several units were vanquished. Julian's space marines made headway in one area but Paul's galards - the equivalent to tanks - threatened a flank of defensive forces protecting Julian's commander. The galards nearly obliterated one of his outer defensive groups. Advantage Paul.

Cheeseboy Games began filling up for the Friday Jarls Magic Tournament. Paul said, "Let's leave it here. I've got to do

8

the tourny." Julian shrugged. Each took his commander and placed an eight-sided die to mark its position and status. *More time to plan my strategy.*

Paul asked, "This weekend?"

Julian nodded. This match started two weeks ago and would continue at unspecified times. The schedule was casual, winning or losing was anything but.

Walking out of Cheeseboy Games, Julian strode toward the end of the strip mall. He didn't notice the stores he passed, or for that matter, any part of his walk. Thinking about plan B for his space marines, he almost walked smack into the glass window of King Kool's Pizza Palace. Without hesitation, he spun right and started down the walkway. About halfway down on the left, he opened the door to Dylan Shrugged Used Books, one of his favorite hideaways. The dusky smell of aged paper greeted him. So did Robert, the proprietor, behind the counter.

"What's up, Julian?"

"Nothin." But he gave a slight upturn of his head in Robert's direction as he proceeded to the back. *Why am I most comfortable around grownups? Robert, Paul, Mr. Granderson. College will be a different story.*

Robert didn't add anything. He knew that Julian usually had nothing to say.

At the back of the store, he headed to the science fiction section. Main order of business, peruse the "Z's" in case anything new from his favorite author, Roger Zelazny, was on the shelves. To his delight, he found *Jack of Shadows*. He pulled out the soft cover book, turned to its back and read the hook. *The world of half-science, half-magic sounds great.* But he didn't need to be convinced. He gobbled up everything Zelazny wrote. At a buck fifty, it wouldn't make a dent in the money his parents left him for the weekend.

Three books farther to the left he noticed a small gap. Julian took a half step down the aisle and saw a small copper-red hardback recessed slightly from the rest of the books on the shelf.

There were no markings on the spine. Not a title, not an author. *This is freak.*

He reached up and grabbed the peculiar hardback for a closer look. It felt slippery and appeared brand new. It was six inches tall and quite thin. Both front and back covers as blank as the spine.

Julian opened the hardback and his eyes widened as he stared at the most beautifully colored and intricate space scenes he had ever seen. The inside cover showed a nebula, opposite a trio of galaxies. *Cool.*

The photos were glossy, realistic, and vivid. More vibrant than anything he had seen in astronomy books or online. Still looking for a book title, he turned to the first page to find, printed, in bold simple letters, *Beyond the Known Universe*. The back of the title page was blank, no copyright or other information. Opposite, he was greeted by a short list of eight chapters. The first was 'Let there be Light'. Julian saw the chapter was about the Big Bang and the very beginning of the universe. *Oh sure, I get it.*

He closed the book, thinking how odd the blank cover. It was not science fiction. It was science. Julian reached to put the book back and suddenly stopped, arm frozen in mid-air. *What's goin' on?*

He found himself taking the book, tucking it under his arm along with *Jack of Shadows. Ok, some real science for Spring Break. I can go for that.* No matter if he didn't understand some of the math. Diagrams and text filled much of the book, and he could follow most of what he already read.

Julian handed the two books to Robert. "The red book doesn't have a price."

Robert turned the book back and front, and even looked inside. "I don't remember this. Where'd you find it?"

"In the science fiction section." Julian squelched his surprise that Robert took no notice of the stunning photos inside, no notice of the lack of a title on the cover.

"Well, it isn't in the best condition. But it is hardback." Robert looked up at Julian with a warm smile. "How about a buck fifty like *Jack of Shadows*?"

The book looked brand spanking new to Julian. *Weird.* Nevertheless, he nodded his head in agreement.

+++

At home, Julian found a note reminding him again of the rules, along with some redundant tips for safety. Home alone for first time over an entire weekend. *Hell, it's three nights. They won't be home 'til Monday.* The note included, "We trust you." *Is that some kind of a warning?* And, "We will celebrate your birthday when we get back." Sunday would be his sixteenth birthday. It didn't faze him that his parents would be away. As usual, the note ended with a quote: "responsibility is a sign of trust." *Blech.* Julian took this not as a burden but as freedom borne of good decisions.

I'm gonna order all the delivery pizza I want. Blast the music, play Gattica, read, maybe go to the skatepark or a movie. No real friends to have over. Fine by me.

+++

Sitting cross-legged on his bedspread, he kept his sneakers on. *What they don't know won't hurt them.* He thought *Jack of Shadows* was in his hands, but to his surprise it was *Beyond the Known Universe.* Julian opened the book and immediately noticed the middle few pages were the color of burnt orange and did not lay flat. *They are old. I don't remember this from the bookstore.*

Opening the book to the odd pages, handwriting greeted him. Script with precise, neat penmanship.

I should write this before it is too late. First, this world has two faces. One face always sits in the sun.

11

Wasteland, turning into molten lead at the Hot Pole. The other is in perpetual darkness. Tundra, turning into the Kelvin Sea. A continent, Kelvin Land is believed to lie at the Cold Pole. Ninety percent of the planet is a cerulean ocean, mostly boiling or frozen as the case may be. The main continent, paisley shaped, contains a swath of land between the light and dark side. A 'Goldilocks Zone'. Habitable.

The rest of the page showed a crude map of the continent. Terrain features: forests, mountains, rivers, and some marks that Julian could not identify were sketched in. *This person is an explorer or a scientist.* Many locations were indicated on the map with strange names. Like Zhon Jeul, Sayll, and Kolsnikh-Yal. The continent itself was called Edrym. But the map was incomplete; one end of the land remained hidden. Julian turned the page and reconsidered his scientist idea with what followed.

The eight moons confer special powers to the different races. You must learn them all. You must master their intricacies. The black moon rises. I must hurry. The struggle between Nova'h and Yetzer-Xie rages. I have done the calculations. The time of Weynonovar Ha is drawing near. I am out of time. I must do what needs to be done.

The next two lines were set apart and written in large print rather than script. Julian felt compelled to sound the odd words aloud. "SKETOOCH EBOY ALLOKAM JENNOFIO MEELOOCH."

Phffft! A mysterious oval 'picture' appeared at the foot of his bed, stretching from the floor to the ceiling, a good ten feet from side to side. *Huh?* He looked behind to see if a projector was the source. No projector. *What the hell?*

The scene featured a close up of a dirt path, wide and curling up and around the bend of a steep hill like a spiral staircase. The soil was a rich, deep, chocolate brown; the path lined by tree trunks at irregular intervals. The bark varied from light ash to soft cadet blue, providing stark contrast to the ground. The edges of the phenomenon, a full foot in width, were an intricate gold inlay of runes upon a background of bottle green. There was no thickness to the 'painting', as he now thought of it. It seemed surreally brushed upon the very air. *Totally weird.*

He reached out tentatively to touch the phenomenon. At the last second, he pulled back, wondering if the image was somehow made from lasers that would slice through his flesh. *Is this a wormhole? Crap! I'm being drawn in.* Between nerves and suspicion, Julian panicked. He looked down at the book and spoke the final line. "MEELOOCH JENNOFIO ALLOKAM EBOY SKETOOCH."

Phffft! The 'painting' disappeared. Julian stared through the space where it once stood and saw the closed door of his room. *This is crazy.* His mind stayed blank for a few seconds until the doorbell rang. He shook his head vigorously. *My pizza!* He dropped the book on the bed, dashed through the spot where the portal had been, and taking the stairs two at a time, hustled to the front door. *What does that picture mean?* It was all a blur.

Julian opened the front door only to find a delivery man. "Delivery for Patricia Byrne." Julian, still in a daze, looked stupidly at the tall man in brown. *Of course, mom's pseudonym.*

"I'll take it. Oh. Sign here? 'Kay." Two rectangular packages, some four feet by six feet, but only two inches or so thick, leaned against the side of the house. Julian carried them into his mom's studio. From the shape, Julian surmised that these were two pieces of art. Probably his mother's own work, now framed. One package had a rip revealing an eye with a purple iris. *Who's this? Mom only does real people.*

The doorbell rang again. A dour-faced pizza delivery boy greeted him. Julian gave the guy a five-dollar tip because it was his parents' money. If the money were his, he probably would have stiffed the poor shlump.

He cranked up his father's sound system. His father played jazz trumpet and the stereo was *sick*. He by-passed tech trance, rap, and synthpop to grab some older heavy metal. Metallica. As he sat down to eat his pizza the room pulsed, nearly shook, with the volume he set. *I'm killin' it.*

Julian grabbed one of his dad's beers. *I can get away with it. Gotta try sometime.*

He wolfed down the pizza and sipped down the beer without a single thought in his head. Slightly buzzed, he acted as if on auto-pilot. He paced for much of that evening, feeling a strange attraction, and also dread, directed at the stairs to the second floor, to his room, to the book. He did not understand it, nor did he choose to dwell on it. Mind fuzzy, the cold, grey leather couch became his bed for the night, music still blasting.

+++

When Julian awoke in the morning, his head throbbed and it felt like a dog had taken a giant crap in his mouth. A soda helped with that. He turned off the stereo, still disoriented and confused. He sat at the kitchen island, eating a muffin, trying to clear his head. Not knowing why, he grabbed his board and headed to the skatepark.

When he returned home, Julian felt like something important, terribly important, happened while skateboarding. He just knew it would come back to haunt him. But as he tried to remember, his gaze settled on the stairs. He remembered the book. He remembered the 'painting'. He remembered the dread. Feeling as if he were sleepwalking, he went upstairs.

Julian knelt on the end of his bed and opened *Beyond the Known Universe* to the beckoning page. He hesitated, then read the words aloud. "SKETOOCH EBOY ALLOKAM JENNOFIO MEELOOCH."

Phffft!* The portal appeared before him once again. *Shit.* With shallow breath, he bent forward, drawn to the quiet richness of the scene. He teetered, tried to right himself without success, and lost his balance. Still clutching the book, he fell in.

Chapter 3
Ambush

Julian found himself sprawled upon the chocolate-colored dirt of the path. He glanced behind, but the portal was gone. The ground smelled of musk, and the sound of footsteps came from around the bend. Julian grabbed the book, leapt to his feet, darted across the path, and wedged himself behind a tree against the hillside. *Holy shit!* He held his breath. The footfalls were many and sounded close.

Three tall men strode past the tree. They wore chainmail armor, gray, rough-hewn trousers and hazel leather boots. Each carried a longsword, hanging from his belt. Ivory was their skin, and their silver hair hung in two long braids down their back. They passed no more than a couple yards from Julian's hiding place.

Like, awesome... Can they see me? His muscles tensed.

A scarlet cloak trimmed in hunter green nearly touching the ground came into view. A woman of royalty. She could be nothing else with her fine features and regal countenance, and she stood as tall as the men. Julian guessed six feet like his father. Her hair was not braided but fell in lustrous waves to the middle of her back. Julian realized that her silver hair was not a sign of age, sparkling even in the shade. *Impossible.* The majestic lady stopped and turned abruptly to face him.

"What is this?" Her voice was stern but polite, and the men in front halted, turning to face the teenager as well.

He could only gape.

The queen opened her cloak revealing the same military garb as the men, including the sword. She gestured to the somber men to stay put, took a few steps toward Julian and crouched to bring her face to his level.

"What curious manner of human are you? Eyes the blue of Al'uah, long hair of the Halili and the color of the golden Kem'nesh? And strange garb, a tunic the purple color of the power of Ava'cynh?"

Julian managed to speak. "Where…am I?"

"You are on Naspia Dor, the sacred plateau."

"I don't understand any of this." *What the hell is goin' on?*

The queen paused to look at him closely. She could tell he was alarmed and smiled gently. "I am Queen Aemiluria. What is your name?"

"Julian."

"J'liánh, you are obviously not of Edrym."

The stunned teenager realized that she was not speaking English. And neither was he. The sounds were fluid and of an odd tone, yet he understood it. That is, all but the peculiar names.

"You come from behind the Tree of Ages, however I do not know why."

Julian gathered himself to a modicum of composure. "How did I get here? I've never heard of the Tree of Ages. How do I get back?" And as he said that, he remembered the book held behind his back. He brought it out and stared at a supple, leather-bound volume with unfamiliar but elegant gold letters on a background of neutral brown. The borders of the book were also trimmed in gold. *Its changed. Oh shit! What now?*

Aemiluria gasped. "Where did you get that?"

"From a…" Julian could not come up with a word for 'bookstore' in this strange language. He opened the book and the writing resembled the letters on the cover. "I can't read this. I need to read from this to get home. The book brought me here."

Aemiluria whispered, "May I?" and reached for the tome.

Julian hesitated for a moment then handed it to the Queen, still holding a corner.

She tugged slightly and he let go. She looked the book over. Front, back, and inside, treating it as if priceless. "This is the tome Nchaud-Zel from the time of Tamiel. Scholars from W'lkyndh Hold may be able to decipher the language." She handed the book back to Julian.

I have to hold onto this! "Can we go there? I mean, I don't belong here." *At least I want to find out **how** to go back. Maybe I could stay awhile. This place is crazy. Crazy cool.*

"J'liánh, Eswar will see to it that you may go back from where you came. Of that I promise. Perhaps there is a reason you were brought here."

"Then let's go see this Eswar right away."

Aemiluria smiled. "I will get you to the High King. But not now. We have wounded that must be attended to, and dead to be honored. Cthomechdul rises. We need to leave Naspia Dor. My people and our allies must descend the plateau. When we arrive at camp, we can discuss this more." She looked up the path. "Iniqui! Come and look after J'liánh."

A young girl emerged from the throng of these silver haired people who'd come down the path to gawk at him. He heard the word *Ava'cynh* again among their whispers. Iniqui seemed his age with Aemiluria's features. There could be no doubt this was the Queen's daughter. The same full mouth and oval eyes the color of plum. *She's cute. Like that matters – she's the queen's daughter.*

"Come J'liánh," ordered Iniqui impatiently.

Julian stood stupefied. The silver-haired people passed, four or five abreast. He noticed that some limped or hobbled. Men and women supported each other in blood-soaked clothes. But what held him frozen were the other beings comingled in the army. Lithe hunter-green skinned creatures with fine features of exquisite beauty, with leaves in their wispy brown hair, and some with aquamarine gossamer wings. Mixed in were shorter, heavily tattooed humans with blue skin and slanted eyes. As Julian tried to absorb the details, a noise broke out.

"K'rai! K'rai!"

"Shyro!"

Unmistakable sounds of clashing metal erupted from the far side of the path.

Julian flinched. *Oh shit!*

Aemiluria jumped to her feet to face the noise and a line of four guards shielded her, weapons ready. Some of the soldiers in front of the guards swung swords high over their heads, other swords slashed sideways.

What the crap?

The black heads and shoulders of the hideous forces opposing them towered over the Queen's warriors. Liches with skull like faces and long tangled, faded yellow hair growing out of their boney scalps. Scraggly yellow beards came forth from their faces. *Monsters.*

Two blue warriors ran wildly down the winding, tree-lined path away from the fight, arms flailing, screaming nonsense. The liches inched forward. *I'm trapped! There's nowhere to run.* Then standing tall, *I'm not gonna to run.*

"S'rrinha!" Aemiluria cried out and a long silver scepter appeared in her left hand, her sword in her right, down at her side. She held out the scepter, at eye level, canted sideways. Her left leg thrust forward, feet apart as if braced against some unseen force. Queen and scepter, still as a sculpture. Iniqui shoved Julian back against the hillside and took a fighting stance at her mother's side. The Queen's scepter glowed with a silvery halo.

Julian was dumbstruck — the scene was much too fantastic to elicit true fear. "Iniqui. What's goin' on?" He stashed the book in the back of his waistline. *Is this real?*

Iniqui ignored him, all her focus on the fight.

Warriors surrounded the eerily silent liche force. A silver-haired combatant fled from the fight down the path, eyes bulging. Another silver-haired swordsman dispatched the closest liche, driving his sword directly into the fiend's face. With the crunch of bone, its eyes popped out.

Holy shit! This is not a video game. The screams, the grunts, the cries. The sour stench of sweat and blood — it's... it's gross. And Julian put his hands to his ears, his face twisted in a grimace as he stood transfixed.

The wind whipped into a howl. Metal clanged upon metal. Two silver-haired soldiers flanked one of the beasts, hacking away, bringing forth maroon blood that soaked its tattered grey robe. Torn chunks of flesh revealed bare bone. The liche fought back, up to the moment he crumbled in a heap of dove-grey flesh and robe, yellow hair, and cream-colored bones.

The fighting was indeed genuine, only some seven yards from him. Sounds punched the hollow of Julian's stomach. The all-too-real commotion of battle, shook, but did not break, the tough guy part of his self-image. *I am the cat that walks by himself and all places are alike to me. I will come out of this stronger. That is, if I come out at all.*

A spear *thunked* as it lodged itself into the hillside a few feet from Julian's head. He ducked. *Oh my God! Am I the target? Or was that meant for the Queen?* The reality of the moment continued to gnaw its way into his perspective.

"Shyro!" Another liche was cut down. The Earth teenager saw a blue swordsman leap into the air and with a flash of his sword, an action too swift to obey his ideas of the laws of motion, took off the last liche's head. Noise of metal clashing and war cries ceased, leaving only the moans of the wounded and the shuffling of the army. Aemiluria ran forward asking questions. About the fight, about the ones lost, about the injured.

A voice exclaimed, "It is done! Anything up the hill?"

The answer, "There was no attack save where you stand."

Aemiluria shouted, "Down the path! Quickly! Cthomechdul rises." Iniqui grabbed Julian by the arm and pulled him forward with the throng.

"Like, what was that?" The Earth teenager asked,

"Sneak attack. Be quiet! We must get off Naspia Dor."

Julian, keeping pace with Iniqui, overheard comments from the crowd.

"... distracted by J'liánh ... put the *Fear* into us."

"Thank H'rol she was on the far side of the path."

"... lost Ra'jhan, Fjolti ... enchantment of *Quash* ... S'rrinha"

Julian and Iniqui hustled forward toward the front of the walking army. He saw the two blue warriors who had run away, rejoin the group. *They are accepted without hesitation.* He took a quick look back and saw several bodies being carried over combatants' shoulders. He caught more snippets of conversation.

"... never before struck on the path ..."

"... a suicide ambush ..."

+++

As Julian emerged from beneath the canopy of leaves that had been a roof over the path, the sky was revealed. *Oh shit!* He stopped abruptly, causing someone to bump into him from behind.

"Come." Iniqui commanded.

But Julian stepped to the side and away from the moving army, his eyes awestruck by the sky. The air in his lungs escaped in a low whistle as he took in the deep cobalt-blue heavens, and colorful orbs hanging there. The rich coppery-orange sun was directly in front of him, some twenty degrees from the horizon, a perfect melted marmalade contrast to the sky. Julian's eyes fixed upon one, then two, then three moons scattered across the cobalt canvas; one lavender, one quicksilver, one cornflower blue. *All the moons are larger than mine.* The lavender was twice the size, and the silver moon gigantic, at least three times the size of the Earth's. *They seem to fill half the sky.*

Iniqui poked Julian in the shoulder.

He pulled away. "Shhh. Gimme a sec."

The sun shone strongest, but the moons glowed as well. *This is eerie, like being inside a giant planetarium.* The dark rich earth, a field of tall golden-brown grasses, the strange cobalt sky. *It's fantasy.* The sounds of the soldiers were loud around him but Julian heard nothing. He felt like an oyster trapped inside a shell of multicolored glass.

"J'liánh! J'liánh! *Look* at me!" Iniqui barked and broke the spell.

22

"This is dope! Totally mind-blowing." Julian knew that dope was probably not in their language, but it must translate for Iniqui into something comparable.

"You are truly not from Edrym."

Edrym? Edrym. Oh yes, from the map in the book.

Julian turned to see that the green-forested path descending from Naspia Dor blocked his view of nearly half the heavens. "No. I'm from a place called E'rth. You know, I read words from this book. Some kinda portal opened and I fell through. The book — it's changed here in Edrym. If I could read it, I bet I could get back."

Iniqui asked him the details of finding the book and going through the portal. Julian provided the full account. He turned to face her. "I must see the scholars, or meet Eswar, I'm not sure which."

"The High King Eswar is my father. We are the Khalil. Bespoken to I'rnh Alon, the silver moon. You met my mother, Aemiluria."

"So, when can I see him?"

"First we must return to camp. Cthomechdul rises."

"Cthomechdul?"

"The blood-red moon. Even now it is partly above the horizon in the west. The view is blocked by Naspia Dor. When Cthomechdul is fully in the sky, the lava giants will join forces with Yetzer-Xie. We will be safer in camp."

"What does—"

"Enough! Follow me. The camp is not far." And Iniqui turned her back to Julian walking alongside the rest of the troops. She expected him to follow obediently.

He paused momentarily, *I'll be lost on my own,* and scampered to catch up with her. *Oh shit. Still, I am the cat that walks by himself and all places are alike to me…*

Chapter 4
Strength and Speed

Less than a half hour later the tall grasses gave way to a dense forest. The soldiers plunged directly into the thicket. The smell of pine and bark followed Iniqui and Julian as they walked through the woods. They came upon a large glade spotted with tan and rose-colored, rectangular tents. Iniqui guided Julian to one near the middle where a gnarled, older looking blue-skinned blacksmith hammered a glowing sword upon an anvil.

"Hjerim, this is J'liánh."

"Ahh, I have heard news of a stranger." Hjerim looked at him casually, without alarm.

"Look after him." Then to Julian. "I shall send Gjallimé with some clothes. You must *not* wear that." She pointed to the boy's t-shirt.

What's wrong with my shirt?

"Gjallimé will acquaint you with our customs." And with a swish of her silver hair, Iniqui turned her back and walked away. Julian looked slack-jawed at the space where she had stood.

Hjerim spoke. "Don't let her aloofness fool you. Iniqui is as passionate as the scarlet rose and her temper flares easier than kindling catching flame."

Hjerim was a head shorter than the Khalil. *The blue women on the path were taller than the men. Hjerim looks older than the blue people I saw during the descent from Naspia Dor.* Intricate lined tattoos covered every inch of exposed skin.

Hjerim caught Julian staring. "We are the Hassjidar. Bespoken of Calixto, the blue moon."

Bespoken?

The Hassjidar were lean like the Khalil but more muscled, with harsh angular facial features. The irises of their slanted eyes matched the cobalt hue of the sky. Their hair was tightly curled, the color of fern, and trimmed short. Hjerim's movements seemed somehow wrong, with sudden starts and stops. And rapid in-between.

Hjerim noticed Julian's questioning eyes and explained. "Hassjidar have Boshnjaku, the power of *Speed*. The power is modest but can be greatly enhanced by the enchantment of *Speed* conferred by an Eptizar, a sorcerer, using the Talisman of Mitha."

Julian practically hollered, "I saw a blue fighter wield his sword faster than I could imagine."

"Then Ken Noru or S'rrinha must have been using the talisman."

"You know, I overheard the name S'rrinha. I also overheard something about *Quash*. Who or what are they — what does it mean?"

"Ken Noru is the Hassjidar Eptizar, a sorcerer. S'rrinha is the sorcerer for the Irulahna, the nymphs. One must have used the enchantment of *Speed*, the other the enchantment of *Quash*. Both get their energy from the blue moon."

The conversation was interrupted by a group of Hassjidar, each piling their arms in a heap inside the Smith's tent. Some used long, heavy, two-handed swords, while others favored two smaller, lighter blades, one for each hand. Several placed swords of various types and a shield on the pile. They each looked intently at Julian, some with a scowl, others bright-eyed. A few were not taking sides. There were as many women as men and they seemed to range in age from young like himself, to elderly adults.

After the group passed, Julian muttered, "It seems that I may have, umm…, played some role in the ambush on the path. You know, like maybe a spy."

Hjerim did not look up from his work. "I heard you saved Aemiluria by drawing her to the side of the path away from the attackers."

"I don't see how there's a connection at all, you know, I just arrived. But if my appearance did play a role, like, what would that role be?"

"Three things cannot be long hidden: the sun, the moons, and the truth." Hjerim doused the sword he was working on in a bath of oil with a sizzle. "J'liánh, hand me a claymore from the pile."

Julian bent his knees and took a two-handed sword by the thick hilt. He used his legs to lift, only to find himself a foot in the air floating softly back to the ground. *Wha...?* "Holy shit!" The steel claymore in his hands was not heavy. Julian took the sword in his hand and parried in the air.

Hjerim said. "You are left-handed."

Other than the hilt being too large for Julian's hand, the sword felt fine, perhaps a little light. He thrust the sword forward and swung it from side to side. His motions seemed quick, as if he held nothing. He jumped hard and lifted more than two feet off the ground, landing gently.

Hjerim watched all of this with a cautionary eye. "J'liánh. How is this possible?"

"It reminds me of seeing...." The word for astronaut was not in this language. "Seeing men walk on the moon."

"What do you mean, walking on the moon?"

"Hjerim, I'm not from this world. On my world, E'rth, we have but one moon, and men have, you know, walked upon it."

"How could that be?"

"It doesn't matter. What matters is that the gravity here must be less than E'rth. Hey, what's the name of this place"

"I heard that you are an outlander. We are in the realm Edrym. How can you move like that?"

Julian handed the claymore to Hjerim. "My muscles are better than yours, giving me strength and quickness."

"Swifter even than the Hassjidar." Hjerim exhaled with a trill.

"Hallo," said a young Hassjidar entering the tent. "I'm Gjallimé. You must be J'liánh."

"Hey. Look what I can do!" Julian grabbed another claymore from the pile and cut the blade through the air, back and forth, as fast as he could. He jumped high into the air, landing with a smile. *I'm dope.*

"You will make a great warrior." Gjallimé remarked.

Hjerim added, "We must make a custom sword for you."

Julian gathered himself. *Weird. How do I know how to walk and move without bouncing? Maybe it comes with being in this world, like knowing their language.* He stood, feet apart, leaning on the claymore, point on the ground, vertical, in front of him. "I'm not a warrior. I need to go home." *Thanks, but no thanks. No on the bloodshed.*

"Right now, you need to get out of those clothes." Gjallimé handed a sack to Julian.

Julian crossed his arms. "Yeah? Like, what's wrong with my clothes?"

"Well, your strange tunic is the color of Ava'cynh, and the rest looks foolish. We will keep your clothes ready for the time of your return."

"Ava'cynh?" Julian looked down at his t-shirt. It was purple with a black and white logo of the game Gattica.

"The color of the purple moon, Z'th, is worn only by a Champion. I do not know the meaning of Ava'cynh combined with a symbol in Klaiwohaya and Ihl."

"What?"

"Klaiwohaya the white moon and Ihl the black moon. Your new clothes are in the sack." Gjallimé pointed to a hanging tarp. "Change over there."

"It makes no sense to me. Iniqui said you would explain things, names themselves don't explain anything." *The bizarre words fly right by me.*

"Later. Change!"

Julian's new clothes consisted of grey pants, a plain sienna-brown, snug and supple tunic and heavy black boots rising to mid-calf. He wore a leather satchel, large enough for the book, just behind his left hip. *Where's my chainmail?*

+++

Outside the camp a group of eight wraiths, mauve with yellow eyes and strong beneath their flowing, tattered robes of maroon cloth, joined forces with the liches who had followed Aemiluria's army. This small force, operating aggressively outside the conditions of Ravoq-Ma or the call to Naspia Dor, was unusual. Nothing was as usual now that the Overlord of Darkness, Zhokul, arrived from the dark pole across the Kelvin Sea. The draugr, a freak at almost seven feet, provided Yetzer-Xie with a relentless, impassioned leader. Skinless with exposed, taut dark-grey muscle and crimson eyes, Zhokul intimidated even the beings of Yetzer-Xie.

The surprise ambush on Queen Aemiluria during the descent from Naspia Dor derived from the Overlord of Darkness's crafty but merciless mind. He thought of his people, the draugrs, wraiths, liches, banshees, lava giants, and yellow humans as his children, many of whom were scurrying in small platoons to spread Zhokul's reign of terror across Edrym.

One of this newly formed force of wraiths and liches was off scouting the Nova'h camp. The rest spoke in quiet sour tones. An Eptizar was not with them to wield power. They would use the basic special abilities imbued in each of them, as best they could. They were small in number, so they looked for a weakness to exploit. Yetzer-Xie could scheme and have patience. The wraiths and liches were waiting for their moons to rise.

+++

Gjallimé stood maybe an inch taller than Julian with far fewer tattoos than Hjerim. He was naturally boisterous and quite amiable as they walked through the camp. Gjallimé explained to Julian that Edrym was a realm locked in conflict between Nova'h and Yetzer-Xie, a conflict constant throughout the ages.

"Like Good vs. Evil?"

"I suppose so. Nova'h, Good, is the side of the Khalil, the Hassjidar, the nymphs, and others you have not yet met."

Am I Nova'h? "So, Yetzer-Xie is Evil?"

"Yes. The liches swear allegiance to Yetzer-Xie together with a host of other beings including a race of humans, the Ja'tasarr, Bespoken of Gobanh', the pale-yellow moon."

Julian looked up. He saw the black, white, and lavender moons, all full, and scattered across the sky. A shamrock green moon was rising in the northwest. He remembered the book and asked about the eight moons. Gjallimé told him each race had a power. A power that is enhanced when its moon was in the sky. Like *Speed* for the Hassjidar when the blue moon comes out. Or like *Fear* for the banshees when the yellow moon hung in the sky.

The directive from the book rang in Julian's head. *You must learn them all. You must master their intricacies.* Apparently, the moons were always full, which did not fit Julian's understanding of physics. The sun, less bright than his, continued to hang at the same spot in the sky that Julian first observed. *Of course, one side of this world perpetually faces the sun, the other side, the darkness of space. The sun will not move in the sky unless I travel east, toward it, or west, away from it.*

The notion of a day was not foreign to the dwellers of Edrym. Gjallimé explained that a day was 27 hours, which corresponded to one revolution of the white moon. Edrym's night was considered to be the ten hours the white moon spent on the dark side. That made for a long, 17-hour day. Julian was in for a shock when he asked how they kept time. The beings of Edrym had two hearts and two independent circulatory systems. One heartbeat varied with exertion the same as Julian's. The other smaller heart kept a steady beat and provided the beings of Edrym an accurate internal clock. *Dope!*

Julian wondered whether he would get home before his parents. He wondered if he would survive.

"Hey! Lemme show you Ns'rullah." Gjallimé broke into a run as they approached a pen of unusual horses sporting large nostrils and long, thin legs. Gjallimé hopped up on the first rung of the fence and stroked one of the animals that came near.

"Ns'rullah is a Domo, the swift and tireless horses of the Riders, who come only from the ranks of the Hassjidar. I became a Rider last year. Edrym is normally a five-day ride from tundra to desert but I can make it in under two!"

"Tundra to desert?"

"Edrym becomes a land of tundra and cold as you ride west and the sun sinks in the sky. Ride west too far and the air freezes in your lungs. Ride east and the sun rises in the sky until the fertile land gives way to desert. Ride east too far and the air burns through your lungs."

Another blue teenager approached them, his curly green hair falling to his ears. "Gjallimé, why are you with this outsider. Perhaps Yetzer-Xie favors him."

Gjallimé tensed and retorted. "He was found under the Tree of Ages. I have been assigned by Iniqui to teach him our ways."

The blue teenager mocked a bow. "The Princess herself. Huh. I will be on my way."

Gjallimé was about to address Julian when Ns'rullah whinnied. Gjallimé retrieved sugar cubes from his pocket. "Are all the beings of your world fair-skinned and spotted?"

"Not everyone is fair-skinned or with these spots, called freckles. Dude, what's the deal with this Naspia Dor?"

"Sometimes the minor moons eclipse. When so, the Seal of Nova'h—"

"Seal of Nova'h?"

"I can't explain it. You must see for yourself."

Julian rocked back on his heels. "Oh."

"When the Seal of Nova'h appears upon Naspia Dor, the forces of Nova'h must defend it against Yetzer-Xie. The forces called upon are only the ones summoned by the eclipsed moons."

This is a full-blown fantasy land. Is it real or am I dreaming? What's my role?

"The most recent battle, Waykenim, was called with the eclipse of the pale-yellow moon in front of the cornflower blue;

and the lavender in front of the silver. Waykenim called the Hassjidar, of the blue moon, and the nymphs who receive energy from the blue and green moons. The Khalil were summoned by Z'th, silver one. The Yetzer-Xie forces were the Ja'tasarr, humans Bespoken by the yellow moon, the liches of yellow-black, and the wraiths of yellow-red."

"Hey, what are wraiths?"

"Mauve-skinned abominations fighting for Yetzer-Xie. They glide across the ground with no feet, and spill melon-colored blood." Disgust flashed across his face.

White, blue, and green were the moons of Nova'h. Black, yellow, and red of Yetzer-Xie. Humans are bespoken by only a single moon while creatures are bespoken by two. For Julian, this was all turning into a blur. *You must learn them all. Well maybe not all at once.*

A proud Gjallimé addressed Ns'rullah. "That is all the sugar there is." The Domo bobbed his head in protest. "The Chart of the Moons for the next thirteen days are entrusted to the Riders to take to all Nova'h Holds."

"I can guess what The Chart of the Moons is, but, you know, where does it come from?"

"The scholars at W'lkyndh Hold prepare them." Gjallimé turned to face Julian with all seriousness. "The knowledge of which moons are visible at any given time is of vital importance. Each combination affects the balance of power. Special combinations invoke the most serious of circumstance."

"Yeah, like what?"

"Such as an eclipse, of which Waykenim was an example. But when the three moons of Yetzer-Xie are alone in the sky, the black, the yellow, and the red; with no other moons visible, it is called Ravoq-Ma."

"And what does that mean?"

"Ravoq-Ma is a perilous time for the forces of Nova'h. Fierce, powerful attacks erupt, enhanced by sorcerers of Yetzer-Xie."

"Like, how often does that happen?"

"Too often for my liking. The next Ravoq-Ma is in three days."

Who says I have to learn this? It's not my problem.

The blue teenager's cobalt eyes locked with Julian. "Be wary of shimmer storms."

"What's that?"

"Powder-blue fog-like storms that pop up with no warning. If you are riding, your horse will run away. Most who enter never return."

"Sounds supernatural."

"Tis indeed." Gjallimé slapped the rump of the Domo and hopped off the fence. "Come." He said solemnly. "Let us help build the funeral pyres." Then with a grin. "Put your strength to good use."

Julian grimaced. "Do I need to?"

"I cannot force you. But it will help the perception of you as part of the Nova'h force."

"Oh. Okay." Julian conceded, and followed Gjallimé to the northwest corner of the glade. The forest was barely a few trees deep in this direction. They walked through, emerging onto a vast plain of tall golden-brown grasses.

Gjallimé pointed to the plain and said, "The grasses are Kem'nesh. Your hair is that color. Why do you wear it that way?"

"What do you mean?" Julian asked.

"Well, your hair is long and flowing like the scholars, the Halili. But then on one side it is cut short like the body of the manticore. Allies of Nova'h, Bespoken by the green and white moons."

As Julian wondered what the manticore looked like, a nymph approached. She was not much taller than he, fair, and with bold splashes of color; aquamarine wings, hunter-green skin, and soft brown hair. Her eyebrows and lips were cornflower blue. Her gaze upon him twinkled, but as she was about to pass on his left a metallic glint appeared in her hand. Her arm swung toward his neck and Julian saw the knife. *What the...*

He ducked to his right knocking Gjallimé off his feet. The nymph spun like a dervish. Julian didn't have time to be afraid. The attacker followed up her slashing motion with a backward stab. Julian reached for her knife arm, but her stab was a feint. He failed to grab her arm, only managing to knock it off course. The knife scraped his hip leaving a rip in his pants and a line of blood.

Then she was upon him, catching him off balance. As he fell to the ground, the air deserted his lungs with an *uhffff*. He finally secured her wrist keeping the blade away from his body. A scowl twisted her face. His left hand grasped her waist. Julian was too quick and too strong for the now spitting nymph. Gjallimé was up, reaching for her knife hand. Julian and the nymph rolled over and over, becoming a tangled mess. The nymph switched the dagger to her free right hand. They rolled up on her right arm and the knife sunk deep into her gut. The nymph's breath escaped with a guttural shriek.

Chapter 5
Killed by Bare Hands

Gjallimé gasped. "J'liánh, are you all right?"

Julian looked at the superficial wound on his hip and nodded, not quite ready to speak. He pulled himself to his feet and looked down on the unconscious body. The nymph's knife stuck in her stomach as she lay in a growing pool of sea-green blood.

"S'rrinha! Here!" Someone shouted in the crowd that started to form.

Gjallimé stared in disbelief. "This is impossible."

Making her way through the crowd that encircled the scene, S'rrinha's authority showed in her square shoulders, straight back, piercing gaze, and head held high. She was Eptizar, sorcerer, the wielder of power for the nymphs. Earlier that day, on Naspia Dor, she was just princess S'rrinha, but Yetzer-Xie had killed her mother. Now she was also Queen.

The assassination attempt she had ordered failed. S'rrinha fought hard not to reveal her disappointment. *Perhaps his appearance here on Edrym had nothing to do with mother's death.*

She held an ankh made of bone and did not ask what happened, but rather knelt down by the attacker holding the ankh to her own breast. The whispers in the crowd grew silent. S'rrinha closed her eyes and placed her other hand on the shoulder of the nymph lying in a growing pool of blood. She did not speak, but concentrated and tried to invoke the power of healing. The body under her fingers grew colder. Weeqq, the green moon, was but a sliver in the sky. The wound was too deep and the nymph aggressor had gone into shock. S'rrinha could not draw enough power.

"Mneri is dead," S'rrinha announced grimly. "What happened here?"

Julian could not exercise his vocal cords, so Gjallimé described the events. Two witnesses added their observations, confirming Gjallimé's telling. Aemiluria arrived in time to hear the accounting of Julian's speed and strength.

S'rrinha stood, turned, and put her hand on Julian's injured hip. The warmth of her touch surprised him but he stood frozen. Her gaze shifted to his eyes; they probed his soul. He shivered. The bleeding stopped.

She released him. *This Julian has special abilities. What shall I do with him?* "You will heal rapidly now." And S'rrinha moved through the crowd and back to the forest.

I have killed with my bare hands. It mattered not to Julian that it was in self-defense and an accident. His head spun and nausea consumed him. He sank to his knees, put his hands flat on the ground, and rested his head upon them. *I should be home. Why am I here? None of this would have happened.* Tears streaked down his face as he turned to Aemiluria. "Why?"

Aemiluria leaned down and looked at Julian with gentle eyes. "I do not know for sure. Some believe that your arrival is a bad omen. That you brought about the ambush on Naspia Dor." Aemiluria stood tall and put her arms out in the air, palms open, fingers spread wide.

"Harken. I have spoken with Iniqui and Hjerim who have spent time close to J'liánh. They sense no Yetzer-Xie in him. Some of you may not know that J'liánh was found at the Tree of Ages. This also attests that he bears no favor from Yetzer-Xie. I believe his appearance pulled me away from the ambush. I believe he bears favor from Nova'h, that he was brought to Edrym for a purpose. We shall travel to Sayll and council with N'ttala-Toor. I have spoken. Let all those who harbor doubt come forward."

And no one did.

+++

Aemiluria pulled Julian aside and told him they would hold a Truth Council to understand this attempt on his life. "J'liánh. Princess Iniqui and Prince Corwin will join myself, Ken Noru, Eptizar of the Hassjidar, and S'rrinha—"

"S'rrinha, who tried to save Mneri, after the attack?"

"Yes, she is Eptizar, and now Queen, of the nymphs. We will convene to discern the meaning behind the attempt on your life. Discussion of the paths you could take will be of paramount importance."

Paths? Other than getting me home? "What are Sayll and N'ttala-Toor?"

Patience and reassurance described Aemiluria's gaze and tone of voice. "I shall explain everything to you, after the Truth Council."

"When?"

"In the morning. After you have some sleep." Her eyes tightened. "I have heard the account of your coming to Edrym. Do you have anything to add?"

"Iniqui told you the details of my acquiring and using the book?"

"Yes."

Julian stared blankly. "Then no. Nothing."

+++

Gjallimé took a stunned, lethargic Julian to help prepare the last of the funeral pyres. S'rrinha appeared briefly as they lit the pyre for her mother. A peek of wild anger snuck through her counterfeit deadpan countenance. The glow of the fires seemed out of place with the sun in the sky. Visible were the black moon, and the green, white and silver. Julian did not know what that meant and did not ask. The smell was more than that of burning wood. A pungent stench penetrated his psyche and cramped his stomach. It was a smell Julian would never forget.

+++

37

Julian did not sleep well and the nausea followed him as he came to his feet. Last night's violence, last night's death, differed from the ambush. It did not seem like a video game at all. His body still shuddered with intermittent spasms. *The question is, what am I going to do about it?* He could not come up with an answer. Gjallimé, Iniqui, and S'rrinha might be his age but they grew up with real bloodshed, real suffering, real death. Head hung low; his shoulders slumped. *The High King Eswar cannot fix this.* He had been wrong to put all his confidence in Eswar, wrong to put all of his confidence in Aemiluria's promise.

Last night he was numb and did not speak up. This morning he wished differently. *I should've screamed. I should've insisted. I know my path. I gotta get the hell outa here. My path is for you to send me home!*

+++

Julian sulked in Gjallimé's tent, thinking back on the night, when he heard countless footfalls and the cacophony of many people. He threw back the tent flap. The source of the commotion was a crowd of Khalil, Hassjidar, and nymphs, all with their backs to him, not far from the tent. Julian heard gasps of bewilderment and wonder. The crowd peeled apart, half to each side, still agog, and he saw why they gathered.

The equine eyes caught him first, and they were the same steely-blue as his own. The intelligent eyes looked purposely into his, as the steed finished its walk four paces from where he stood. A horse unlike Julian had ever seen. His mane and tail were the purple of the moon, Z'th. Purple against a striking coat of ink-black gleaming in the ever-present sun. And the hooves were as silver metal. But more than anything else that made Julian gasp was the fiery dance of the mohawk mane and ragged tail. Purple flames flared out of the top of his hooves as well. The animal reminded him of the legendary Nightmare from his role-playing

38

games. Except for the purple. Julian felt only pride and honor from this stallion which he decided to call a nightsteed.

Gjallimé sprang from the crowd. "J'liánh! Is he not magnificent? When he passed by the other horses they bowed. I tell you; they dipped their heads to the ground! And he walked straight to *you*!"

Xorn, the Khalil priest emerged from the crowd. He watched as Julian approached, placing his hand flat beneath the animal's muzzle letting the steed lower his mouth to rub against his hand, breathing warm, moist air from his nostrils.

These purple flames aren't hot. Julian took a step closer and the nightsteed nestled his head against his shoulder. He patted and rubbed the magnificent black neck. Julian felt a bond unlike anything he ever experienced with an animal.

"Is he mine?"

Xorn answered, "He is as much yours as you are his. This is no ordinary wild steed of the plain. He has not spent his life under the skies of Edrym. His birthplace is beyond the purple moon. He has come here for a time to be your companion."

From out of the crowd, "A name! A name! He must have a name!"

Xorn walked up and put his hand on the nightsteed's nose but he looked at Julian. "His name is Dor'ossoss." The crowd jabbered. Xorn held his hands up. He gazed up at the sky. "Dor'ossoss. Dor'ossoss, The Guardian. Because he will help J'liánh stay on the one true path."

Chapter 6
A Warrior Begins

Julian helped break camp as Aemiluria approached.

She asked, "J'liánh, what are your thoughts about Dor'ossoss?"

He hesitated, then spoke the truth. "It feels as if he is a part of me. I don't understand it." *He makes me feel special, important.*

Nodding her head Aemiluria continued. "J'liánh, the Truth council lasted through the night. I cannot reveal all. However, we feel strongly that your arrival helped save my life. I have come here to offer you a choice."

Send me home.

"If you choose, we will put together a security force to take you directly to W'lkyndh, the Hold of the high elves, where the scholars will translate the book so that you may return directly to your world. The journey may be perilous because Ravoq-Ma, the time of the Yetzer-Xie moons, will manifest itself during your travel."

Three days if I remember Gjallimé. I can't make it home before my parents. Shit.

Your guards will hold vigil in the forest, Ad-Nykal, during this period for protection."

"What's my other choice?"

"We travel to Sayll, the Hold of the Nymphs, for S'rrinha and her people must go home now that the battle on Naspia Dor is over. We will reach Sayll before Ravoq-Ma is upon us. Accompany us and meet with the soothsayer, N'ttala-Toor. He will help you understand why you are here. And we shall deal with Ravoq-Ma behind the walls of the Hold."

"I don't believe in soothsayers."

Aemiluria tilted her head and gave Julian a soft smile. "J'liánh. It will take some time, some period of adjustment, for you to get used to the ways of Edrym. I know it is vastly different from your world. Have not your eyes already beheld wonders which you would never have believed?"

Can't deny that. He nodded.

"N'ttala-Toor will earn your trust."

Julian paced back and forth. "And what happens after meeting with your soothsayer?"

"That will be up to you."

"How long a delay for my return to E'rth?"

"The trip to Sayll will add two days. But you will be much safer in Sayll during Ravoq-Ma. The presence of Dor'ossoss already speaks of a purpose for your coming to Edrym. I will not mince words; I am eager to find out what N'ttala-Toor will uncover."

I'm so lost. What can help me make this choice?

"I'd like to talk to Gjallimé."

"Make it quick. The Hassjidar head west toward their Hold, Methedriel. Gjallimé will travel ahead in his role as Rider, to spread word of your decision and the events since your arrival."

+++

Julian found Gjallimé grooming his Domo. "I'm told that you'll be riding to Methedriel with my decision."

"What did the council say?"

Julian explained as best he could. "How do I know what to do? What would *you* do?"

Gjallimé stopped his grooming. "What is meant to be will always find a way."

"Oh. You're a big help." And he poked Gjallimé in the ribs. Gjallimé feigned a punch back. In spite of the seriousness of the moment, they grinned at each other and continued the mock fight until laughter consumed them.

42

Dor'ossoss found his way up to Julian. He took hold of the stallion's head and looked him in the eye. "If only you could tell me."

Dor'ossoss stared back.

"Gjallimé, what do you think of the nymph soothsayer?"

"N'ttala-Toor's wisdom is legend."

Julian paused. *These people believe I'm here for a purpose. It's only a two-day delay. I can't get back before my parents get home either way. They'll worry about me... but I want to know what this is all about. I seem to be special here in this crazy cool place. It's exciting. I need to know more.* Julian did not want to think about being homesick. He did not want to think about whether or not he was concerned with Ravoq-Ma. *I am the cat that walks by himself and all places are alike to me...*

He made up his mind. "I will go to Sayll. I will meet with N'ttala-Toor."

The cries of "K'rai!" and "Shyro!" erupted once again, this time from the far side of the field outside the forest. Julian and Gjallimé sprinted toward the noise. It appeared that Yetzer-Xie forces had launched a small assault on the very edge of the camp site, in the tall, golden grasses. They had already departed. The attack left the bloodied dead bodies of four nymphs, one smaller than Julian. A dead wraith was among the bodies, impaled through the chest, its sticky insides spilled along the Kem'nesh, smelling of rotten eggs. *At least they got one.*

Gjallimé's eyes grew wide, and he pointed skyward. "Look! The red, black, and yellow moons are in the sky. Only the white moon, half setting, keeps it from being Ravoq-Ma. Why were we not prepared?"

Xorn was among those who responded quickly to the battle cries. He took out the Chart of the Moons and looked within. "This moment was brief. Look, I'rnh Alon rises." And the silver moon could be seen as a sliver above the horizon. "Yetzer-Xie has never attacked with their powers so briefly in the sky. And in conflict with one of Nova'h's moons. This is something new."

S'rrinha arrived and surveyed the scene. She looked up defiantly. "When is Xrarreth?"

Xorn checked. "Xrarreth occurs in four days with the setting of Ihl, the black moon."

Gjallimé leaned in and whispered to Julian. "When the moons of Nova'h, the white, green, and blue, and the silver moon of the Khalil are the only moons in the sky it is called Xrarreth. In four days, this combination will present itself."

S'rrinha held up the talisman of Mitha which provided the enchantment of *Speed*. The crowd grew hushed. "I say the time has come to change our tradition. I say that it is time to take full advantage of Xrarreth and *attack*." S'rrinha knew this group of onlookers could not change the code of the forces of Nova'h. That would take the High King and sorcerers, the Eptizars.

With raised eyebrows Julian mused. *I guess she's wants to fight back.*

"If you are in favor of taking the fight to Yetzer-Xie then tell your Eptizars. Now, attend to the dead and get back to work breaking camp."

The Earth teenager and Gjallimé headed toward the Domos. It was time for Gjallimé to gallop to Methedriel in his capacity as Rider.

Julian asked, "What's S'rrinha talking about?"

"Nova'h defends." Gjallimé answered. "Nova'h defends the Seal on Naspia Dor when required, and defends the Holds and citizens of Nova'h at all times. Nova'h does not take the fight to the forces of Yetzer-Xie, even when the moons favor them. During Xrarreth the people of Nova'h reinforce the Holds, strengthen the enchantments, and hold their festivals."

"I don't understand."

"S'rrinha is upset with the death of her mother on Naspia Dor. However, to act like Yetzer-Xie, is to become as Yetzer-Xie." Gjallimé paused to let that thought sink in. "Mneri's attack on you last night was baffling. Was she acting by herself, in defense of Nova'h, misguided as that may be? Or was she acting on behalf of S'rrinha? King Eswar will confront S'rrinha and have an answer."

They reached the pen of animals. "I can dally no longer. Ask Iniqui. I must ride." He put his hand on Julian's shoulder. "May N'ttala-Toor grant you good tidings. I will see you again. Godspeed." Gjallimé mounted, took the reins of his Domo, and rode away.

"Godspeed." Julian said as he waved after him. He was glad the words escaped his heart. He really did wish Gjallimé a safe Ride, realizing he knew nothing of the dangers that would present themselves to a Rider. Julian would miss his blue companion.

+++

The nymphs and the Khalil formed a long procession on their way to the nymph Hold, Sayll. The multitude of steeds without riders reminded Julian of the funeral pyres. *To act as Yetzer-Xie is to become as Yetzer-Xie. S'rrinha may go down that path.* He forced himself not to think of the grim aspects of this world and concentrated on Iniqui as she rode toward him on a unicorn, an animal nowhere near as remarkable nor as powerful as Dor'ossoss. Julian bent forward and stroked his nightsteed's neck as Iniqui pulled alongside. The purple flames of his unruly mane were cool to the touch. Riding the steed felt natural, as if he had been riding all his life. And the stallion somehow made Julian feel welcome in Edrym.

Iniqui said. "J'liánh, I will ride with you."

"Don't do me any favors. I'm fine by myself." Julian nudged Dor'ossoss ahead a few paces. *I am the cat that walks by himself and all places are alike to me.*

Iniqui caught up. "I apologize." She flashed Julian a small smile. "Truce. I have been distraught about the attempt on my mother's life. I do not mean to let it cloud my mood. I should thank you for drawing her away from enemy fire on Naspia Dor." Iniqui's countenance softened. Gone was the stiff, haughty way she normally carried herself.

"Okay." Julian could not help but notice the smile made Iniqui rather pretty. "I'm blown away by your world. We got off on the wrong foot. Truce it is."

Iniqui looked at Dor'ossoss with awe and admiration. The nightsteed was a full hand taller than her own mount and moved with exquisite grace. "Dor'ossoss is truly regal. Idrazel, my own unicorn, does not match the power he exudes. And I have never seen the color of Ava'cynh on any beast."

"I gather the color of Ava'cynh is purple."

"Yes. His purple mane and tail. And coming from the tops of his hooves. Like the moon Z'th, they represent unparalleled power."

Julian's brows tightened. "Unparalleled power?"

"The lavender moon does not favor Nova'h. Nor does it favor Yetzer-Xie. All of the inhabitants of Edrym gain power from Z'th. Each individual gains a unique, distinctive *Enhancement*. It is said to reflect their true heart, their true nature."

"So, when the purple moon is in the sky, all are imbued with power?"

"Yes. Each uniquely, but in a small way. So it has been since the time of Tamiel, since the last time the full power of Z'th has been harnessed with The-Key-that-is-Lost. It is the most powerful talisman in all of Edrym. Or it was, until it was lost. Perhaps Dor'ossoss can tap into the power of Z'th."

"How will I notice this?"

"The next time Z'th is in the sky, play close attention to Dor'ossoss. He will let you know."

"And what of the silver moon? I understand it, too, does not take sides between Nova'h and Yetzer-Xie." Julian relaxed in Iniqui's presence for the first time.

"True. Only the minor moons take sides. Both Nova'h and Yetzer-Xie forces find their innate abilities enhanced by the silver moon. However, Yetzer-Xie lacks a talisman to amplify this. We Khalil take our power from I'rnh Alon, the silver moon, and have the scepter of *Enhance*. We were once neutral, but we sided with Nova'h shortly after the time of Tamiel."

"And what power does the scepter give the Khalil?"

"It is a small power, but we can *Enhance* the enchantments from other moons of Nova'h."

"So Aemiluria was doing this during the ambush on Naspia Dor?"

"Yes. Because the silver moon was in the sky, she exercised the enchantment *Enhance* using the scepter. S'rrinha called upon the power of *Speed*, and Ken Noru invoked the power of *Quash*, both from the energy of the blue moon. My mother made them stronger."

"I saw the power of *Speed* in the rapid motions of a blue soldier in the fight. What is *Quash*?"

"*Quash* is very powerful because it counters *any* of the Yetzer-Xie enchantments. Vr'dan, the Eptizar of the liches, was down the hill, nearby. She put the power of *Fear* into our troops, derived from Gobanh', the yellow moon. The power of *Quash* countered it. Otherwise, many more would have fled." Iniqui found she hadn't the courage to add that her mother could have died without it.

+++

Julian learned from Iniqui the yellow moon could invoke the power *Weakness* as well as *Fear*. However, each Eptizar could only use one talisman and harness one power at a time. Beginning to get his bearings, he paid closer attention to the world around him, instead of being so focused on himself. The black moon, he noted, was by far the fastest, spending only six or seven hours in the sky. It looked to be a little larger than the Earth moon. Julian remembered the black moon conferred the power of *Death*. Lucky for Nova'h, no Yetzer-Xie possessed the talisman for *Death*. The other power of the black moon was *Infect*. During the recent eclipses of the Waykenim battle on Naspia Dor, the black moon was not present, so the warriors descended the path with wounds, but not illness. He couldn't remember the rest. Iniqui rode ahead to speak with her mother, leaving him alone with his thoughts. *How am I supposed to remember all of this?*

Julian's mind wandered back to Earth, before this strange adventure. There was something unnatural about the way the book came into his possession. Aemiluria said he was *brought* to Edrym. *By whom? How? Why?*

The events of the skateboard park back on Earth, the day he fell into Edrym, broke into his memory like a burglar on a heist. He was alone that morning, carving, grabbing air, both frontside and backside. Sometimes throwing in a lip grind. He would crossbone one pass then throw an ollie to a fakie. Every so often he threw in his hardest trick, a backside 360. The long side of his hair would fly wildly and he would shake his head to keep it out of his eyes. No one else in school sported Julian's unorthodox hairstyle. He was a loner in looks as well as attitude.

Two of the bullies from school showed up. *Time to have some fun.* Julian knew the unwritten rules of skateboard etiquette. Pausing at the top of the wall, he took off on paths that would interrupt their strongest, fastest carves. Staying within the rules, he timed things perfectly so as not to interfere. He would, just barely, put in jeopardy the path to their best runs. He did this as often as he could, taking pleasure in his craftiness. It reduced his ability to get his own best runs in, but that was a small price to pay. Whenever they looked ready to start things with him, even though they knew better, he would back off for a while.

This game continued for a spell. Then, while waiting at the top of a wall, he noticed the full moon hanging directly over a church steeple. A planet, probably Jupiter, floated visible in the daylight sky just to the side of the moon. If not for the moon, he would never have seen the planet. *A planet in the daylight sky...* Julian lost interest in his little game, in skateboarding altogether. *This is something important...I just can't put my finger on it...* He had then abandoned the park for home. Home to the book. Home to the portal.

Julian snapped back to the present, to the change in rhythmic motion of his stallion's stride. They were stopping. He had lost track of time. The steady sun hanging in the sky gave him no clue. *Have I made the right choice?* Dor'ossoss gave no protest to their trek to Sayll, so maybe this was the right path. Of all that was bizarre and quixotic about Edrym, the nightsteed seemed the most real to him. If he trusted anything, he trusted Dor'ossoss.

The cobalt sky left Julian somber. The silver moon, I'rnh Alon, loomed spectacular, more than three times the size of the Earth's, giving the impression of a giant lagoon of liquid mercury carved out of a velvet cobalt canvas. On the opposite side of the sky Weeqq glowed, a green lantern partially hidden by trees. High in the sky, Klaiwohaya, the white moon reminded Julian of Earth but did nothing to shatter the aura that he was a stranger in a strange land.

Iniqui came next to him. "We are going to stop. The warriors will train. Come."

The Khalil and nymphs paired up and fenced with wooden swords. Iniqui sparred with a nymph. A tall, intense Khalil man came over and handed Julian a wooden longsword with the handle whittled down to fit his hand.

Julian protested. "But I'm not a warrior."

The Khalil man looked at him gravely, "Failure to prepare, is preparing to fail. My name is Jr'esh and I am swordmaster. Come, I will start with the basics."

I can refuse. But I don't want to. What am I doing? He couldn't answer this with any clarity. *Training could be fun. Better than all this riding. It's like living one of my medieval war games. What the hell.*

Attack, parry, cross-step, lunge, retreat, flick, block. And again.

Julian's balance and coordination impressed Jr'esh.

It takes balance and coordination, and a bit of daring, to throw a backside 360. Staying firmly on his feet continued to be his major problem. When he floated, he could not move as quickly nor strike with power. The adrenaline of the fight countered whatever unconscious ability he used to walk normally, without a bounce in his step. In combat he must concentrate not to push vertically against the ground.

Jr'esh said. "Being of the left hand may prove beneficial…once you are accomplished with arms. Very few on Edrym are thus, so you will present a unique challenge."

The procession stopped once more for training before they camped for the night. Jr'esh paired Julian with a young adult Khalil, Rafnh. He instantly recognized the look on Rafnh's face. *What is so special about you?* He had seen that look often in school. Julian called upon all of his strength and swiftness. Even with poor technique he knocked Rafnh hard to the ground. Repeatedly. *Hah! Take that you piece of crap.* Jr'esh stepped in and resumed his lessons. Julian did not miss Rafnh's look of disgust as he walked away.

The members of the group who were not combatants attended to the horses, distributed food and drink, and performed other necessary tasks. Their noise added to the grunts and banging of wood from the sparring. No one really rested much.

The purple moon rose after the second training session, and Julian did not need to look for a change in Dor'ossoss. The nightsteed's body pulsed with electricity. He pawed at the ground and shook his great head. As if he expected something. Julian feared the animal was waiting for some kind of signal, or worse, perhaps the signal needed to come from him. The power in Dor'ossoss made Julian apprehensive to learn the what and the how. *I'll ask Iniqui.* And with this thought, as if by magic, the steed settled down. Julian placed his hand on Dor'ossoss's neck. He could still sense the power.

The camp was a simple affair. After a satisfying meal of unknown meat, bread, and what Julian would call vegetables, all tasty, he was invited to sleep in Jr'esh's tent. He thought of his mother and father as he drifted off to sleep. *If only they could see me now.*

Julian awoke during the night, still uneasy, trying to make sense of it all. *When will I get home? Why am I going along with all this? True, it is magical. It's intense and dope! And I'm treated as someone almost supernatural.*

It was too bright for sleeping, even inside the tent. *Of course. The sun is still hanging there in the sky. In roughly the same position, on the right. We must be traveling north.* He arose, went by provisions to get a treat for his steed, and made his way to Dor'ossoss.

"How ya doin' fella?" Julian asked as he stroked the nightsteed's nose. "You don't truly belong here either." He took pleasure in believing the stallion was there only for him. The feeling came easily as it stoked his ego. Reaching into the sack from provisions, he broke what was akin to an Earth carrot into chunks. Dor'ossoss obliged and Julian felt the animal's warm breath from his nostrils and the rough whiskers of his mouth as he happily gobbled up the treat. Dor'ossoss shook his head up and down for more. Julian had developed a closeness with the extraordinary animal that made him feel safe.

Julian practically jumped when S'rrinha appeared at his side. Her voice was not hard and commanding as he heard earlier. "So, I am not the only one who could not sleep." Her eyes were as green as emeralds.

Julian's mouth did not work right away and S'rrinha's unicorn ambled up beside Dor'ossoss. Before he could get any words out, S'rrinha asked if he could spare some carrots for her unicorn, Sh'rrikh.

"Of course," Julian composed himself and gave her a couple.

Embraced by an easy wind, S'rrinha fed her unicorn. "I wanted to apologize personally for Mneri's attack. From what we could discern, she did not know you were found at the Tree of Ages. She must have thought you were a threat." Her emerald eyes said I'm sorry.

Julian answered. "There's confusion about my role in the ambush. Heck, I don't know if I even had a role. Totally. I didn't intend to have a role. I came here by accident."

S'rrinha's voice remained soft. "That remains to be seen." She took her next carrot chunk and held her open palm near Dor'ossoss's muzzle. Her hand touched Julian's and her eyes asked the question. He nodded and let S'rrinha feed the nightsteed. But that barest touch, along with her husky voice and sultry gaze made him uncomfortable and somewhat light-headed. Julian found himself staring at her mouth and pulled his eyes away.

She turned to face him directly. "He is a glorious animal." She paused briefly. "I will leave you alone with him now." Julian caught a small smirk on her lips as she turned to walk away. As if she had accomplished something.

+++

During the second day a combat game, Nevinrynh, replaced training. Jr'esh said, "Come J'liánh. Today we learn other aspects of battle."

"Like what?"

"Teamwork, strategy, scouting, taking the right angle to intercept, and leadership to name a few." And Jr'esh took Julian to a nymph. "Fenianh, this is J'liánh. He plays his first game today." Fenianh nodded, and Jr'esh hastened away.

Fenianh gestured for Julian to come closer. "Today we defend the silver banner. We target the green and blue banners. All banners are a mile away from each other, forming an equilateral triangle." And he put a silver headband on Julian's head.

Nevinrynh reminded Julian of Capture the Flag, with three teams. Fenianh told Julian that each of the three groups would consist of a team of twenty-one players, each wearing a colored headband. Today they played on foot, in a plain of tall Kem'nesh. The grass enabled the players to remain hidden in a crouch. Participants became visible while fighting or running.

Julian asked. "How do we win?"

"By protecting the last banner that remains safe. I'm putting you with the right advance defensive group. Three of you will hide about a third of the distance to the green banner."

Julian wanted to be in the offense, but this was his first time and he must learn. "What do we do?"

"Scout for attacking troops, and engage as the first level of defense." And Fenianh introduced Julian to an adult female Khalil. "Mb'ntth shall serve as your lieutenant," he said. Then he turned and walked toward another group with silver headbands.

"So, you are J'liánh, the being from a different world."

"Umm, when does the game start?"

"Nevinrynh is much more than a game, it is training, and individuals retain their score which is recognized as achievement. It is told that you are fast and strong, that Jr'esh himself has trouble challenging you while coaching your swordplay."

I'm good!

Julian heard a woeful horn.

"Ah… the game begins. Follow me."

Julian took his wooden claymore and shield and fell in behind Mb'ntth along with another Khalil warrior. They proceeded a third of a mile along the right side of the imaginary triangle defined by the placement of the three flags and hunkered down, watching. Eventually some forms emerged far to the left and forward. Muffled sounds of conflict reached them. The combatants fought too far from Julian's group to discern who was fighting. Regardless, it was not their responsibility. Time passed. *This is boring.*

Two soldiers with blue headbands popped up at what appeared to be the center of the battlefield, jogging toward the silver corner. *They attack our flag!*

Adrenaline raced through Julian. "With my speed I can reach them before they advance much further!" He was already running as he uttered these words.

"Halt!" This from Mb'ntth. "They are not our responsibility."

Julian was calculating an angle to intercept the attackers. "I can handle this by myself!" And off he went.

His intercept path was too direct, so he adjusted during his sprint. Now, he was upon them, wooden sword slashing. The first blue banded soldier was touched and fell to the ground, followed swiftly by his partner. Julian raised his claymore in triumph, turning to see his group overwhelmed by four more blue bands. "I'm coming!" He shouted.

Out of position, even Julian's speed failed to allow him to join the fighting at his silver flag, now being attacked from two sides. Minutes before he reached his unit, the enemy shouted. "Shyro!"

Fenianh stood up and brushed himself off as Mb'ntth approached. Both glared at Julian.

Fenianh barked, "You abandoned your position."

"I took out two—"

"We lost. Your assigned position was overrun without your presence in the group."

"I—"

"This is a team game."

Mb'ntth added, "I wouldn't want you on my team."

As shame swept Julian, his entire unit turned their backs to him and walked away.

Oh crap. And he stood alone.

At the gathering after the game, he continued to be ostracized. Gjallimé returned, finally found him, and explained how Nova'h works as a whole when fighting. Slapping him on the back, Gjallimé expounded with his usual glee, "Now you know."

Do I? Will I? I am the cat...

"Come let's eat."

During subsequent games Julian took no singular action. The other warriors accepted this apology.

+++

When not playing Nevinrynh or training, Iniqui often rode with Julian. She found she enjoyed his company, even though she got impatient with all of his questions. Iniqui wondered why she had dismissed him on their first meeting. On the fourth bout of training, Jr'esh pitted her against the teenager from Earth.

"En Guarde!" Iniqui faced Julian with two wooden short swords held at her shoulders, tips pointing forward. "And now you die!" She lunged with her right blade while using the other to keep Julian's wooden longsword to the side

Her words stunned him. Only his quickness allowed him to leap back unscathed – his sword now free to put in middle guard.

Iniqui circled. "So. Accounts of your quickness are true." Even while speaking she launched a volley of diagonal attacks with the edge of each blade, moving relentlessly forward.

His mouth agape, he witnessed her dexterity and ferocity.

"Ha! You wilt."

Apparently, she used verbal insults to distract her opponent. *Or is she like this only with me?*

His training with Jr'esh had not advanced further than wielding a single sword. Although his longsword gave him a reach advantage, his left arm felt useless. Up to now, his quickness and strength provided him with enough benefit to defeat his training partners. He gathered himself and responded with a riposte.

Iniqui laughed. "Your technique is sloppy." He tried a feint followed by a slash. "And obvious." Iniqui had now gauged his quickness and used an empty fade to draw him forward where she parried his sword enough to land a powerful blow on his right arm. With steel she would've severed the limb. He conceded.

She chuckled. "I will not go so easy on you next time. When your skill matches your innate abilities, you will be most formidable."

Julian responded with a mock bow.

He soon put in a request with Jr'esh for a shield. Julian would later find out Iniqui was one of the best swordsmen in Edrym.

Chapter 7
Soothsayer

Sayll bustled. A small town of natural beauty, completely embedded in the forest, B'jnh. A double wall of fireproof-treated hardwood encircled the town using massive trees as structural support. A clear indication that the enemy must be kept out. Steel bands a foot-wide wrapped vertically around the walls to strengthen them at about twenty-yard intervals.

Some of the trees thinned out in the city proper, but the remaining ones acted as component parts of the structures. The shops, houses, and trade buildings were made of wood, with windows, doors, and other features trimmed in lively colors.

Looks can be deceiving. These are warrior nymphs. There are deadly weapons in those buildings. Nevertheless, Sayll enthralled Julian. The colorful, tightly packed structures lining the streets, many with a second story, gave him the impression that he was inside a honeycomb of square cells. The gentle buzz and sweet smell of the open market elicited the impression of a lively, peaceful community.

After a tasty meal and quick cleanup, the members of the Truth Council took Julian directly to the modest, but artfully adorned, central complex. It had the feel of a castle without the battlements. *This fantasy land becomes more fairy tale or medieval with every turn.*

The meeting with N'ttala-Toor was *not* to be delayed because of the coming of Ravoq-Ma. Julian was led to a small chamber. As they walked into the dark room, incense smell assailed him. His companions fell silent.

+++

N'ttala-Toor was not what Julian expected. The soothsayer was a young man, perhaps mid-twenties, taller than most of the nymphs, and astoundingly handsome or beautiful. It was hard to choose between the two. Like nymph males, he bore no wings, but nevertheless looked androgynous. Julian stared; mouth open. N'ttala-Toor glided up to him and put his hand on the teenager's shoulder. Julian expected some kind of a shock or something, but there was none.

N'ttala-Toor hesitated only briefly, "J'liánh, you come from a world with just one moon, of white, the size of our yellow moon. Your people are ignorant as to the power it confers." His eyes were looking directly at Julian, but they seemed lost, as if seeing nothing at all. "You are an ally of Nova'h, of that there can be no doubt. And you have another name, a powerful name. H'rol, the Creator." And there was a hushed murmur among the onlookers.

OMG! My middle name, Harold.

"You come with the book, Nchaud-Zel, from the time of Tamiel. The book brought you here to Edrym. It is not clear how you acquired it."

"I like got it at a store."

"No, not that. The book's appearance on your world, called E'rth, is a mystery."

"Is there like a prophecy or something that foretold of my coming?" Julian was thinking of the science fiction and fantasy he read.

"No. I did not see your coming and that in itself is strange." N'ttala-Toor put his hands at his sides, straightened, and the look in his eyes became clearer. "I may have a way of discovery." He motioned Julian to the back of the room where the scent of rosemary incense grew strong enough to make his eyes water. The soothsayer pointed at a small pedestal shaped table of jade streaked with veins of silver and gold. On the table were an abundance of small smooth stones and tiny wooden rods. The stones were lavender and the sticks were the coral of the oceans on his home world.

"J'liánh, grab what you can from the table. Cup them in both hands." Julian took as much as he could and shivered, he thought from the cold of the room.

"Now. Toss them there." N'ttala-Toor pointed at a depression in the floor, shaped like a half circle, a few feet away against the back wall. The semi-circle and the smooth alabaster wall behind it boasted many hues.

The room grew silent as Julian gently tossed the contents of his cupped hands into the depression. To his amazement, they separated into six groups of six items each. Before he could ask how that happened, N'ttala-Toor nodded his head and spoke.

"There. The first group of six Adaa, rod-rod-rod-stone-rod-stone. **Conflict. Danger.**" He paused and Julian felt a small chill. "Next. **A Clustering. A Mass Gathering**. And there, stone-stone-stone-rod-rod-rod. **Greatness. A Hero.**" The fourth Adaa was **The Wanderer**. The fifth was **Youthful Folly**. The final Adaa evoked a gasp from the members of the Truth Council.

"Rod-stone-stone-rod-rod-rod. **Taming Great Power.**"

Julian clearly heard a whisper from Aemiluria, "The-Key-that-is-Lost". The words sounded a refrain throughout the group.

N'ttala-Toor raised his arms out horizontal from his body, hands open with palms up. Without turning around, he said, "Yes, The-Key-that-is-Lost, Kjobaaj."

Julian finally found his voice. "Wow. What does it all mean?"

N'ttala-Toor turned to Julian. His deep, smooth voice exuded wisdom and kindness. "The **Conflict** or **Danger** may have something to do with a **Mass Gathering**. Such as the double eclipse battles on Naspia Dor. You could have the makings of a **Hero** in that fight. Or perhaps you become a **Wanderer** with no tribe, or maybe that is what you already are. Even if you emerge from wandering, **Youthful Folly** could stand in your way from being a **Hero**. And most important, you may discover the missing piece of The-Key-that-is-Lost and wield the **Great Power** that has been missing.”

“These stones and rods foretell my future?” Julian asked with wide eyes and raised brow. He had already witnessed N’ttala-Toor knowing more than he possibly could about Earth and the means by which he found himself in Edrym, but he was still reeling with what the reading said. “Maybe I should toss them again.”

“No. H’rol only guides one toss – results in only one separation into Adaa. Did I tell you how many stones and rods to pick up? No. Six Adaa of six is a powerful sign in and of itself. Is this your destiny, laid out before you, as the moons in the sky? Not exactly. The Adaa reveal only likely possibilities. A path is uncovered. Some or all may come true. The **Hero** seems to be in conflict with **Youthful Folly**. Nevertheless, you may have it in you to **Tame Great Power** with The-Key-that-is-Lost. This is a most significant development here in Edrym.”

Julian protested, “But I gotta get back to Earth. I’ll be missed. It’ll cause quite a problem.” *My ass will be grass.*

“Edrym and your E’rth experience a time dilation. For every day you spend in Edrym, about one hour passes on your E’rth. You have been gone at most, four hours. Is that significant?”

Julian hesitated. *How much can I believe? If true I could stay here maybe two months. Three weeks or so is probably better.* He surprised himself by going along with it all. *N’ttala-Toor is freaking me out. But I find that I believe him.* “No, I won’t be missed for several days. Of my time.” Julian looked at Aemiluria, then at Iniqui. They believed. And they looked at him with great anticipation.

“What is this Key-that-is-Lost? What does it mean?”

“Kjobaaj has been lost since the time of Tamiel, the time of the book, Nchaud-Zel. The Key is by far the most powerful enchantment in Edrym. It is said to give the bearer the power of what is true in their heart, provided that he or she is imbued with the power of Ava’cynh. You were found wearing a tunic the color purple of Ava’cynh.” N’ttala-Toor directed his next question at the members of the truth council. "Has J'liánh demonstrated any such capacity?"

Julian interrupted. "Why is the power so important?"

"Ava'cynh confers the ability to use the true nature of one's heart multiplied a hundred times over with the Key."

The members of the Truth Council talked together in hushed voices. They turned to N'ttala-Toor.

S'rrinha spoke, "It is unclear. J'liánh's adept and ruthless response to the attempt on his life could have been influenced by Ava'cynh."

Julian exclaimed, "That was self-defense. How could that be related to Ava'cynh?"

N'ttala-Toor explained. "One's devotion to one's self would augment self-defense."

"The low gravity on Edrym has given me great strength and speed. And everybody's instinct for self-defense is natural!"

"That may be so. What else do you hold in your heart?"

"I...I don't know. The same as everyone else."

N'ttala-Toor just shook his head. "I see."

+++

Julian and Iniqui walked toward the eastern corner of Sayll. Julian was perplexed by the soothsayer's ritual, and sullen about N'ttala-Toor's comments. He tried to search his feelings for the answer to what he held in his heart. *I am the cat that walks by himself and all places are alike to me.* Maybe N'ttala-Toor was right and he was selfish.

Iniqui respected Julian's mood and walked in silence. She did not tell him where she was taking him.

"Iniqui, isn't self-defense an instinct? Why would it mean that I'm selfish?"

"Self-defense *is* natural. Ava'cynh could be working through that part of your character, however that does not necessarily define all of you."

61

"I chose to come to Sayll. I'm trying to find out why I'm in Edrym and what to do about it." *I have adopted the style of language here in Edrym. Adopted? I would never say that.* They passed nymph vendors in the street. "What do you think?"

Iniqui brushed her silver hair back from her face. "Sacrifice should be a noun in your vocabulary, and it should be a verb in your life."

Julian rolled his eyes, more annoyed than upset. "Great, more quotations. You all sound like my parents." He found Iniqui a difficult target for his animosity. "Well, what do you make of all those predictions about my fate?"

"Actions are the seeds of fate; deeds grow into destiny." Iniqui tried to deliver that deadpan, but couldn't hold back a wry grin.

Julian nudged her. "Oh, I see. You're giving me the business."

"Our fate hides among our free choices." They both broke out in belly laughter.

They were still chuckling and smiling when Iniqui stopped in front of a Smith's shop.

"Gjallimé sent a Rider ahead with specifications. The nymphs are not the masters of weaponry like the Hassjidar, but it is time that you have more than a wooden sword." With that, she led Julian inside.

A heavy-set, middle-aged female nymph greeted them. "Ah, you must be J'liánh. An honor to meet you. Here try these." She handed him what appeared to be a two- handed claymore, but shorter and less wide, made of blue steel, with a leather-wrapped grip.

Julian took the weapon in his left hand and brandished it in the air. "This is awesome. My hand fits perfectly." He politely did not mention that it seemed to him that the custom sword, so attractive in his hands, could possibly have been a little longer and heavier. Next, he was handed a massive shield, precisely matching the length from his chin to his knees. It was larger than Julian expected, but that would give him more protection. Its weight was well suited to Julian's strength.

Julian pranced about, vanquishing some invisible foe. "How did Gjallimé know my size?"

Iniqui smirked. "Well if you hadn't noticed, you two could be twins."

Smiling wide, Julian tilted his head. "Sure. If my skin were blue." The two broke into hysterics. The smith grinned, assuming this was some personal joke.

+++

Iniqui led Julian, sword and shield in hand, through the colorful streets of Sayll. He continued to play at fighting. He was showing off with motions that were lightning quick.

"J'liánh, your training is paying off; your technique has advanced well, though it is still a bit sloppy." Iniqui said this with all seriousness, but with a grin nonetheless.

Not acknowledging the insult, Julian queried, "Where are your weapons?"

"Hopefully we will not need them. We are to work in the field infirmary being put together in the town square."

Julian let his sword and shield fall slack at his sides, and his face went slack as well. "What? Well, I think I'm ready to fight." He did not want Iniqui to think of him as a coward.

"This is Ravoq-Ma and slicing flesh, human or beast, is not the same as slicing air."

"What will Ravoq-Ma be like? How long will it last?" The teenager was rethinking his bravado and wondered whether working at the infirmary might suit him well after all.

"A shitstorm will break loose. We will be at our weakest and they will be at their strongest. We fight to survive the two hours before the green moon rises. Ihl, the black moon, sets shortly thereafter."

"What will happen?"

"Only H'rol knows."

H'rol, the Creator. Julian flashed a thanks-for-nothing smirk.

As they walked through the streets Julian noticed the nymphs and Khalil were creating stockpiles of building materials and weapons at strategic intersections. There was one such cache in front of the infirmary when they arrived at the town square.

"Iniqui, are we manning the field infirmary because we're young?"

She turned and gave Julian a somber look. "Not in the least. Nymphs and Khalil a few years younger than we are will fight as needed. They are trained and eager to help allay the bloodshed they have witnessed all their lives. No, we will not be in the fighting because of your potential. The word of N'ttala-Toor is taken sedulously. As a matter of fact, The-Key-that-is-Lost, and your role, whatever that may be, is far too important."

"And you are assigned to look after me?"

"Not exactly." She blushed. "Of those qualified, I volunteered." And Iniqui went about familiarizing him with his duties.

She volunteered to be with me? A tingle rippled down his spine. *I like it. I like it a lot. But I'm not going to tell her that.*

+++

On the eve of Ravoq-Ma the first clouds Julian ever saw rolled in and drew the curtains of the night. *This is the first darkness I have seen, an eerie mask - but at least I should sleep well.* He walked alone to visit with Dor'ossoss. *Can you help me know what is right? Am I to be a hero at Ravoq-Ma? Or do I stay with Iniqui at the infirmary? Will I survive?* That thought was a surprising, hard slap in the face. *Death? How is it that I am caught up in this?* Dor'ossoss continued eating, providing no indication he was aware of Julian's musings.

As he strode toward the quarters he and Gjallimé would share, S'rrinha appeared silently at his shoulder. He looked into eyes that seemed to him a mixture of hard and sweet.

"N'ttala-Toor is not the only one of my kind with the gift of Sight. Ever since I became Eptizar, ghostly apparitions sneak into the eyes behind my eyes."

Julian halted and turned to face her.

"I see us fighting with valor, side-by-side. I see the Eptizar of *Infect* crumble to the ground. We look around and are alone. You gaze at me with victory splashed across your face and declare with strength: 'The best defense is a good offense'. Is that a saying from the wargames you play?"

"Yes, it's a strategy. How do you know about Gattica?"

"So, it is true."

"But doesn't *acting* as Yetzer-Xie, lead to *becoming* as Yetzer-Xie?"

"I see more. I see us laying with each other." And with a gleam in her eyes, she receded into the gloom, not giving him a chance to respond. She wanted to have Julian as an ally in her upcoming schemes. S'rrinha was sowing seeds.

The Earth teenager's mouth was agape, while his heart raced.

Chapter 8
Ravoq-Ma

Young nymphs took to the trees before the onset of Ravoq-Ma. They encircled Sayll, high in the treetops and waited. An observer west of Sayll saw them first. Liches and lava giants pouring in toward the Hold. The nymph signaled with a bird call. The signal was repeated making its way both to the Hold and to the other young nymphs in the trees. Many then made their way across the treetops to the area of the coming onslaught, while others remained on the lookout for another attack.

When a dozen nymphs were over the advancing horde, they took out their bows and rained arrows upon the forces of Yetzer-Xie. These weapons of Sayll were small and lightweight. Although their aim was true and their adversary barely ten yards beneath them, only a scant few of the thirty-some liches fell. An arrow to the eye slowed down one of the twenty-three lava giants. That was the extent of the damage.

The lava giants were almost eight feet tall, thick as small tree trunks, hairless, with a flat cranium and leathery skin the color of rust. Some of the creatures threw lava balls at a section of the outer wall. In spite of its fire-retardant treatment, the flames lapped along the wood and eventually the section of wall between the steel bands burned. Several more lava giants continued to assail the fire laden wood, each with a lava ball made from its own flesh. Others waited to use their one lava ball at the inner section. Liches brought forward a short battering ram to assault the fire weakened wall.

Inside the Hold, additional building material was rushed to the scene. During the fifteen minutes it took to get through the outer wall, The Khalil and nymphs reinforced the inner wall and quickly built a funnel of two nearly parallel walls abutting the steel bands, forming an alley narrowing inward.

The nymphs in the trees continued to take down as many of the enemy as they could. During the Yetzer-Xie assault, several of the nymphs began to feel nauseous and weak, some more than others. Pox erupted from their skin and several fell, only to be slain on the ground. The Khalil and nymphs working the building efforts were stricken as well.

"They are using *Infect*!" was the cry that sounded out among the forces of Nova'h.

+++

At the infirmary near the town square, Julian carried a makeshift stretcher bearing a moaning Khalil female who couldn't have been much older than he, to the area of fighters suffering from boils and fever. "What can be done?" He yelped at the nymph coming to tend the patient he had just brought in.

"Not much without the green moon in the sky. We try to keep their temperature down and give them lots of fluids."

"Why are there so many more ill Khalil than nymphs?"

The nymph nurse applied a cold compress to the infected Khalil's forehead. "We have *Heal* as our innate ability. Even without Weeqq it affords us some protection."

Julian didn't dally; he and his young nymph partner trotted back toward the skirmish with the empty stretcher for the third time. As he approached, he saw Nova'h soldiers in a half circle, two or three fighters deep enclosing the opening of the walls built to funnel the enemy toward them in single file. A lava giant rushed thru the opening, hacking downward with his black, iron battle axe. An audible crunch ensued as the blade cleaved and crushed a Khalil combatant's shoulder. The Nova'h warriors at each side of the opening slashed at the giant's ankles and thighs bringing him face down where Nova'h swords from those in front thrust into the monstrosity's head and back, killing it. The giant's initial blow severed the arm, killing the brave Khalil. Soldiers in the second line pulled both fallen bodies away from the funnel opening. These two were but the top of a heap of several fallen fighters. Bodies and body parts from both sides clogged the opening.

A pair of liches leapt onto to the pile, pushing forward, swords flashing. The Nova'h strategy of quick attacks from the relative safety of the edge of the walls was efficient, but keeping the path clear of the dead was perilous. The warriors pulling the bodies away were defenseless. Whenever the opening was obstructed, more liches would clamber on the shoulders of others and come over the top of the side walls.

The forces of Nova'h did not have sufficient numbers to engage the fiends effectively along this three-sided front. Smashing them as they emerged over the top was relatively easy, but some of the creatures scrambled over unscathed. Pockets of nymphs and Khalil, in groups of twos and threes, were engaging these on open ground inside the Hold.

Julian saw a lone Khalil soul being beaten back by a liche. A young nymph, she couldn't be more than eleven, snuck up behind the creature and plunged her short sword into its kidney. The liche bellowed with pain, arched and slashed backward with his sword. The young nymph ducked and missed being beheaded by a hair's width. The Khalil exchanging blows in front, seized the opportunity and gutted the creature.

The giants were not nimble enough to scale the walls. The few who failed to use their lava balls to breach the outer walls surrounding the Hold, lobbed the hot globs onto the Nova'h forces. Young fighters, maybe a dozen, hung back from the melee at the opening and rushed in throwing buckets of sand on the flames.

Infect took its toll. Khalil, and even nymphs, were weakened from the illness, compounding the burns and battle wounds causing injury and death. Reinforcements, directed by Aemiluria and S'rrinha, were barely keeping up with the onslaught.

"Find another partner!" Julian shouted at the Khalil youngster helping him with the stretcher. He took off as fast as he could toward the town square. His heart pumped with fury and his head spun, at the thought that occurred to him.

"J'liánh!" Iniqui called out with alarm as he grabbed his shield and sword from a pile of weapons close to where she was assisting triage at the field infirmary. "What are you doing?"

He deserted the infirmary, her mouth fell open as he sprinted back to the fight. He could do something the others could not. Putting down his sword, he pushed his way through the Nova'h beings at the very front of the funnel opening. Using his shield as a canopy he jerked the wounded, dead, and dying bodies from the pile out of the way with one hand. He was strong enough to pull even the lava giants this way. His other arm could withstand the beating of the steel upon the shield, but would the shield itself withstand the drubbing?

Julian crouched this way at the center of the storm enabling the swordsmen of Nova'h to dispatch the swarm that poured through the gap. He was vaguely aware of war cries, but they seemed in the far-off distance. At one point a sweltering heat engulfed him, the air scorched his throat and his left foot was awash with pain. He withdrew even more under his shield, grateful for its size. A shower of sand fell from the edges of his shield and more sand put out the fire burning his left boot.

For Julian, time stood still, lasting an eternity. Finally, he heard the cry, "Weeqq rises!" S'rrinha held high the ankh of bone and invoked *Heal* across the onslaught. The forces of Nova'h began to resist the pox giving them more strength.

Shortly after, "Ihl sets!" erupted with a cheer. Eventually the forces of Yetzer-Xie grew weaker and retreated, their swagger dissipating, their numbers no longer able to pressure the fighting men, women, boys, and girls defending Sayll.

The blows upon Julian's shield ended and the bodies ceased to appear before him. However, he remained crouched, still hypnotized, still waiting. A hand shook his shoulder and a husky voice declared, "J'liánh. It is over."

Julian looked around at the carnage and commotion in a daze. The scene before him hadn't registered yet.

Again, words broke through his self-imposed isolation, "J'liánh. Come quickly. She is calling for you." Stupefied, he followed the Khalil. When he saw Queen Aemiluria lying on the ground, body covered from neck to toe in a blanket, black splotches on her neck, Julian abruptly snapped back into the world.

"Come." Aemiluria's voice cracked. Her face twisted in pain, but her eyes were clear and commanding. "Sit by me." Julian sank cross-legged and his heart sank as well. "Come closer." And although speech was a struggle, her mouth was turned upward in a small but proud smile. He scooted up forward not far from her face. The black on her neck was like soot. Withholding a grimace, he certainly did not want to see what was under the blanket.

"You fought with valor."

"I didn't fight—"

"Hush. You were part of the battle." Her face stiffened again as she continued, "And your actions were selfless and crucial to saving lives."

Julian remembered how regal she had been coming around the bend on Naspia Dor. He remembered that she accepted him, defended him. And his eyes welled up. *This can't be happening.*

Aemiluria brought a burnt hand out from under the blanket and placed it upon Julian's knee. Her body heaved. Biting his lip, and gripped with sorrow, Julian did not know what to do. The Queen added, "Remember you arrived by the Tree of Life, you may well be under its protection. But do not let that make you careless."

Running footfalls marked Iniqui's arrival. She knelt and gently lowered herself upon the Queen's covered torso, her arms gripped her mother's shoulders, and she buried her face in the long, ruffled, silver hair strewn along the ground. She closed wet eyes and her faint voice whispered. "Mother."

The Queen turned her head towards her daughter and Julian observed blood oozing from her ear. "Let me see you." And Iniqui rose up to her knees to catch her mother's gaze, her face white and frozen in a state of shock. Her cheeks, lined with tears, which flowed salty on her lips. She sat back upon her legs.

Pain seized Aemiluria again, but her eyes never wavered. "Bless you my child." Her eyes looked back and forth between Julian and Iniqui. She spoke to both of them. "We are all connected. We are all bound to one another."

They both began to speak but the Queen's body pitched once again, and this time she squeezed her eyes tight. They opened again without fear, without panic, without pain. "Go to Eswar. You must discover what the Adaa you tossed with N'ttala-Toor foretell." Julian would later marvel at the strength of this woman.

Aemiluria brought out the silver scepter from under the blanket. An unconscious spasm passed through Iniqui as she saw it. Finally, with certainty, she knew what this meant. "Iniqui. You have the strength to wield this with great power." Aemiluria paused and peace washed over her face. "Take care of your father." She inhaled a labored breath and gazed at Julian. "Take care of each other." With that she went limp, eyes staring blankly up at the unfeeling sky.

Iniqui murmured. "Leave me alone with my mother."

+++

Julian walked aimlessly through the streets of Sayll. A lava ball had landed directly in Aemiluria's chest. Iniqui would become the new Khalil Eptizar. His body shivered; he could not believe she was gone. *This world is dangerous. This is crap.*

He passed a row of razed buildings, later learning that two liches made it into Sayll proper and did unspeakable things before being overpowered. *Horrible.* This was not the cheerful city he had been introduced to. Head down, Julian watched as his boots shuffled listlessly beneath him.

An agitated S'rrinha caught up to him. "J'liánh, a Rider has arrived with alarming news. In nine days, Enhendendor arrives! All the moons of Edrym will eclipse. The battle on Naspia Dor will include all the armies of Nova'h and Yetzer-Xie."

Julian stared blankly. He wanted no part of another fight.

72

“You will be a hero!”

He spat out. “How can you know?”

“I’ve heard of your strength and speed. In training, Jr’esh has never been so impressed. And the Adaa with N’ttala-Toor—”

He turned solemnly and walked away.

“I see you as more than you seem to be...” The words faded behind him.

Chapter 9
The Bejeweled Dagger

*What am I supposed to do now? I want to go see the scholars at W'lkyndh and find a way home. But as she died, Aemiluria asked me to go to the Hold of the Khalil, to meet with Eswar. And now, in nine days Enhendendor calls for a titanic battle on Naspia Dor to defend the Seal of Nova'h. I remember the Adaa I threw with the soothsayer N'ttala-Toor; one said **Mass Gathering** and another **Greatness**, a **Hero**. Is that my destiny; to be a hero at Enhendendor? It's true, I'm extra fast and strong. Could I be that special? Then again, the Adaa showed **Youthful Folly** and **Danger**. What does that mean? Does any of it mean anything all? This world is all too intense, there's too much pressure. I'm not sure I'm ready.*

Julian sat by himself on the steps of a curio shop in a far corner of Sayll. As he had walked the streets, the nymphs that passed him paused briefly and gave him a silent bow of their heads. He made no acknowledgement of the gestures, and did not stop to think how rude this was. With Aemiluria dead he wasn't sure he deserved any recognition for his actions.

He did the math. It was early Saturday night on Earth. *I should be reading at home. Alone.* A sudden wave of nausea came over him and he staggered to a side alley. He was racked with dry heaves, as still pictures, in black and white, flashed through his consciousness. Severed body parts and hacked torsos filled his vision as his body tried to expel the contents of his stomach. No color, no motion. Just picture following picture of the horrors of the fight. At least he didn't see the dead and dying faces, at least he didn't hear the anguished and frightened screams. Julian realized there was no relief coming. He gasped between the heaves that doubled him over on his knees. He wished he had eaten something earlier so he could truly vomit and maybe stop this agony.

A hand touched his shoulder. Terror gripped him as he imagined a liche who remained on the loose come to skewer him. He was ready and willing to give in to the fiend when he heard a melodic voice close to his ear.

"It will be all right." The voice soothed and comforted him. A voice he recognized as that of a nymph.

Julian's dry heaves finally subsided. A small cloth appeared below his face, he took it and wiped spittle dripping from his mouth. He turned his head and saw a deeply wrinkled nymph face with a prodigious nose and penetrating eyes.

"Come. Come inside. You look pale."

He was led through a curio shop to a small table in the rear. The elderly nymph sat him in a chair and draped a damp towel over his head. Thankful for the peace and quiet, Julian's mind became blank.

After some time, the towel was removed, a bowl of hot soup appeared on the table, and Julian was told to eat. The soup was extremely spicy with hints of mint and orange peels. When finished, he looked up expecting the old nymph to be sitting at the table across from him. He searched the emporium, only to find him dutifully dusting a glass case.

Dark, heavily grained wood shelves filled the shop. They occupied each of the five walls. Tens of free-standing open shelves stood throughout the store. There were musical instruments and masks, jewelry and wooden boxes, baubles and glass thingamajigs, paintings and many strange and beautiful objects Julian could not name. Three entire open shelves in the middle of the store were filled with items of bright primary colors that could only be toys. The prize collection, displayed at the front of the emporium, was a large variety of knives and swords of all types, some simple, others of dazzling artistry adorned with jewels.

He slowly walked and gawked. The elderly nymph glanced upward, but said nothing, returning to his cleaning. Julian was thankful for the nymph's behavior. At times he got tired of the stares, of which his odd haircut seemed to bring the most curious reaction, perhaps because it was something they could relate to. *Color of Kem'nesh, the tall golden grasses. Long like the Halili, except for one side buzz cut. Halili, the elf scholars that can get me home.* He was tired of the endless questions, many concerning his audience with the soothsayer, N'ttala-Toor.

Julian wandered around the shop, strangely afraid to touch anything. He came upon a small handsome dagger that held him spellbound. The dagger's grip bore unusual and ornate metalwork. And two blazing opals.

"Go ahead. Pick it up," said the elderly nymph who suddenly appeared behind him. "It is named Ilzjur. Forged in the Kholsnikh-Yal mountains by the Borgakh, bespoken to the black moon, at the time of Tamiel. Ilzjur goes through bone like butter. First made for the Earth Jarl, warrior king of the Borgakh, who no longer exist. It is weighted for throwing, and reportedly was used thusly in the assassination of Sigil, the Borgakh Eptizar, using poison upon its tip. Legend has it that it next fell into the hands of the Khalil during their bloody attacks on the banshee."

Julian turned Ilzjur over gingerly, testing its balance and admiring its beauty.

The old nymph continued. "Legend holds that the Khalil warrior who possessed it fell in love with a banshee. She took it from him and killed him, thus starting the shift of the Khalil from neutral to Nova'h. Later it was kept by St'lggar in the time of the Kings and he was the first to sleep with it at all times. Lore would have it that an unspoken pact is made between Ilzjur and whomever agrees to own it. But what that pact is, which side it favors, or with what consequences, is never known except to its owner. And so it passed from one to another, many of them prominent figures in the history of Edrym, to be used in nefarious ways, only to be lost at the same time that The Key, Kjobaaj, was lost. Ilzjur was recently returned by Kanh-apal-apli, who did not want to serve it."

"Who is Kah-apa…lapi?"

"He is known as the Wanderer, a Snow-Jarl, and the last of his kind since ages past."

Julian's heart skipped a beat when he heard the name, because he remembered **Wanderer** was one of the Adaa he threw with N'ttala-Toor. But he didn't say anything.

Instead, he asked, "What will you do with it?"

The nymph replied with a shrug, "For now I will display it. I do not know its future; of which it seems to write its own." With that said, the old nymph paused, then his somber face broke into an enormously wide, wrinkled grin. "Where are my manners? Welcome neighbor! I am R'qanar, proprietor of the grandest curio shop in all of Edrym!"

Caught off guard by this transformation Julian stared blankly.

"Can I interest you in one of these fine instruments of song and dance?" R'qanar picked up a long, thin wooden gizmo that became a large corkscrew for the final third of its length, and contained holes along the first half of the wood. He promptly put his mouth to the beveled end and as his fingers magically caressed the air holes, he played a sweet melody, a lively and happy contrast to the horror of Ravoq-Ma. A black cloud lifted from Julian's sentiment; such was the power of the tune.

Without a breath between, a brass horn found its way into R'qanar's hands and from it poured a soulful, exaggerated scale.

"My father plays. He's quite good. But alas, I do not."

"J'liánh, what is it that vexes you?" The fact that R'qanar knew who he was, but never made any fuss about it, did not escape him.

"I wish there could be two of me, so one could go home and the other could go see Eswar."

R'qanar winked and replied, "Make a wish in one hand and do something constructive with the other. Then squeeze them both and see which one comes true."

For Julian this seemed to suggest that he could choose equally, and he chose his overriding wish, to go home. His thoughts were interrupted by the subtle whoosh of the shop door opening. A familiar blue face shined at him.

"J'liánh!" Gjallimé crossed the room in quick strides.

"Gjallimé. You're back!" The two greeted each other with a friendly shove. "This is R'qanar."

"Good beginnings." They said at the same time using the Edrym idiom for 'good to meet you'.

Gjallimé held Julian at arm's length with both hands, "Have you heard? Have you heard about the coming of Enhendendor!"

"I've heard."

"I was the Rider that brought the news. I was entrusted to bring it through the hazards of Ravoq-Ma!"

R'qanar jumped in. "What did you see during Ravoq-Ma?"

"Nothing. I was instructed to lie flat and hide in Kem'nesh until it passed. I have been told of what happened here in Sayll including J'liánh's heroics."

Julian shook his head, "I did not—"

R'qanar interrupted, "The Yetzer-Xie force was not as large as we feared. I was among those who were prepared for a second attack. Scouts stayed in the trees spread out around the walls. But a second attack never materialized. We were lucky there were not more of them. Although, on the other hand, we did have a contingent of lava giants to deal with."

Julian's eyes widened. "It could have been worse?"

"Indeed," said R'qanar somberly.

Gjallimé broke the uneasy silence. "J'liánh, I have been assigned a new task. I am to stay at your side. Now we must go to N'ttala-Toor; for he has sent for you."

Julian nodded and the two departed for the castle. He did not forget to thank R'qanar for the soup, the kindness, and most especially the music that had raised him out of his melancholy.

+++

It would be some days before all of Nova'h learned the reason the Yetzer-Xie raid on Sayll was smaller than expected. Most of the Yetzer-Xie forces attacked the Nova'h Hold, Sneprttai, isolated in the far south of Edrym. The Hold was home to the efreet. The largest assemblage of Yetzer-Xie during Ravoq-Ma ever seen on Edrym assailed in ferocious waves, coordinating between lava giants, wraiths, draugrs, and banshees, led by the Overlord of Darkness, Zhokul himself. By the third wave's onslaught, Yetzer-Xie overran the efreet, beholden to the white and silver moons. The Hold was sacked and pillaged and razed. The flames licked the sky and the banshees howled. The efreet were no more.

+++

On the way to the castle Gjallimé gave Julian a wry smile. "So…. You certainly are the center of the storm."

"Nothing is for certain yet. N'ttala-Toor said so himself."

"That is not what I'm talking about." And Gjallimé continued to give him a sly look.

"I have no idea what you are getting at," muttered Julian with a frown.

"Come on. Come on. Speak your truth."

Julian pulled his eyebrows together in a quizzical glare.

"You and Iniqui. You have been seen a lot together. Do not tell me that you are as stupid as you look with that hair."

Julian shoved Gjallimé with both arms.

Gjallimé didn't give up that easily, "She is mighty fine." And the grin reappeared.

"It's nothing like that… but then again, she *is* hot." Julian raised his eyebrows in an attempt to show that he knew all about sex.

"Hot? Why do you use that word?"

"Oh. Yeah. It's E'rth slang for sexy and attractive."

"So, have you got a girl on your home world?"

"Not really." He was ashamed to admit. "No. No, I don't."

80

"Then go for it."

"Are you, like, nuts? She's a princess. Not that her bod isn't killer… Hey don't talk what you don't know."

"My Pris could kick her ass." Gjallimé retorted with a winner's nod.

"Pris?" And Julian squeezed his face in an exaggerated grimace when he repeated himself with a you've-got-to-be-kidding me tone. "Pris? What kind of name is that?" He rolled his eyes." "She must be some pig!"

Gjallimé jabbed Julian with a sharp elbow.

"I mean dog." He bounced away laughing.

Gjallimé threw his shoulders back. "You obviously would not know beauty if it bit you in the ass." And he scowled and walked ahead.

Julian knew Gjallimé didn't exactly say *bit you in the ass* in the language of Edrym – but it was the equivalent. "Okay. Okay." Julian scrambled to catch up. "Tell me about her."

"J'liánh, she is as fair as the blue moon. She is no less than a waltz and a 'Hano. And she can fight like a cornered beast. I do not get to see her much, what with all my Riding."

Julian grabbed Gjallimé's arm. "Hey, we can get someone else to be my bodyguard…or companion…whatever it is you are."

Gjallimé flashed a genuine smile. "No, I was just joking with you. It is an honor. Really."

Julian did not want to admit he was secretly glad.

+++

The muted rumbling of the running lava giant and liche force that had attacked Sayll, crystallized for Zhokul at about the same time he saw them. They arrived at the Qeobl plateau west of the Ad-Nykal forest to join the Overlord and his army of banshees, wraiths, and other lava giants who had obliterated the efreet. Ravoq-Ma had passed. Cthomechdul shone dull red, the only remaining Yetzer-Xie moon in the cobalt sky.

The Overlord of Darkness spoke over the sound of the roaring bonfire and buzz of voices. "Look! Our brethren approach. They join our celebration from their assault on Sayll."

"Krai! Krai!" from Zhokul's warriors.

"Krai!" as the Sayll raiding horde reached the bonfire.

The Overlord bellowed, "Come. Welcome. Drink the spirits I have brought." For he had been confident enough in his attack on Sneprttai, to carry liquor with the troops.

Yetzer-Xie creatures regaled in their individual battles adding rabble to the crackling of the orange, yellow, blue and red growing fire. Buoyed by drink they sought to outdo their comrades in tales of valor. Banshees bragged to liches; wraiths bragged to lava giants.

A liche who had returned from Sayll stood and shouted. "Comrades, our attack on Sayll nearly brought them to their knees. True, the forces siphoned off for the attack on the efreet cut into our numbers." He scanned the crowd. For the moment he failed to grab their full attention. "Though our losses equaled theirs, we have reason to celebrate! Queen Aemiluria *fried and died* from a direct lava ball hit!"

Slowly, a cheer spread through the crowd. "The Queen is dead! The Queen is dead!" A chanting flew on the breeze of burning wood. "Btamnk 'hm torha torha ch'manah 'hm b'rha b'rha yeekh 'hm k'rha k'rha." Yetzer-Xie soldiers stomped and danced, turning individual circles next to the glow of the fire. "Btamnk 'hm torha torha ch'manah 'hm b'rha b'rha yeekh 'hm k'rha k'rha."

A banshee accidentally knocked over a wraith. The wraith jumped to his feet and threw punches at the offending banshee, who fought back. The throng cheered the fight, not picking sides, but delighting with every blow. Liquor flowed. Hooting and howling drowned out the noise of the fire.

"Enough!" Zhokul's angry thunder startled the raucous mob.

A lava giant intervened in the ongoing fight, knocking the banshee and wraith to the ground.

"Enough!" All souls stood still and quieted, such was the fear the Overlord elicited. "The time for celebration has passed. Yetzer-Xie shall band together as a fighting force this land has never seen. Enhendendor draws near! Every one of the moons will eclipse in the sky. I have seen it!"

A reluctant cry, "Krai!" erupted into full-throated exclamation. "Krai! Krai!"

"Go forth to your Holds. We have eight days to train and power our enchantments. Harbor no doubts. I shall devise the best strategy and lead you to victory!"

+++

"It is useless to argue!" Iniqui shouted above the voices of Xorn, S'rrinha, and the nymph priest, Talen-Jei. Only the soothsayer, N'ttala-Toor, remained neutral. "Eswar shall decide!"

Julian only half listened. S'rrinha sat opposite, dressed in a tight-fitting fern-green gown displaying ample cleavage. She occasionally flashed Julian a coy smile. Her bosom heaved with each breath causing Julian to fidget in the opulent chair within the inner chamber of the Sayll castle. The oval room was the only place on Edrym that Julian had seen to be even the least bit luxurious. A mosaic ceiling loomed high overhead, fifteen feet above the thickly-carpeted floor of cherry, coral, and teal.

With the vaulted ceiling, Iniqui's voice reverberated with command and everyone quieted. "So. Back to you J'liánh. What say you?"

Julian shifted in his seat, but delivered his answer with conviction, "I will go to W'lkyndh, get the book translated, test the portal, and affirm my ability to get home. In case there is any difficulty, I want to be able to work with the Halili immediately to find a solution. If the time dilation that N'ttala-Toor believes is correct, I will not be missed on my home world, so I vow to come back and take audience with King Eswar." He felt quite pleased with his answer.

A palpable disappointment blossomed in the room, but Iniqui settled the uneasiness quickly. "Very well. Gjallimé, you take J'liánh. Dor'ossoss and your Domo can make the ride in less than a day—"

A murmur broke out among those present.

Iniqui spoke over the noise. "I know. I know. It is risky, but it does not make sense to split the Khalil into two groups to provide a full escort. They will rely on speed." She turned back to Julian. "My people are prepared to depart in two hours' time. We will push the pace and make it to Zhon Jeul in two days. We leave eight Khalil too injured to travel, here under S'rrinha's care."

S'rrinha nodded. "Weeqq rises and I will invoke the full power of *Heal* once again. Most of the wounded should make it. Although some with loss of limb."

"The Riders already carry the news of Enhendendor to all Holds of Nova'h. We meet again in seven days at the encampment below Naspia Dor, on the northwest side as Edrym law dictates. Our brethren, the K'narikh and the efreet in the far south, should arrive a half day later. Spend whatever time available preparing weapons, training, and powering the enchantments. Eswar and the War Council will decide which enchantments we take into the campaign. Morale is of the essence, the entire army of Yetzer-Xie will be waiting for us on the southeast side."

Julian knew Iniqui mourned deeply for her mother, but she didn't show it. More likely she wouldn't show it, and couldn't show it. For the new Queen must appear strong.

Chapter 10
Kidnapped

Julian walked alone toward the stables while Gjallimé ran back to get some sugar cubes. He studied the parchment Gjallimé provided. It contained the color, name, and enchantments for each moon.

I should have had this long ago. I'm starting to recognize the names of the moons, but I need to know a whole lot more about the enchantments. He thought back on the enchantments he already witnessed, *Fear* (yellow moon) and *Enhance* (silver moon) at the ambush; *Heal* (green moon) after the attempt on his life; *Speed* and *Quash* (blue moon) also at the ambush; and *Infect* (black moon) at Ravoq-Ma. Each minor moon imbued power for two enchantments, leaving *Death*, *Weakness*, *Mind Shield*, *Blind*, *Strength*, *Shock*, and *Trample*, as Eptizar powers he was unfamiliar with. He vowed to learn them one at a time.

A second parchment was equally informative; showing the races of Nova'h, their moons of power, and the names of their holds. He didn't recognize the green race of humans, nor the manticore or efreet. *What's a manticore? What's an efreet? I'll have to ask and do some more studying.* The liches, lava giants, and draugrs were Yetzer-Xie races he was familiar with. *What more does Yetzer-Xie have?*

"J'liánh." R'qanar appeared beside Julian while his focus was deep in the second parchment.

"Oh. I didn't see you coming."

"Well, I can see you have a lot to study." The curio shop owner's lips drew into a line. "Don't try to understand everything at once. It will come to you." And that wrinkled face broke into a happy smile. "I want to give you something." The old nymph reached into his jacket and pulled out the wooden spiral instrument he played earlier. Before Julian could object R'qanar added. "I know. I know. You do not play. This is a piece of Edrym I want you to take back with you. You may present it to your father."

"But—"

"No. Take it." He scampered away before Julian could protest.

+++

Julian was brushing Dor'ossoss when Gjallimé returned with a small sack of sugar cubes. They gathered all the supplies, mounted, and walked through the Sayll streets. Many nymphs were rebuilding the outer walls as they approached the front gates. Nevertheless, they stopped to wave to Julian and he waved back. Dor'ossoss rocked his regal head back and forth, his ink-black coat gleaming.

Gjallimé was unusually quiet as they passed through the B'jnh forest. When they reached the end of the trees, the plain flowing with Kem'nesh appeared before them. The blue teenager spoke. "W'lkyndh is west and a bit south. As we ride the sun shall fall closer to the horizon and it will get cooler." Gjallimé turned his Domo to the proper direction, dug in his heels and started off with a canter.

When Julian did the same, Dor'ossoss reared high off the ground, his front hooves clawing at air. The nightsteed would not follow Gjallimé. Julian clutched his saddle hard to avoid being thrown. Gjallimé heard the neighing, saw the commotion, and headed back.

Julian, still holding tight, exclaimed, "I don't know what's gotten into him. He's never acted this way before." He secured a tight grip, stroked the animal's withers, and spoke soothingly to him. "Easy boy. Easy boy." Dor'ossoss did not stop rearing up on his hind legs.

Julian carefully dismounted when all four of his stallion's silver hooves were firmly on the ground. His manner changed to

86

stern. He held the reins and tried to pull the steed in the direction Gjallimé took toward W'lkyndh. "Come now. This minute."

Dor'ossoss stood steadfast, eyes afire.

Julian approached the nightsteed, who lowered his head until they were eye to eye. He engaged the surly stallion in a staring contest, a contest he could not win. When his eyes began to burn, Julian exploded. "Damn it! We are going this way!"

Gjallimé chuckled catching Julian's attention. "I've never seen you angry. Sorry, but it is comical to see you engage in a battle of wills with this incredible beast." The blue teenager bent forward trying to stifle laughter.

"Damn it, Gjallimé. I could use some help here. Get some of those sugar cubes."

Gjallimé pulled himself together and said with all seriousness, "That probably will not do any good." The last remnants of his grin faded. "J'liánh. Dor'ossoss is The Guardian. And W'lkyndh is obviously *not* your true course."

Julian took hold of that great muzzle and shook it gently, affectionately. He bowed his head and Dor'ossoss did the same, until they were touching forehead to forehead such that the purple fire mane was inches from Julian's head. No heat, just the cackle of fire dancing. They simply stood that way for a while. "All right. All right. We go to meet Eswar. We go to Zhon Jeul." The nightsteed pawed the ground and whinnied.

+++

"Wake up! Come quick!"

Julian sat up lethargically and the narrow strip of cloth wrapped around his eyes fell into his lap. Gjallimé was already on his feet, speaking with the nymph who poked his head into the tent.

"Get up J'liánh!" Gjallimé was shaking him. The nymph was gone.

"What time is it?" The sun's glow permeated the inside of the tent. They had proceeded northwest from Sayll and the sun hung lower in the sky, but it was ever present. *Are we breaking camp?*

"It is the middle of the night. We are going to the horse's pen, but we are not to wake the others."

I wish I had a watch. He was still weary from the twenty-hour travel of the previous day. Nevertheless, he stood and asked, "What's goin' on?"

"I do not know. Come and let us find out."

Julian and Gjallimé emerged from their tent and headed to the temporary pen the Khalil had erected. When they arrived, Iniqui, Xorn, and Jr'esh were already there. Though their voices were in near whisper, they were arguing.

Iniqui was upset and fiercely determined. "We must go after them." She implored the others. She turned to Julian. "J'liánh, Idrazel has been taken. The camp's western guard was found decapitated."

Dor'ossoss paced back and forth, however he did not come to Julian which was strange. "How would any Yetzer-Xie take Idrazel without commotion?"

Gjallimé pointed to a half-eaten, peach-colored, roundish fruit on the ground. "Look! Liel, their favorite. They must have imbued the fruit with a potion like Thania, making the horses dazed and confused."

Xorn looked at the ground, "There are multiple tracks leaving from the back of pen where the fence has been dismantled. Only Iniqui's unicorn is missing."

Jr'esh butted in, "It is a trap. What else could it be? Why else would they have only taken Idrazel? They expect Iniqui to pursue. We cannot risk it. And we cannot afford the time to attempt a rescue. Only eight more days till Enhendendor."

"I refuse to abandon Idrazel. From the tracks there cannot be many of them. My people will follow."

"There will surely be more Yetzer-Xie at the trap. Only a few were sent to abduct the unicorn," Xorn's forehead creased. "Certainly, the Khalil will follow you, but I agree with Jr'esh, we cannot waste the time. Idrazel means much to you, I know, but I beg you to reconsider.”

Gjallimé rocked back on his heels. “My Domo can overtake them rapidly. And Dor’ossoss can keep pace carrying both J’liánh and Iniqui. The three of us should go.”

Julian asked, “Can Dor’ossoss and your Domo ride?”

“Domo are immune to Thania and I would be surprised if Dor’ossoss took more than one bite. Look, they pace while the rest of the animals do little more than rock back and forth.”

Iniqui’s countenance brightened and she spoke with authority, “They could not have left more than five hours ago, shortly after we set camp. We can overtake them quickly. I cannot fully take my place without Idrazel.” She put her hands on her hips. “Jr’esh, at daybreak, continue on to Zhon Jeul. We will catch up to you. My mind is set. Thus, it is so.”

“And what if you reach them after they have set the trap?” Jr’esh rocked on his feet.

“I put my fate in H’rol.”

H’rol, the creator. If I remember it right.

+++

Dor’ossoss could indeed keep pace with Gjallimé the Rider. They agreed there could be no plan until the kidnappers were spotted. Iniqui’s arms encircled Julian from behind, hugging his chest. He was keenly aware of her warmth and the pressure of her breasts upon his back. Within minutes she rested her head on his shoulder. Her sobs were quiet but Julian could hear them nonetheless. More than that, his body felt the shudders that belied the quiet of her mouth. *With this loss, she finally mourns her mother. I will not mention it.* A pang spread inside his chest as if the world spun too fast. *Aemiluria welcomed me to this world and told the others to accept me. I owe her.*

Gjallimé pulled to a stop and looked through the spyglass. Iniqui still rested against Julian but her sniffles had abated. Even the stop of the chase did not bring her to full awareness. He felt

89

warmth throughout his core, as her softness clung to him. Gjallimé shook his head and they continued onward; the tracks still evident beneath them.

"Do you know where we are, where we are heading?" Julian asked.

"Aye. As a Rider, I know this land well. We are traveling almost due west, Zhon Jeul is to the north and W'lkyndh is to the southwest. We will soon approach the dark forest Cyrodilh and further west the river Leywyn-Pah runs above ground."

"How long have we been in pursuit?" Iniqui awake now, sounded in charge.

Gjallimé glanced her way, "Just under two hours." Julian was continually amazed how they kept track of time so precisely with their second heart.

Keeping her voice low, Iniqui said, "With our speed we should be upon them soon. We do not want to run over them or fall blindly into a trap. Stop and use the glass."

As they pulled up Julian folded his arms across his chest and slowly shook his head. "Iniqui, we have been using the spyglass periodically. The last time, just minutes ago" Iniqui did not acknowledge him, rather took command and released her hold around his torso.

"Shhh. Keep your voices down." Instructed Gjallimé. "I have detected the glow from a fire but I am not able to see any of our enemy. Cyrodilh stands before us. Let us move forward at a measured pace."

Julian squinted his eyes but could not see the glow. However, the horizon looked less than smooth ahead and to the left. He surmised it must be Cyrodilh.

It did not take long before Gjallimé, keeping his eye on the glass, brought them to a halt. Julian could finally make out the fire's glow.

"Idrazel is there." Gjallimé whispered. He handed the spyglass to Iniqui and when finished, she passed it to Julian.

A lone draugr sat on a log, facing them across the campfire. Four horses and Idrazel appeared to be tied to the same log, not far away. The Kem'nesh gave way to the trees of Cyrodilh.

"I presume the other three draugrs are sleeping, hidden by the Kem'nesh," continued Gjallimé as Iniqui and Julian took their turns with the spyglass. "It is nearly daybreak…"

It's odd that daybreak is an Edrym term, even though the sun maintains its position in the sky. "…let us dismount and come up with a strategy."

"What the hell is that?" Julian caught sight of a skeleton-like creature and shuddered. It had no skin, exposing thick, black muscle, white ligaments, and ash-grey bone. But worse were the soulless eyes that seemed to stare directly at him. He reminded himself that the monster could not see him at this distance.

"That is a draugr, bespoken by Ihl."

"But I thought creatures had two moons."

"Draugr are the undead humans of the black moon."

"If they are undead then how do we kill them? By chopping off their heads?"

"That will work," chuckled Gjallimé. "But they have vital organs although not the same as you or I. Just above the waist on the right side is an especially vulnerable spot."

And what is its innate power?" Julian asked with sarcasm.

"*Death.*"

"*Death?*"

"*Death.* The mind is assaulted first. A weakened mind will affect the entire body. Also, you will bleed out faster, your organs will shut down easily, and not much adrenaline will come to your rescue when injured."

Julian tried to swallow, but his mouth was dry. He glanced at the sky and Ihl was not present.

"Gjallimé added. "The black moon is not in the sky, so the draugr's power is lessened."

There was only Cthomechdul casting a dull, blood-red hue upon the land. "I'm not going to ask what the *enchantment* of *Death* would do."

Iniqui cleared her throat, glared, and took over. "J'liánh, you are the fastest. Circle behind the guard, first using the trees for cover, then crawling through the Kem'nesh. When you feel close enough, rise up and use that speed to take out the guard from behind."

"Sure, I'll just cut off his head." *Anyway, that's the plan. I may need to improvise.* Julian pondered his role as the first to attack. *Okay. I'm up for this.*

Ignoring Julian's remarks, Iniqui turned to Gjallimé. "You take a position well to the right and wait for J'liánh's charge. The need for stealth cannot be overemphasized. I will approach and hide on the left. When J'liánh strikes we will rush toward the campfire and take on the others as they rise."

"What if the forest is the trap and I find it to be full of the enemy?" Julian tried to sound unafraid.

Gjallimé answered, "We must hope not. I think they would choose the spot where the river comes close to Cyrodilh for an ambush. That is the path I often Ride through. They are probably expecting a full contingent of the Khalil, and that narrow pass would be an ideal place for a trap. It is more than a half-day's ride away."

"It'll be difficult to crawl through the Kem'nesh with my shield."

Iniqui reached into her boot and brought out a dagger. "Take this."

Julian looked at the weapon, befuddled. *Jeez, that's great.* "What does it mean that only Cthomechdul is out?" *I think I got the name right.*

"Enough!" Even in a whisper Iniqui's anger was obvious. "Gjallimé and I will reach our positions before you can get behind the draugr. We will wait for your rush and take them by surprise. Now go!"

+++

Not more than twenty minutes later, Julian, Iniqui, and Gjallimé rode directly toward Zhon Jeul. Four dead draugr lay hacked and bloodied in the Kem'nesh behind them. The rescue went without complication. The draugr on the log had turned and was just beginning to rise when Julian cut him down. Hellsbane got stuck between some ribs. The next two draugrs were dispatched before they armed themselves. The only embarrassment was when Julian tried to throw the dagger at the last draugr rushing him and it struck by the handle instead of the blade, bouncing off harmlessly. With a running leap and thrust of his sword into the back of the creature's neck, Gjallimé finished the job forthwith.

The Earth teenager gasped. "You've saved my life!"

Gjallimé beamed. "Then you must follow the Law and return the favor. Someday." Gjallimé extended his arm, Julian took a forearm-to-forearm grip, and Gjallimé pulled the Earth teenager to his feet. And thus, their bond grew stronger.

As they gathered around Idrazel, Dor'ossoss, and Gjallimé's Domo, Iniqui hastened to give each of the boys a quick peck on the cheek. A warm flash erupted within Julian making him dizzy. He cared not that she also kissed Gjallimé. She had kissed him! And the presence of her lips upon his cheek lingered sweetly. Before he could regain his composure, they mounted their steeds.

Idrazel, under the influence of the drug, could only manage a fast trot, so Iniqui rode between Julian and Gjallimé who kept their animals in pace with her drowsy steed. Julian realized he missed the press of Iniqui upon his back.

They wanted to put as much space between them and any possible Yetzer-Xie force that may have been preparing for a trap. Sooner or later the Yetzer-Xie soldiers would find the dead draugr at the campfire. They might pursue them.

Iniqui quipped, "If you two were any noisier back there, you could have awoken a sleeping troll."

"And if you were any worse with the blade, we would have all been skinned alive." Julian flashed a nasty grin.

Gjallimé joined in, "My father warned me about depending on the likes of you two."

"Clods"

"Spazzes"

"Frod under my sandals." This from Princess Iniqui. Julian didn't understand but howled just the same.

"Slackers."

"Dickwads."

"Asswipes."

They all broke out in bellowing laughter, driving them to tears, not knowing they were expelling the fear that had gripped them. Julian nearly fell off of Dor'ossoss. Iniqui caught him halfway down. They continued to snicker until Iniqui started to hiccup. That brought the boys to laughter again. After a stern look from Iniqui, they eventually reined it in.

Iniqui decided it was too perilous to stop and rest. They would have to make do on the few hours of sleep they attained in camp before being abruptly wakened.

They rode eastward to intercept the rest of the Khalil on route to Zhon Jeul. Julian learned the trick of sleeping while riding. They each took turns. Although Julian brimmed with so many questions, Iniqui and Gjallimé insisted that Julian tell them about Earth and again how he happened to find a way into Edrym. Julian was too caught up in events to realize that he had made his first kill in battle.

The Khalil force came into sight thru the spyglass and they all rushed to meet it. Iniqui excused herself to talk with the Khalil priest, Xorn, which allowed Julian and Gjallimé to tell and retell the story of the draugrs at the campfire to the others. They were not more than half a day's ride to Zhon Jeul.

+++

A message reached King Eswar about the same time Iniqui, Julian, and Gjallimé rejoined the Khalil forces. The messenger informed Eswar that Kanh-apal-apli asked to meet him at the pit of the four pillars located south, just outside the Hold.

94

Alone, Eswar descended into the dark sub-basement beneath his weapon room. The torch he carried revealed a narrow path with smooth, rock steps and walls. Each step took two strides to cross and it continued that way until he reached the twisting tunnel. At the fork he went left and quickly ran into a dead end. Eswar searched the wall for the small cross shaped slot hidden by natural features. He used his key and leaned hard against the heavy secret door. Beyond, he crossed the large circular room to the steep and narrow steps on the opposite side. At the bottom he used his key again and walked out under the blue and silver moons.

"You knew about this hidden passage." Eswar looked up to the large, sullen man of ice covered in extensive body armor sitting on his chocolate-colored horse. "What brings Kanh-apal-apli out of the wilderness?" Eswar stood tall and proud, not in awe, regardless of the fact he looked up to peer into the eyes of the Snow-Jarl. The King of Edrym was more than an equal to Kanh-apal-apli.

The Snow-Jarl stroked his legendary horse's neck as he responded. "There has come a powerful Alzjerja to the land of Edrym." He used the ancient word that meant both cyclone and gladiator. "The Alzjerja has clouded my sight and I know little about it, except that it has shifted the balance to Yetzer-Xie. I have come to warn you, the outcome of Enhendendor is in doubt. Ravoq-Ma saw the complete eradication of the efreet."

At the mention of the loss of the efreets of Nova'h, shock jolted the King but he forced himself not to show it. "And what made you break your neutrality to bring me this news?"

Kahn-apal-apli ratcheted down his baritone to a hush as if he might be overheard. "There is another new force in the land, Elzjer, who is on his way to meet you now." And this time he used the ancient word for storm and warrior. "The Alzjerja is hindering my sight, but I have a strong suspicion that Elzjer has an essential role in finding the final piece of The-Key-that-is-Lost."

"The Riders have brought me news of Elzjer. His name is J'liánh and he is not of this world. Yet he sides with Nova'h."

Kanh-apal-apli nodded his head slowly in agreement. His eyes remained piercing and steady. "King Eswar, there is a small thicket of Brygul trees that exist only near the tundra to the northwest of the Z'ngil-Toth mountains. Their wood will make strong your bows, tripling the power of what you have now."

Kanh-apal-apli gave directions to the thicket, then without a word of farewell, he turned his great horse and cantered away, leaving Eswar standing alone under the cornflower blue, and quicksilver moons.

Chapter 11
King Eswar

Zhon Jeul stood imposing, embedded within the foothills of the Kholsnikh-Yal mountains. A massive stone gate served as the only entrance. The streets and buildings were hewn from the beige and sand colored mountain itself, like orderly and embellished caves. The city was a fortress on the outside and a bustling town on the inside.

This seems like the safest place to face Ravoq-Ma.

Gjallimé was his animated and amiable self as they took their mounts to the stable, but the sixteen-year-old Earthling didn't hear a word, he was so humbled by the soaring heights of the mountain that held the city in its belly. They brought Idrazel to the stable as well, since Iniqui had gone immediately to see her father. Julian walked silently as Gjallimé gave him a cursory tour. They stopped at a café and to Julian's surprise they were served mead while he waited to be summoned by the King.

+++

The castle façade was massive, with ornate balconies reaching five stories high. For several hours, Julian waited to see Eswar in an intricately carved, yet simply decorated antechamber. He was taking a much-needed nap when a Khalil guard awakened and guided him through the great hall to a small room in the rear.

King Eswar leaned on a magnificent, polished wooden desk, examining a parchment scroll. Julian fidgeted in silence while he waited for the King to put the parchment on the desk. Eswar was thinner than most Khalil and this rendered his face gaunt, highlighting the wisdom in his green eyes. Eyes that looked directly and slightly bemused at Julian.

Eswar wore black pants tucked into black boots studded with silver, and his chainmail was brighter than any Julian had seen. He possessed the same ivory skin and silver braids of all Kahlil men. He wore a black cloak clasped at his neck with a silver rose. Each forearm was encircled with a band of steel and he wore gloves of scaled silver. A thin black belt held a glittering silvern dagger, its hilt inlaid with onyx gems. His countenance was noble. There could be no doubt this was Aemiluria's King.

Julian straightened up to his full height. Although he was about a foot shorter than Eswar, the easy and generous bearing with which Eswar carried himself did not make Julian feel small.

"I thank you, J'liánh, for assisting my daughter in the recovery of Idrazel." And so it began with graciousness. Julian stopped moving his weight from one foot to the other.

Before he could respond, Eswar took his dagger and held it out before him at eye level. He held the dagger's hilt between his thumb and the first two fingers of his right hand. The tip was pointed down.

"When you grab this dagger, I suggest you avoid not only the tip, but even its edges which are exceedingly sharp and will slice your flesh." And with that he let go.

Julian's hand darted forward and snatched the dagger from its fall just one foot from Eswar's outstretched hand. Julian grasped the flat of the blade without touching the edges, the steel, cold against his fingers. He did not examine the dagger, instead he tossed it gently in the air, with one flip, and re-grabbed the flat of the blade. He then handed it back to the King, hilt first.

Eswar did not acknowledge this display of the teenager's skill. He casually returned the dagger to his belt and asked, "May I see Nchaud-Zel?"

Julian obliged. Eswar handled the book with the same care as Aemiluria. He returned the book forthwith.

"Are you a hero?"

Julian jumped in his skin. There it was, the simple question that hung in the air since his mystical encounter with N'ttala-Toor. No one had asked him directly, though he had noticed the question in their eyes.

"I…I don't know."

Eswar waited calmly, patiently, as both confidence and doubt danced across Julian's face.

Julian blurted out, "But I am prepared to fight during Enhendendor." *What am I saying? Have I been swept up in all of this? Has my ego gone crazy? No…part of it is ego, part of it is like a row of dominoes – each causing the next to fall. But part of it is something else altogether.*

Eswar responded with steadiness and empathy as Julian stood spellbound in the moment. "Jr'esh and Iniqui have spoken well of you." The King crossed his arms. "I have counseled with N'ttala-Toor and I understand his hope. **Conflict** and a **Mass Gathering** are certainly upon us. And the **Wanderer** has gotten involved. These three predictions appear to have come true."

Taking a deep breath, he continued. "However, I cannot afford to rely on future sight when it concerns defending Nova'h." Eswar turned his head slightly and stared at a deep purple banner on the wall. "I never have and I never will. It is too important." With a composed face and probing eyes, he looked back at Julian. "J'liánh, you may choose your own path." Eswar stopped to give the teenager a chance to speak, but Julian remained silent. The King continued with somber deliberation. "We are all put to the test…. But rarely at the time or under the circumstances that we might anticipate. It is yet to be written what role you may play here in Edrym."

We are all put to the test. Death. It should be impossible. But here it is real. Iniqui, Gjallimé – I want to stand with them. Most of all it's the sense of worth, of being special. Eswar puts me at ease like no other except Dor'ossoss, he makes me feel truly as Nova'h. Julian stiffened to attention, "My lord, I choose to fight."

Eswar pressed his lips into a thin line. He reached out and placed a firm grip on Julian's shoulders. "I welcome you wholeheartedly into the fold. I know this a difficult thing you undertake." His eyes locked onto Julian's. "I would ask one thing of you first."

"Name it."

"On the way to Methedriel you and Gjallimé break off from the army and ride to W'lkyndh to meet with the Halili scholars. Test the portal and ensure your ability to get home. With your speed you will catch up with us either at Methedriel or on the ride to Naspia Dor."

"But—"

"Dor'ossoss has kept you from this path once before. Test him again. With your mind at ease about the path to your world, I gain a better warrior." Eswar did not mention that he feared that Edrym intoxicated the teenager. Only with one foot in both worlds did the King wish for Julian to make this choice.

+++

The next morning, preparations were complete and the Khalil army headed south to Methedriel. There they would acquire more chainmail and weapons for the army's newest members and join up with the Hassjidar. Training breaks now included two on two combat because in the fight to come, often they would be standing shoulder to shoulder.

After a period of training Julian rode to catch up with Gjallimé when he spotted Iniqui riding towards him, opposite the flow of the march. Her father was at the front of the procession and this was a rare instance she was not by his side. A crimson cloak flowed majestically around her, held by a silver clasp in the shape of a rose like her father's. She wore bronze wrist bands and crimson gloves. Her hair was full and gleaming, making her lovelier than Julian had ever seen.

Iniqui pulled up alongside Julian, Dor'ossoss gave Idrazel a quick muzzle to muzzle hello. Julian wished that he could do the same. Iniqui looked regal in her crimson, but Julian sensed melancholy. Her face lacked the playful petulance she often

100

showed when they were together. Nor did she wear her hard mask of command and arrogance.

Iniqui's voice was measured, "Is it true?'

"Is what true?"

"That you are leaving Edrym."

"What?" The question angered Julian. "Who told you that?"

"My father says that you go to open the portal to your world."

"I go to *test* the portal, not to use it. I have pledged myself to your father to fight on Naspia Dor."

"Oh." Iniqui blushed with embarrassment. She caught hold of herself in an instant, gave a curt nod, and changed the subject. "Father was taken with Dor'ossoss. He said they got along well."

"When did he see Dor'ossoss?"

"Before he met you. I am sure it was part of his assessment."

+++

Dor'ossoss did not offer protest when late on the second day Gjallimé and Julian split from the group and rode at top speed nearly due west, to skirt the eastern most regions of the forest Cyrodilh. Gjallimé explained he had chosen a slightly longer route because he did not want to ride through a risky pass ideal for an ambush. The same location he had feared when they rescued Idrazel.

Beyond Cyrodilh they turned southwest towards W'lkyndh, riding on a wide path of chocolate earth, cutting through the Kem'nesh. Their one-day journey was uneventful.

W'lkyndh nestled in the foothills of the Z'ngil-Toth mountains, almost as safe as Zhon Jeul. High elves opened the gate readily to the Rider and his special companion. Gjallimé asked for sleeping quarters and Julian did not protest. For safety they had not rested along the way.

Gjallimé and Julian proceeded to a massive stone circular stairway and followed an elf up one level.

Julian asked. "Where exactly are we going?"

"To the Chamber of Souls." The elf's face remained slack..

"What is that?" From Gjallimé.

"Hey, will the Halili be there?"

"Patience."

Their path took them down a narrow hallway, second door to the left, and inside a cavernous room of rock, with chairs, tables, and two elves, a male and female, both with distinctive hair. The same black hair as the others, but long and swept across their head from a part on the side. Shoulder length. Julian could see the resemblance to his, except he was buzz cut below the part on one side while their hair hung to the shoulder on both sides.

"Ah, welcome J'liánh and Gjallimé." The female elf approached. "I am Amarhee." She gestured toward the other elf. "We are Halili. May we see the tome?"

Julian retrieved the book from its carrying pouch and handed it to the female elf. "Ah, indeed. This is the tome Nchaud-Zel." She glided back with it for the other elf to examine. "Come sit with us. I understand that you found it in another realm, and you, yourself are from that place."

"Yes. But it changed after going through a portal to Edrym."

"How did you acquire this treasure?"

"You know, I purchased it for reading. I bought it from a store. On E'rth. My home world."

"I see. I see."

"The language in this book was of my land, except for the two incantations that open and close the portal." Julian opened Nchaud-Zel to the appropriate page. "These two lines were not in E'nglsh, but used our alphabet so I sounded them out as best I could. The first opened the portal; the second, with the same unusual words in reverse order, closed it."

The Halili nodded. "Except when I fell through. Then the portal closed on its own and the letters all changed. The look and feel of the book also changed. I'm pretty sure I need to be able to read the incantations to get home. I was told you could translate."

Amarhee did not look up from the book as she spoke. "Do the people of your world wear their hair as you do, half like the Halili?"

"No, I choose to be different."

The other elf caught Amarhee's eyes. "Perhaps that is how he was able to read the incantations."

"It matters not." Then to Julian. "Let me translate." She took some parchment and a pen and began writing." She quickly finished with the two lines indicated, handing the parchment to Julian.

Julian's hands shook as he rose and faced a blank wall of stone. He read the first line and the portal appeared before him, looking like a picture in the air once again. His breath escaped with a whoosh. He could see his room on Earth. Looking back at Gjallimé, whose mouth gaped, Julian explained. "I'm just going to go through and come right back." Then addressing Amarhee, "May I have Nchaud-Zel? I'll need it to return."

A wide-eyed Amarhee obliged, exchanging the tome for the parchment.

Julian took the book and steadied himself. He carefully took a step into the portal, but his foot found resistance in mid-stride. He tried to reach through with his hand and felt a cool, hard surface where the portal stood. *Shit!*

With angst in his voice, he exclaimed. "I can't get through! I can't get through."

"Try holding the parchment."

He did, with the same result. Julian pushed at the portal with the flat of his free hand, trying different sections of the rendition of his room, with no success. He then tried with both hands like a mime feeling out an invisible wall, but this wall was a portal to his bedroom he could not use.

Amarhee stood and felt the cool, hard surface of the portal for herself. "Leave the tome. We may need to translate the words to those from the time Tamiel, a time-consuming task. Come back in three days and we will have the proper translation."

The other Halili spoke. "Or there could be another reason you cannot go through. You may not have completed your task here."

My task? Could it be true? Who knows? "I need to be able to go home. Please help me."

"We will."

I could stay and wait. Or... Julian thrust his shoulders back. "I go now to fight on the sacred plateau, Naspia Dor. I will return afterwards."

"H'rol be with you."

H'rol the Creator. "Come on Gjallimé, let's catch up with the others. I think perhaps this battle is my destiny."

+++

On an otherwise uneventful one-day ride to Methedriel, Gjallimé's hold, they easily outran a group of three banshees. Gjallimé thought back to his encounter with Kahn-Apal-Apli, traversing the tundra in the far west while carrying the base circle of The-Key-that-is-Lost. *If only I had my domo then. The fight would not have been necessary.*

Enthusiasm welcomed them to Methedriel. Villagers were already proud of Gjallimé as a Rider, and now as escort to this

104

rumored warrior from Earth. The domo and night steed were taken to be washed, groomed, and fed.

Structures in the Hold showed a combination of wood, slate, and steel. Julian's amazement at the intricate carvings in the slate was topped only by its pervasive use. *So, this is where the blue humans, the Hassjidar, dwell. I wonder where the blacksmith Hjerim works. He didn't judge me when I first arrived.* He chuckled to himself. *That makeshift smith shop was where I first learned of my powers. How naïve I was.*

To Julian's surprise, Gjallimé led him directly to a large, busy smith shop, featuring several work pits, only to find Hjerim hammering steel.

"Hjerim my old friend!"

"Ah, Julian. I greet you with more than a warm feeling."

A wide grin on Gjallimé's face, indicated he knew all about Hjerim's quizzical remark. The three stood in awkward silence. Hjerim grinned with Gjallimé.

Come on with it already. No sooner than this thought occurred, Hjerim walked them to the back of the shop. On the wall, hung a magnificent claymore and a dazzling shield. Hjerim first brought down the unusual sword. The edges of the claymore from point to forte shone a golden hue. The grip was leather and the guard curved, with a blue gem on one side, green on the other. Four shiny, black stones were embedded in the forte, along its axis. They gave the claymore contrast to the gold edges making Julian think of death. Silver steel around the stones displayed intricate carvings in tight chevron and angular lines. The effect could only be described as spectacular.

"Well?" Hjerim's chest puffed outward. "What do you think?"

"It's a work of art as well as a weapon." *The grip appears to be sized to fit my hand.* "Why are the edges golden?"

"It is a new d'rrn-steel alloy. Stronger and easily honed to be razor sharp, more than any other. I recently created it. For you." Hjerim stood with legs wide, crossed arms, and a gleam in his eye. "Be careful, the new alloy edges are razor sharp. You must name the sword."

"Hellsbane." And the teenager was proud of his selection.

Julian picked up Hellsbane with his left hand, noticing black stones and hewn pattern on both sides. A beam of light danced upon the blade like quicksilver. He tested the weight, and experimented with slashes and thrusts, even parrying a non-existent foe. "It's perfect! I love the extra length."

Gjallimé spoke. "It suits you."

Hjerim retrieved the shield from the wall mount. "Here. For your right arm."

The same goldish edges. Large, from my chin to my shin. Good weight. "So, I can slash, as well as thrust?" Julian swung the shield as if attacking with the edge.

"Yes."

Offense as well as defense. I like it. The entire face of the shield was an elaborate pattern of large, medium, and small spiral shapes. Majestic.

Gjallimé remarked. "You will make a handsome entrance when we get to the War Council at the foot of the sacred plateau, Naspia Dor."

Chapter 12
War Council

After the last of the Nova'h forces arrived, when the sky held only the quicksilver moon, Eswar called for the War Council. Located in a capacious tent, the large table stood in the shape of a cross. The Kem'nesh was covered with a paisley rug of maroon and peach and aquamarine, though many smaller highlights of other colors gave it a dazzling contrast to the plain tan tent. The Eptizars and generals of each race took their seats, except for the manticore who sat on their haunches. N'ttala-Toor, Xorn, and Julian took their seats as well.

Eswar rose from his seat. Although the congregation of races were not his subjects, he wore the mantel as High King, garnering their respect. He looked at them for a moment or two, graver than usual. "My friends," he began, "My friends and races of Nova'h. You have all answered the call of Enhendendor. This has not occurred in seven generations. The Seal of Nova'h will rise in fourteen hours, and I must tell you that our task is far more difficult than usual." He paused and scanned the crowd. "Zhokul, the Overlord of Darkness, has returned to Edrym."

Loud mummers and groans could be heard as all present stirred. Some sat back in their seats as if hit by a gust of wind. Eswar let the commotion settle. With a white face, N'ttala-Toor stood up. "This indeed does not bode well. I felt something changed in the land, but could not discern the details. I assumed it was J'liánh. The fact that Zhokul was able to block me speaks of great power."

"Does he have *Death*?" shouted someone.

Eswar did not hesitate. "Yes, he has the obsidian *Death* pentacle."

By now, several members of the group stood. Julian could feel terror as a palpable presence. The babble of voices picked up once again.

Eswar raised his voice above the noise, "Quiet! Sit down. Listen to what I have to say."

"How do you know? How can you be sure?" Asked Xorn.

Eswar waited until silence enveloped the tent. "Kanh-apal-apli has seen it."

There were a few gasps at the mention of the Snow Jarl's name. Julian overheard snippets of whispered conversation.

"...no one has seen him..."

"...legend says..."

Eswar motioned once again for everyone to be silent. All in the tent obeyed. Stunned, they hung upon his every word. "Now. It is true that the presence of Zhokul will inspire the Yetzer-xie horde to fight with more ferocity and brutality than we have ever witnessed. It is true that he will be commanding them, guiding them. Losing the efreets is damaging. Their champion, Par'mth, a force to be reckoned with as you all know, will be sorely missed. I am sure he dispatched untold number of the enemy before they overwhelmed him. Most distressing of all is losing *Quash*."

The crowd began to twitch.

"However, Kanh-apal-apli has also furnished me with their troop alignment, including the positioning and enchantments of their Eptizars. In short, we will have advance knowledge like never before. We shall be able to discern their initial strategy from the formations and placements of their enchantments. So, we can devise how to counter them."

With this, scattered applause broke out.

A tall, aged, golden-skinned being with pointed ears and long black hair stood up. She was Dhov'nh, Eptizar of the Llaholleri, the high elves. Her face was narrow and proud. "I have brought the orb of *Mind Shield*!" And she held up a sphere that was the color of smoky fuchsia. "*Death* starts with the mind and then works its will on the body. We shall have some protection from *Death*!" The others knew Dhov'nh was Nova'h's most powerful Eptizar.

Iniqui stood up and hesitated a moment. It was her first time as Eptizar addressing the group. "And I have the scepter of *Enhance* to strengthen the *Mind Shield*!" She glanced nervously at her father.

Due to the nature of these interruptions, Eswar allowed them. He knew all too well that morale often swings the balance of a conflict. The King let the wave of confidence wash over the gathered leaders. Before nervousness could return, he motioned with his hands for all to sit. "Our enchantment strategy, indeed our entire strategy will come later. First then, let us reckon our strength. Let us begin with our largest force, how many do the K'narikh bring?"

Ib-Amel, General of the K'narikh rose. To Julian it looked like she was wearing a disguise. Her olive-green skin matched her olive-green garb and her olive-green hair and eyes. She was human, bespoken to Weeqq, the green moon. She and her kinsmen were stocky, square-jawed and medium height. She proclaimed in a deep and rich voice. "The K'narikh regular army numbers 1,100 and the Elite another 350."

She sat down and Taa're, the K'narikh Eptizar, rose and displayed a nickel signet ring of intricate design with a bright square emerald of the deepest, purest green. "We bring the enchantment of *Strength*."

Jr'esh rose next. "The Khalil bring 850." He threw back his shoulders and barked, "And they are *all* Elites!"

The crowd chuckled and many applauded, for although the Khalil were great swordsmen, they could not match the K'narikh Elites. But such was Jr'esh's pride, and they loved him in spite of it, for he was indeed the greatest trainer in all the land.

And so it went. Stenvar, General of the Hassjidar led 685 blue soldiers and an additional 50 spearmen. Gjallimé spoke proudly of his blue brethren, claiming they carried the finest weapons in all of Edrym, crafted in the armories of Methedriel.

Julian remembered that no hooves ever touched the sand on Naspia Dor; all forces from both sides would be on foot. Ken Noru raised the totem of *Speed*. It was forged of polished pewter that shone like silver and was studded with five blue star sapphires, the most handsome of the enchantment relics Julian would behold.

An imposing blue warrior wearing a violet tunic, the first Champion Julian ever encountered, bounced to his feet. Everyone present chanted, "Shyro! Shyro!" He was Vr'Vachal and proudly announced, "My Hoosforanh number forty-three!" The others stomped their feet and pounded the table in fervor. Julian suppressed a snicker. Forty-three seemed like an insignificant number to him, until he later learned that each could out-fight three of any other soldier. The Hoosforanh were by far the finest combatants that would risk their blood on Naspia Dor, which was attested to by Jr'esh.

The high elves could muster but 379, having taken heavy casualties during Ravoq-Ma, two cycles ago. However, Julian recalled they brought the ever-important *Mind Shield*.

I wonder how much Mind Shield really helps against Death.

S'rrinha now carried the bone of ankh, *Heal*, into the conflict. The nymphs added 500 to the campaign. A taller than normal nymph, General S'rratha, announced, "We have 32 new bows, high tension bows with a range at least as far as the lava giant's balls of fire. And arrows strong and true. All recently made from the wood the Khalil supplied, crafted by our artisans working in Methedriel, so they are ready for Enhendendor. The archers are in training as we speak and another shipment of arrows will be arriving via Riders."

"And what is the range of these bows?" asked Barzakh, general of the manticore.

"One hundred yards."

"Outstanding! It is a shame we had no time to craft more."

Last to speak were the manticore. They bore no arms or armor. They had the body of a gigantic lion, the face of a man, and a scorpion-like tail that could slash and pierce as well as poison.

Their flexible tail was indeed formidable. It could reach forward up to two feet in front of their heads. Add to that their razor-sharp claws. They numbered 650, which was 650 more than Julian would want to face. Their Eptizar carried a pendant of copper and rose-colored glass, worn around his neck. It invoked the enchantment *Blind*.

The leaders settled with a feeling of unity and pride.

Eswar rose up again. "Let us not forget J'liánh, whose prowess the trainers say make him a warrior the likes of which Edrym has never seen."

At the mention of his name, Julian perceived uncertainty on the faces of many and hope in the eyes of few. By now they had all heard of the six predictions from the Adaa. N'ttala-Toor's countenance hinted of expectation. *I sense many feelings but none of true enthusiasm. The soothsayer was right about a **Mass Gathering** and **Conflict**. Why not **Hero**?*

Julian asked. "As an outsider, can I participate?"

N'ttala-Toor answered. "The Law allows it. Have you not already engaged during Ravoq-Ma?"

King Eswar took back control of the conversation. "J'liánh, I will place you under the charge of Vr'Vachal to fight with his Hoosforanh, if that is to his satisfaction." To which the Champion nodded his head. A diplomatic response.

What should I expect? I'm confused and don't know exactly what to think.

Eswar continued, "The forces of Yetzer-xie may well be more daunting than anything which we have encountered. But with our advance knowledge and with our new archers, I believe, without doubt, it is *we* who shall have the advantage. It is time for Nova'h to rise up and seize victory!" This last he shouted with all the zeal he could summon.

The tent erupted with an ardent cry of "Shyro! Shyro!" There was true courage and determination in their shouts. The cries did not let up for several minutes.

When calm ensued, Eswar raised his arms. "Begone now. I will send word when it is time to reconvene to go over the plan to defend the Seal of Nova'h. Go and continue preparations."

+++

Julian caught up with Iniqui as the leaders filed out. "May I walk with you?"

"Of course." Iniqui projected all business now, their totally carefree attitude while returning with Idrazel, absent. With her long silver hair tied up, her face filled with color, her straightened shoulders, and battle garb, Julian could not help thinking how regal, radiant, and formidable she looked.

"Why was my name called?" Julian asked, afraid of the implication. "What does he expect of me?"

Iniqui stopped walking and turned to face him. "J'liánh, remember you told me of your game Gattica?" She bumbled pronouncing the word, "I told my father that you were an expert in strategic battlefield planning, especially with multiple unit types."

"You what?!"

"I persuaded him to include you, and believe me when I say it wasn't easy."

"But did you have to call me an expert? I know and understand only a scant amount about your warfare."

Iniqui tried to suppress a sly grin. "Well, I didn't go quite that far."

"What am I supposed to do in there?" Julian asked, exasperated.

"Don't speak unless you feel very confident in what you are about to say."

"Okay. Okay. As long as he doesn't expect too much." Julian considered that he might be good at this asymmetrical warfare. He almost thanked Iniqui but he bit his lip; he did not want to sound too eager.

Iniqui's brows drew toward each other. "I am taking no chances; I truly am of the opinion that you might see something

112

new. We can be fairly rigid in our traditions." This time Iniqui's eyes smiled. "Besides, I thought you would have fun." She quickly sobered. "And what better way to provide you knowledge."

"That reminds me. Ken Noru used *Quash* as a counter-enchantment in your last battle on Naspia Dor. I can see how powerful it is. Why not use it again?"

"Our Nova'h allies, the efreet, were not called during Waykenim, the engagement at the time you first arrived from E'rth upon the path on Naspia Dor. Ken Noru borrowed the cyclix of *Quash* from the efreet. He returned it immediately after the confrontation. The efreet were all killed and their Hold was pillaged during the last Ravoq-Ma. The cyclix of *Quash* should be in a secret place for us to find, but we have not the time to go to their ravaged Hold and search."

"How is it that *Blind* will not blind *our* men and women?"

"The side of the Eptizar that yields an enchantment dictates its targets. If Nova'h wields *Blind*, a negative enchantment, it will only target Yetzer-Xie. When S'rrinha uses *Heal* it affects only Nova'h."

"Ah. That makes sense." Nevertheless, Julian scratched his head.

"It is simply the state of affairs here in Edrym. The same goes when an eclipse calls for a challenge on Naspia Dor."

"Oh. How long until Eswar calls us back?"

"My father has found that too many souls spoil and delay a good plan. So, he is developing a battle-plan for Enhendendor alone. It may take one to two hours. The rest of those he called, including yourself, will return to give suggestions and comments. The plans may be modified to make them final. After that, he will bring all the generals and Eptizars back in and give us our orders. When everyone returns to their area of the camp, the Generals will instruct their Lieutenants and so on."

"How are adjustments to strategy made in the field?"

"Now is not the time." Iniqui's eyes first closed some, then relaxed, along with the rest of her face. "Do not try to be a hero." *For me* was implied.

"Then I shall settle for valiant." *Shall? And valiant? Are these words really coming out of my mouth?* A silent yet respectful moment passed. "How do you feel about wielding the enchantment of *Enhance*?"

Iniqui lifted her chin a wee bit, "I have the scepter. I have been trained. I am ready."

"If you do not mind my asking, what is the range of the enchantment? And will you have forces for protection?"

Iniqui, grateful to return to business, responded. "Good thinking. I knew I was right about you. The enchantment is at maximum effectiveness up to eighty yards, depending on the skill of the Eptizar. And I am very good. The effectiveness falls quickly to just ten percent at one hundred yards. The range of the lava giants is seventy-five to a hundred yards. So, the Eptizar has a slight advantage even if the enchantment is not one hundred percent at the lava giants' full range."

Julian repeated with concern, "Will you be protected?"

Iniqui scoffed. "Of course. All Eptizars are. We are like your Gattica commanders." Her voice softened. "And we stay behind the front lines. I suggest you get in some training, or even a little nap. You will need it."

"Can I ask to be assigned to protect you?"

But Iniqui had already turned her back and was walking away. She did not want to answer that last question.

+++

Julian re-entered the command tent and his eyes immediately went to the map of the battlefield and the painted blocks of wood and colored stones representing races and Eptizars. He stood around the table as did the other advisors called for this crucial task.

Eswar began, "We face a campaign of six fronts." He pointed at each painted block and colored stone as he spoke. "They have positioned the lava giants on the far-left edge of the battlefield where they will have no exposed flank. The enchantment behind the lava giant force is *Trample*. Next are the wraiths with *Infect*. Zhokul himself is positioned just left of center wielding *Death* and he stands behind the army of draugrs."

Eswar continued to enumerate the starting positions. The rest of the Yetzer-xie force was deployed from center to right: *Fear* with the banshees; *Shock* with the liches; and far right, *Weakness* with the yellow humans, the Ja'tassr.

Eswar looked over his advisors, "Zhokul's plan appears to focus on *Death*, placed near the center of the battlefield to reach the greatest number of our forces within its sphere of influence."

"As I would have done!" Ib-Amel declared.

Eswar fired an angry glance Ib-Amel's way. "The lava giants' position on the end constrains the force we send against them. The edge of Naspia Dor in effect removes their right flank. I believe the lava giant army will attempt to race forward using both their lava balls and *Trample* to full advantage. *Death* and a lava giant rush look to be the two main prongs to their strategy." He raised his eyes, "Our strategy is to keep as many forces as possible away from *Death* and the lava balls, and to optimize the use of our enchantments."

No one contested this overall approach. Not yet.

"Let me begin with the most controversial part of my assessment. I propose we send the Hoosforanh to use their speed to intercept the lava giants before they get a third of the way across the battleground. Slow them in their rush, to minimize the effect of *Trample*."

Ib-Amel snickered, "You cannot trample what you do not over-run."

Julian realized that he was assigned to this critical advance and froze. Time stood still. *I fight, and maybe die, in the first wave.* It didn't really register.

It seemed to Julian that Eswar's voice came from a distance. "One hundred Elite and fifty Khalil will join the Hoosforanh. I know this is a small number of troops to confront the lava giants, but small in number, not in capability. I do not want any more soldiers to backup this group just to find themselves vulnerable to lobbed lava balls."

Nervousness rippled among the advisors except for Vr'Vachal who proclaimed, "We are equal to the challenge!" Julian's mind continued to wander.

"The rear guard for all fronts will form two lines, one sixty yards from the Seal, the other thirty yards in front, the last line of defense. The rear guard for the lava giant front will be double the amount for any another front, one hundred K'narikh and thirty Manticore. These warriors shall send three soldiers to intercept any lava giant bursting through our front-line defense, in order to finish them rapidly."

"I see that no Eptizar is assigned to this front." This from Jr'esh.

"You are correct. They are needed to negate *Death*."

Eswar gestured toward the middle. "*Mind Shield*, *Blind*, and *Enhance* will accompany the manticore force sent against the draugrs and Zhokul himself. Our thirty-two archers will remain in the rear of this group in order to rain arrows upon the Overlord of Darkness.

Enhendendor

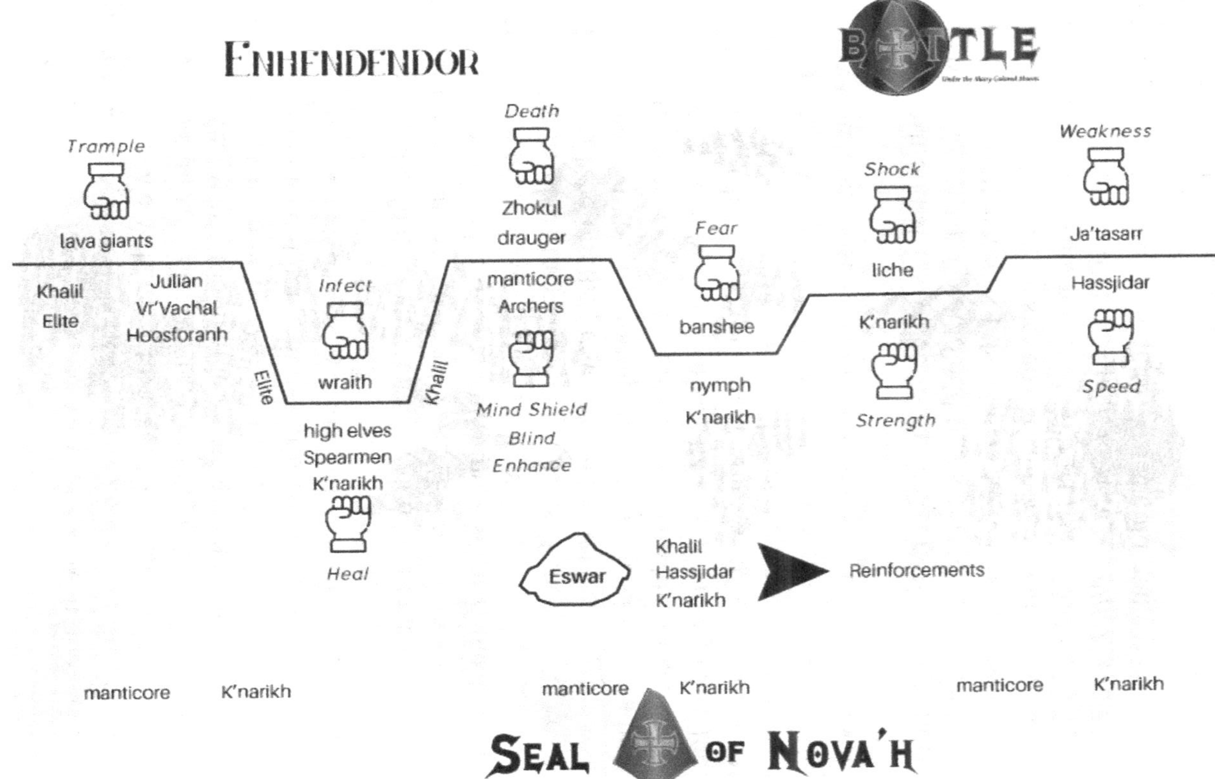

"The Overlord may be very adept with the pentacle of *Death*. Nevertheless, I believe that *Enhanced Blind* should out-range *Death*. We will need to adapt to the actual reckoning, and any counter move Zhokul may attempt after he realizes our strategy. Meanwhile the manticore will engage the draugrs with a hold tactic at the limits of *Death*'s range."

All in the tent hung on Eswar's every word.

"The high elves and nymphs will execute a retreating battle drawing the wraiths and banshees into a killing zone where Khalil shall storm their flanks. This retreat will also put the high elves and nymphs out of range of lava balls and *Death*."

Stenvar used a questioning tone, "What if the wraiths and liches do not press forward into the trap?"

"Remember, they must come at us if they are to reach the Seal of Nova'h before the purple moon has set."

"We will be expanding the front thereby spreading our forces thin." Stenvar offered, pressing on with his concern.

"Which is why we have two lines in the rear guard. Picking off enemies who break through allows us to isolate them individually or in small groups and attack each with an advantage in numbers. We should be able to dispatch these interlopers rapidly. Catching those breaking through is an essential part of our strategy."

Jr'esh added his voice to the conversation. "I believe the strategy to be sound. I would add that some K'narikh will need to support the smaller force of the high elves against the wraiths."

"Indeed. I've assigned a hundred and fifty K'narikh regulars to augment our forces along that front."

Julian gathered the courage to speak. "*Blind* is our biggest advantage. They have no counter. We should make more use of it. Perhaps move it as needed."

Some of the advisors sneered. Eyes rolled. Jr'esh jumped in, "The Khalil on the flanks of the wraith and banshees will draw them into *Blind's* range."

Eswar also came to Julian's aid. "J'liánh, it was a good question. We have always lured as many Yetzer-xie into *Blind* as possible. But to move means the enchantment loses much of its range and power, especially if the movement is fast."

Why did I speak up? He hid his embarrassment.

Eswar referred back to the battle plan not giving anytime for anyone to think about Julian's naiveté. "Eptizars will have a personal guard of ten Manticore and ten Elite. The same for the archers." He added, "It is impossible to anticipate what exactly will play out in the clash in front of Zhokul. Casualties can be expected to be especially high along this draugr front."

If Eswar was unsure of himself, it did not show in his face or tone; both exuded confidence. "On the other fronts I have placed *Heal* against *Infect* and *Strength* against *Weakness*."

Jr'esh spoke up, "I wonder if it might be better to oppose *Shock* and the liche force with K'narikh and *Strength*, while switching the Hassjidar with *Speed* against *Weakness* and the Ja'tasarr. We have no direct counter to *Shock* now that we do not have the cyclix of *Quash*. At least *Strength* can be a partial counter."

Eswar put his hand to his chin and thought. "A good idea. What say you all?'

All either nodded or proclaimed with assent, "Aye!"

Julian zoned back into the proceedings, and gave a late nod.

"Then it shall be." Eswar swapped the appropriate markers of stone and wood. "I will command from the mound, sounding the horn for orders, employing the usual signals. Ensure your Lieutenants know them all. I want a hundred Hassjidar and three hundred K'narikh for reinforcements. Assign a lieutenant to groups of fifty instead of the normal hundred."

I was slapped down pretty hard last time. But I think this idea is very important. The Eptizars play a similar role to Commanders in Gattica. Julian cleared his throat.

"If I understand it correctly," all eyes were on him, as again, he made a suggestion. "When the Yetzer-xie Eptizars move forward to catch up with their advancing forces, the enchantments are weakened and their troops are more vulnerable. Because we have no true counter to *Shock*, I propose a team of Elites use the opportunity while the Eptizar of *Shock* moves, to form a spearhead rushing directly toward that Eptizar and destroy *Shock* or force a retreat. This would be a strictly offensive maneuver, penetrating their lines."

Eswar asked, "This team would choose forward movement over engagement?"

The most important question. "Yes."

Eswar tightened his eyebrows. "The Elite themselves will be more vulnerable this way."

"True. A tradeoff for attempting to get to *Shock*'s Eptizar. A relentless storm offense."

Ib-Amel jumped in, "The Eptizar of *Shock* may have stopped well before they reach it."

"True." Julian clenched his jaw and leaned forward. "They must rush forward even then. And cut down anything in their path. I would even throw a wave or two of arrows at the right time. If it can be spared."

Eswar stroked his chin, eyes focused entirely on the mock battlefield on the table.

Uh-oh. Nova'h defends, does not attack.

For the first time the soothsayer, N'ttala-Toor, spoke up. "This offensive approach is not typical of Nova'h. Especially an approach so aggressive. But I have searched my being and find no resistance to this change. I urge you to make your decision solely on the merits of the tactic itself."

Jr'esh responded first. "I think the tactic offers ample reward for the risk. In fact, I propose we do the same against the Eptizar of *Infect*. Eswar, how many Elites do you think are needed?"

Eswar looked up at his advisors, holding them in a steady gaze. He addressed Ib-Amel directly. "I reckon fifteen Elite for each assault. But this is pretty much a suicide mission, for they will be operating behind enemy lines. What say you Ib-Amel? They are your brethren."

Everyone fell silent. Ib-Amel grasped the ruby medallion around his neck and he rubbed the gem between his thumb and fingers. The tension between anticipation and reticence hung heavy in the air. Ib-Amel turned to Julian with a fixed stare of inspection and contemplation.

Julian's stomach flopped. *Oh jeez. What have I done now?*

"I understand that you fought gallantly during Ravoq-Ma." Ib-Amel's stare did not waver. Nor did Julian's. Not from confidence, but from fear.

"Shyro! We shall prevail!" was Ib-Amel's response. "But I think twenty, not fifteen."

And so it went. The spearmen were assigned as the lead for the high elves. Details were ironed out for each of the fronts. Contingencies were discussed. But Julian did not hear them. *I have sent men to their death. In the moment, I thought of them as game pieces on the board. In this tent, this world - these people seem like a dream. Why was I kept from going home? What have I done?*

Chapter 13
Battle Under the Many Colored Moons

All eight creature types and the four races of humans stared skyward as the final eclipse was realized. The lavender moon in front of the silver. Julian found himself a step behind the 9,000 beings commencing their full out sprint from each side of the flat, goldenrod-colored, sandy surface of Naspia Dor. He caught up with the 43 blue Hoosforanh, Julian's immediate combatant comrades, for his speed was even greater than theirs.

The Hoosforanh's leader, champion Vr'Vachal, led his troops with the war cry of the Nova'h forces, "Shyro!", barely audible over the pounding feet from both Nova'h and Yetzer-Xie forces closing the space between them. Directly in front of Julian, the lava giants.

And so it begins. I'm unafraid. Fear is the death of the mind that paralyzes the body. No, I'm excited. I may die, but I want to rid this plateau of as many evil soldiers as I can. I want to make Eswar and Vr'Vachal proud. And Iniqui. And Gjallimé.

The Hoosforanh ran two deep and twenty-one across. Julian was at the far-right edge of the formation. He glanced behind. A hundred and fifty Khalil combatants ran close, to the left, with less velocity. Well behind both segments of the Nova'h response, the rear guard of manticore and blue fighters stood in wait. Hovering behind the rear guard glowed a towering circular design of corise and luminescent crimson, the Seal of Nova'h.

Oh shit! That shape! Julian's heart took up residence in his throat at the sight of the pattern.

"Dive!" shouted Vr'Vachal.

A hundred lava giants unleashed their one lava ball during the charge. A volley of fire raced toward them. The soldiers in this left flank of the campaign hugged the sand. Over a dozen Khalil and two Hoosforanh screamed as low, flying balls of intense heat scorched them. Foot soldiers rolled and writhed on the ground screaming in pain, attempting to put out the fire feeding on their flesh. Through the acrid stench, two soldiers tried to help the badly burned, but still living, when one of the suffering cried out, "Go! Attack!" Julian saw triage coming for the wounded. Vr'Vachal directed all to continue the charge, and the troop responded. About fifteen heartbeats later, Julian could not help but glance behind as he ran. Injured soldiers were being helped, limping or carried, back toward the rear line.

+++

On the mound, Eswar felt a massive rumbling as the armies charged each other. Once the sides met, the din was shuffling, clangs, huffs, and cries of those who were cut or impaled. The purple moon, Z'th, began to separate from the silver, I'rnh Alon.

+++

Julian swung his custom claymore, Hellsbane, in a short but powerful slicing motion. His first foe, an ugly giant, fell face forward to the ground with a thump. His severed leg teetered over behind him. The creature's black iron battle-axe never had a chance to begin its downward motion, falling harmlessly. As Julian finished the giant with a hack to the neck using the point of his shield, a wraith stormed him, for he was at the junction of the two armies. He dispatched the second monster with a wicked backhand. Such was the power within him.

Beside him, with cries of battle, the Hoosforanh engaged the lava giants one-on-one, two layers deep. They were one of few Nova'h soldiers that could manage such a singular contest against the creatures. The manticore and himself being the others. Further down the line Elite Khalil engaged the rust-colored beasts in groups of two which was advantage Nova'h. One of the beasts threw sand in the eyes of a Khalil, rendering him temporarily ineffective. The second Elite took the opportunity to lunge and lance the creature's chest. Blood flowed upon the land. Grunts and screams were occasionally overlaid by directions from one of the warriors to another. The Khalil caught in solo clashes were being pushed back or slaughtered. Several lava giants breached the front and ran toward the Seal only to be intercepted by manticore and Elite from the rear guard.

+++

The mix of high elves, K'narikh regulars, and spearmen facing the mauve-colored wraiths on Julian's right, intentionally retreated during the onslaught hoping to create a killing zone surrounded on three sides as per the strategy.

+++

Two giants rushed Julian from his left. He used his quickness to flank the duo, allowing him to engage one creature at a time. Hellsbane survived the block of the closest beast's black iron battle-axe. *Thanks to the expert handicraft of Hjerim.* The teenager countered by thrusting his shield forward which shoved the closet giant backwards into the other. Both fell flailing to the goldenrod surface of Naspia Dor, where he promptly skewered each.

"J'liánh! Look out!" came from the Hoosforanh next to him.

He turned to see a wraith with hate painted on its face, brandishing a mace, charging him from the rear.

+++

125

On the other side of the battlefield the Nova'h Hassjidar engaged the Yetzer-Xie yellow skinned humans, the Ja'tassr, three and four layers deep. The enemy's sorcerer, their Eptizar, wielded the enchantment of *Weakness*. This was pitted against *Speed*. The interplay of these two enchantments slightly favored Yetzer-Xie. Hassjidar warriors were able to wield their swords with swiftness, but little power. Kills required several blows. Fortunately, the Hassjidar's speed remained effective in defense, or the yellow humans would have overwhelmed the Nova'h force along this front. Nevertheless, the Ja'tassr force inched forward as Hassjidar casualties outnumbered the enemies'. King Eswar sent in reinforcements.

+++

The K'narikh and liches combat bogged down from the outset. Morale along this front played out based on each individual's success. *Shock* and *Strength* effectively canceled each other. The liches height and reach gave them an advantage, but the K'narikh enjoyed an edge in numbers. In the glow of the moons, a valiant K'narikh soldier, even as he fell dying, sliced off a shrieking liche's leg. Flies buzzed around the mangled body parts that littered the ground.

+++

The focus of Eswar's attention centered on the campaign against Zhokul and the draugrs directly in front of him. Although the distance to the Overlord of Darkness measured over a hundred yards, Eswar shuddered at the sight of the seven-foot, skinless monstrosity. The manticore and draugrs raced toward each other until they stood at the fringe of *Death* and the Nova'h combination of *Blind*, *Mind Shield* and his daughter's scepter of *Enhance*. The three Eptizars braced themselves as if a stiff wind blustered in their faces. Zhokul did the same.

126

At the fringe of the enchantments' power, the skinless draugrs saw blurred shapes of manticore, while the manticore dealt with weakness and, if they ventured too far forward, deterioration to death. Draugrs advancing too far in the direction of the Seal of Nova'h fell quickly to a second line of manticore they could not see. The scrum slogged on this way, with a small sprinkling of losses, as each side fought defensively.

From the command mound, Eswar observed *Death*'s sphere of influence was greater than his enchantments, providing a longer battle front. An angry draugr successfully hacked and killed a tall Khalil soldier along the far edge of *Death*. The opposite edge experienced similar results. Eswar shouted. "*Blind* and *Mind Shield*, move eight yards apart!" The edges of the front fared better this way, but *Death* retained the advantage against each Nova'h enchantment on its own.

The Overlord of Darkness decided to use *Death*'s longer range. He began a tactic of taking three long strides followed by a full stop for *Death* to resume its maximum effectiveness. Because the power and range of *Death* fell during the strides, some manticore who stood fast at their position found themselves enveloped by *Death* when Zhokul held, soon crumpling. Their eyes rolled back until only the whites showed as they hit the sand of Naspia Dor. The draugrs had instructions to avoid a similar potential trap by *Blind*. Manticore retreated, creating an empty zone where both *Blind* and *Death* held sway. Draugrs and manticore soldiers hissed and barked at each other across this space. Except at the edges, where the awkward fighting brought the Khalil flanking the wraiths and banshees to engage in the central skirmish.

Yetzer-Xie progressed relentlessly forward. Eswar unleashed the thirty-two archers to fire shots directly at The Overlord's position, adding twang and whoosh sounds to the cries and clangs of battle. The rain of arrows pinned him, but the supply would not last till the setting of the purple moon signaled the end of the carnage. When the Overlord of Darkness could once again advance, eventually the Nova'h Eptizars would fall into *Death*'s range and would need to retreat.

+++

Nine young lava giants peeled off from the rear line. They jogged along the back edge of the field of combat, toward the center of the contest.

+++

Fear proved effective for the banshee mob against the nymphs and K'narikh. The rear guard stopped the Nova'h fighters who fled in fear, but it took some ten to twelve minutes to regain their composure and rejoin the battle. Meanwhile the banshees pushed dangerously forward. Eswar observed this dynamic and commanded reinforcements as a counter. "Two groups, go to the nymph front! Put on some speed!" He also sent word to Dhov'nh to take *Mind Shield* as a counter to *Fear* along this front. When the reinforcements and enchantment arrived, Nova'h held its ground. Weapons drew shrieks, blood, and guts, and casualties grew.

+++

The separation of the red and green moons, completely ending their eclipse, signaled the onset of the attempt by the attacking Elite squad of twenty souls to rush *Shock* from the space between the K'narikh and Hassjidar fronts. A contingent of K'narikh yelled, "Shyro!" in encouragement. If *Shock* fell or retreated, the olive-green skinned K'narikh would decimate the liche force.

Ja'tasarr soldiers, Yetzer-Xie humans bespoken to the yellow moon, assaulted the Nova'h group on one side, while liches assailed the opposite flank. Elites tried to press forward even while fending off the strikes from the sides. The rested rear lines of Ja'tasarr and liches closed off the Elites up front, surrounding the

128

group. Both *Shock* and *Weakness* took their toll. Nova'h combatants fell dead with deep lacerations, missing arms, and mangled torsos. Some without their heads. Only three Elites managed to escape. The thrust was an abject failure.

+++

Swiveling rapidly Julian split the crazed, rushing wraith in two with a sweeping slice of Hellsbane. The creature's last thought was of its comrades-in-arms. The beast's brethren followed the rest, away from Julian and into the developing trap caused by the high elves' fake retreat.

+++

Wraith forces fell foolishly into the retreating Nova'h trap. The high elves supported by K'narikh and spearmen spilled much blood, and the Khalil and Elites pressed the assault from the sides. Anguished cries of the dying wraiths pierced through the sound of clashing swords, war cries, grunts, and thunks enveloping Naspia Dor. Eswar recognized that of all his Nova'h armies, this front was most successful, even though Yetzer-Xie advanced the farthest toward the Seal.

+++

Julian turned back to the giants. A scowling eight-foot creature swung his battle-axe, but Julian dodged the blow. The lava giant paused, pulling himself to his full height, and backed off, putting some space between the two. His left arm swung in a wide arc. Julian waited until the lava ball was formed and released, before jumping right and high while twisting his body sideways, pulling his mid-section inward. In mid-air he crouched behind the large shield Hjerim had forged. The lava ball hit the shield a glancing blow. This knocked Julian even higher and to the right in

129

the direction his momentum was already flowing. Luckily at close range the lava ball didn't reach its top speed.

Shit. I'm falling.

Julian hit the ground, his new shield taking the full force of the giant's follow up leap and swing of its axe. The force of the blow pounded Julian into the sand, bruising two ribs. While the ugly giant towered over his prone form, Julian curled his legs, and, extending his body, kicked the fiend in the crotch. The monster bellowed. He flew rearwards, landing on its back. Julian pounced, hacking off the beast's head. A blood-shot eye-ball popped out from the jarring blow, rolling on the bloody ground. *Holy crap.*

All moons separated from their eclipses, rendering a sky of eight colored, full moons and the marmalade sun. For the first time, the brightness exceeded what he was used to on Earth. With renewed fervor, Julian advanced against the giant army's now exposed flank. *My side. Something's wrong. A dull ache when I move.* The adrenaline coursing through Julian's body washed out what would've been intense pain. He recklessly brandished his blade and swung his shield edge. His motions – swift, powerful, and true – dispatched three more of the enemy. He found himself in an open space.

Nearby, Vr'Vachal withdrew his sword from a giant's belly. Guts oozed out onto the ground, followed by the thunk of the mutilated corpse. A chunk taken from Vr'Vachal's upper arm exposed red flesh. He circled back toward Julian. Five of his loyal Hoosforanh followed.

"J'liánh! It is time to attack. The new target is *Death* itself!"

+++

As more warriors died or were injured, the coppery smell of blood and anguish covered the land. The rain of arrows that besieged Zhokul came to an end. With dread, Eswar watched the renewal of the Overlord of Darkness's 'stride and hold' assault tactic. Where *Blind* and *Mind Shield* overlapped, manticore on the

130

front line hurried forward to cut down, with great success, the draugrs fighting for the Overlord. Eswar ordered this countermove. Even when The Yetzer-Xie leader stopped, and *Death*'s influence began to expand, the manticore enjoyed a few seconds to retreat from its range. Not all made it. Never-ending fresh draugrs filled in for the fallen. A restless Eswar hoped the draugr reinforcements would run out soon. Nova'h could then engage Zhokul's personal guard.

Eventually the Overlord could not advance into *Blind*'s circle of influence. He stopped after a single stride. Unfortunately, when he held, *Death* reached the three Nova'h Eptizars forcing them back. At least the rate of the advance slowed.

Zhokul kept a close watch on the purple moon moving inexorably toward the horizon. He scanned the battlefield, proud that his children fared well on almost all fronts. The leader of Yetzer-Xie schemed. He would soon spring his next tactic.

+++

The Elite line facing the lava giants, stretched thin from casualties, collapsed. Elite K'narikh and manticore from the rear guard charged those lava giants bursting through the front. The enemies reached each other. A manticore swung its claws ripping through a giant's chest, piercing its lungs. The monster fell to the sand, gasping its last breath. More individual duels ensued. The doubling of the guard assigned to this flank proved necessary and effective. Isolated groups of Nova'h and Yetzer-Xie combatants fought scattered confrontations to the death across the left side of Naspia Dor.

+++

On the opposite side, a group of liche forces broke through the K'narikh ranks and reached *Strength*. With the clang of metal, the bludgeoned Eptizar expelled her last breath. Nobody heard her.

131

The wraith army continued forward into Nova'h's trap. They found themselves under assault from three sides by high elves, K'narikh, Khalil, and spearmen. *Heal* canceled *Infect*. The last standing wraith decapitated a high elf directly in front of him. He found himself with a Khalil fighter advancing toward him from one side. From the other, an Elite K'narikh pressed the confrontation with a thrust of his longsword. The wraith turned to absorb the blow with its shield and was pushed back toward the opposite attacker. The Khalil's broadsword sliced gaping wounds in the creature's back with two quick, strong blows. Blood spewed from its torso, and mouth. A muffled scream formed as orange blood gurgled forth. The creature collapsed to the ground with a thud.

"Shyro!" The entire wraith military on Edrym was now eliminated. The surviving Nova'h warriors on this front either ran to help against the lava giants, or advanced to assist against the edge of Zhokul's draugr force which had pushed forward. The purple moon inched closer to the horizon.

+++

Vr'Vachal, Julian and the five Hoosforanh ran at two-thirds speed to conserve energy, toward the mass of soldiers dueling at the edge of *Death* and *Mind Shield*. They made good time across the empty battle ground where the wraiths had succumbed. Fizzing flies swarmed among the bloodied dead. Seven spearmen and their squires encountered runners, word from King Eswar, and met Vr'Vachal's group along the way.

+++

The nine young lava giants caught up with the front line of the draugr – manticore skirmish. They launched lava balls, smaller but with greater range, directly targeting the two Nova'h Eptizars:

132

Blind, and *Enhance*. Several of the courageous personal guard, and *Blind*, took direct hits, instantly bursting into all-encompassing flames.

"Down!" An Elite guard barked as he shoved Iniqui to the sand, covering her with his shield and body. Two lava balls exploded upon him with a boom. Iniqui scampered out from beneath the heat and fire, spitting gravel. Rolling on the ground extinguished the flames that seared her trousers, the silver scepter of *Enhance* remained tightly gripped. She vowed to seek out this hero's family later, to mourn with them.

Eswar ordered *Mind Shield* to return to the aid of the manticore combatants. Iniqui retreated ten yards and stopped, focusing once again on her power. But the pause left several more of the valiant dead. Yetzer-Xie pressed forward.

+++

In sixteen minutes, the purple moon, Z'th, would set. Zhokul whistled orders and took off in a sprint at a forty-five-degree angle away from the center where Eswar stood, skirting the influence of *Mind Shield*. The effectiveness of *Death* shrunk to ten yards. Frustration crept into the Overlord. *I could cross the remaining eighty-yard distance to the Seal in thirty seconds in an open field.* However, the clash of forces, two and three combatants deep, formed a semi-circle in front of him thus slowing his progress. The struggle shifted to match *Death*'s reduced presence. In a blink, Zhokul and his personal guard caught up to the front.

+++

Eswar's horn signaled for *Mind Shield*, *Heal*, and *Enhance* to come as rapidly as possible to the mound where he stood.

"Quickly. Take a stand at the rear guard. At the intercept of the Yetzer-Xie leader's charge to the Seal. Entrench yourselves and wield as much power as you can."

The three Eptizar's, Dhov'nh, S'rrinha and Iniqui, took off without hesitation. Having a clear path, they reached their position within a minute. They stood perfectly still to maximize their enchantments. But now they were only five yards in front of the Seal.

+++

Opposite, on Eswar's right, three separate struggles continued. For each of these individual wars, the forces had thinned out. Dead lay bleeding on the sand. Groans and screeching nearly drowned out the sounds of battle. The clash between the Ja'tasarr and Hassjidar, augmented by Nova'h reinforcements, raged with increased intensity as Enhendendor approached its end. To Nova'h's favor, the combat had not moved much from its initial position.

The army of yellow-bearded liches surged forward with the elimination of *Strength*. Comparing the estimated rate of advance against the setting of the purple moon, Eswar concluded that Nova'h would prevail.

Without *Mind Shield*, banshees had pushed the nymphs and K'narikh close to Eswar's position. He sent the last Hassjidar, Khalil and K'narikh reinforcements to shore up that conflict. It would have to hold.

Rear guard forces dealt with Yetzer-Xie forces that broke through on any of the fronts. Resigned to the threat of Zhokul's advance, Eswar bolted away to a position directly in front of his three Eptizars at the rear guard. Thirteen minutes till moon-set.

+++

While working their way toward Zhokul, Julian, Vr'Vachal, and their attack group encountered *Infect* and its guard, left alone after the wraith massacre. Vr'Vachal leapt first, crushing the skull of a draugr. Julian and the rest quickly dispatched the others. The *Infect* Eptizar ran, but Vr'Vachal cut him down, the

134

crunching of bone signaling his demise. The Nova'h Champion, in his purple tunic, tucked the *Infect* talisman in his belt. *Good. The pox breaking out on some is vanishing.*

+++

The Overlord and his army charged relentlessly as the Nova'h combatants labored defensively, retreating in the face of *Death*. Some weaker soldiers succumbed, even while backing away. Several banshees and the nine lava giants joined the fray.

The Nova'h second rear guard engaged when the Overlord of Darkness reached within thirty yards of the Seal. The 'stride and hold' tactic had advanced the challenge ninety yards, whereas Zhokul gained forty yards in four minutes with his sprint. Twelve minutes till Z'th fell under the horizon.

+++

A lone lava giant broke away from the melee with the Elite and dashed toward Julian. He hurled his once daily lava ball at Julian's group who had recently finished off *Infect*. Julian saw the ball of fire out of the corner of his eye, ducked, and an unfortunate spearman behind him convulsed and howled as he burst into flame.

The Earth teenager shouted to the others. "I'll take this bastard out." He rushed the fiend. They collided in a mash of weapons. Both were thrown back to the ground, hemorrhaging from cuts, heads ringing. The lava giant suffered a large, open gash to its side. Julian pounced up quickly. He hacked off the monster's arm raised in defense. Followed by a penetrating, bone crunching, fatal blow to the beast's chest.

Z'th had but eleven minutes in the sky as Julian ran to catch up to the others. Zhokul stood twenty yards from his goal.

The Overlord of Darkness weakened and turned his head to see the black moon Ihl beginning to set. Z'th was sinking adjacent

135

to Ihl, but at a slower rate. A black, indigo, purple and lavender glaze smeared gloom across the cobalt sky. *Death*'s influence shrank further.

The spearmen closed to within range and unleashed their fury at Zhokul directly, impaling three guard draugrs. One folded to the ground shrieking a dying cry. The others grimaced and pressed forward. The Overlord of Darkness temporarily slowed. Sixteen yards and ten minutes to go.

Heal, *Mind Shield*, and *Enhance* provided more protection as Yetzer-Xie pushed to the fore. However, they stood six yards to the right of Zhokul's path. Moving to directly intercept would mean diminishing their power.

The Overlord's personal guard joined the semi-circle of action. In Julian's group, two Hoosforanh and six spearmen found themselves caught up with the fighting on the flank. The spearmen lasted less than two minutes. The two Hoosforanh hacked and gored many of the flanking Yetzer-Xie. But still, they fell behind Zhokul's advance.

Eight minutes remained. Eleven yards. The Overlord ordered his forces to slide sideways, clearing the middle for him to press ahead. Ihl vanished beneath the horizon resulting in the edge of *Death*'s impact dropping to five yards. Vr'Vachal and the four remaining Hoosforanh reached the center of Zhokul's path, Julian gaining on them.

"V'nnath with me!" shouted Vr'Vachal, leading with his shield, as he rapidly closed distance to the Yetzer-Xie leader. "Hattrad and Zhuaidh, be still for ten heartbeats, then follow. We engage Zhokul directly, at *Death's* maximum." At five feet he sensed the Overlord's ghastly laugh inside his head as his enfeebled muscles began to give way. His strength of character, and the help of the Nova'h enchantments, afforded him enough strength to block the evil leader's huge claymore with his shield. V'nnath caught the ricochet into his left armpit. The blade reached and crushed his clavicle thus magnifying *Death*, and he perished. The Yetzer-Xie leader took one hand off his claymore to fling aside Vr'Vachal's shield. As Vr'Vachal lunged, Zhokul ripped open his gut. Entrails in one arm, Vr'Vachal sank to his knees and fell sideways, eyes glassy with his death. But their suicide mission slowed evil's advance such that he gained only two yards. The Edrym sky would hold Z'th but seven more minutes.

The next two Hoosforanh fell in under a minute. But not before they imparted a deep gash in the dark muscles of Zhokul's hip exposing ash-grey bone. Eight yards away, Eswar and a single line of warriors stood in front of the Seal, the last gasp of defense.

The Earth lad sped toward the Overlord of Darkness, shield and Hellsbane held high because of Zhokul's height. Julian's heart was crushed, his spirit in despair. He too would succumb to *Death*. As he dashed ever closer, surprise momentarily washed over him. *I'm **not** pure Nova'h! No sense of death or decay assails me!* This bout would be one based solely on skill, strength, agility, and speed.

Julian slammed into the Overlord, leading with his shield, Hellsbane at the ready. Their force nullified each other, his shield and the Yetzer-Xie leader's claymore locked. Simultaneously, Hellsbane cut at Zhokul's hip, exposing more bone. They parried, the teenager alternating strikes and checks between shield and sword. Neither penetrated the other's defense. Except for a shallow wound on Julian's right lower-arm, lessened by his chainmail armor. However, even though the Earth teenager did not retreat, his boots slid rearward on the sand. He lost more than a yard in the exchange. Even with his best blow, the leader of Yetzer-Xie gave way no more than a foot. Looming almost two-feet above the teenager, the Overlord hacked downward with more speed than Julian would have guessed. The teenager blocked, high above his head, with shield and Hellsbane's cross guard forming a wedge, combining the strength of both arms. He still slid back. *I'm losing.*

A silver dagger whistled past Julian's ear, impaling Zhokul's left cheek, buried to the hilt. He barely flinched. His laugh, like a cackle, chilled Julian to the core.

Julian recognized the dagger as Eswar's. With three more yards, the Nova'h last line would experience the sting of *Death.* Four minutes till the dark side of Edrym swallowed up the purple moon. Seven yards for Yetzer-Xie to reach the glowing Seal of Nova'h.

Julian took a risk. Jumping two feet off the ground, watching a bewildered Zhokul, he sliced off an ear.

The stunned Overlord of Darkness roared. "Who the s'lennh are you?"

While settling to the ground Julian swung his shield, razor edge first, in an arc aimed at the monster's mid-section. The Overlord of Darkness stepped back avoiding the shield. But gave back half a yard.

Zhokul bellowed. With compressed swings and berserk rage, he pummeled the teenager's shield, forcing a retreating defense.

He becomes wrath. What can I do?

The seventh spearman picked up an unbroken spear on the sand. Thrown with perfect accuracy, the weapon sank deep into the Overlord's right thigh. Zhokul looked around, landing a killer's gaze upon the spearman, and ripped out the spear, leaving ragged, dangling flesh.

Two minutes. Six yards.

An ear-rattling whistle from the Yetzer-Xie leader called for full retreat. *Time has run out. I know how to win next time.* Minus an ear, dagger in his cheek, exposed bone at one hip, thigh muscle dangling, the Overlord of Darkness loped backwards with a wide seductive smile, beaming at the stunned Nova'h warriors.

Julian stood limp, arms by his side. *What does he know, that I don't?*

Chapter 14
Aftermath

Eswar raised his arms, hollering, "Shyro! Shyro!" The exhausted combatants of Nova'h repeated the cheer.

Many joined the field infirmary to give aid to their wounded comrades after the purple moon set, leaving silver, green and others in the sky. S'rrinha and Iniqui took advantage of their moons, visiting the wounded to provide *Enhanced Heal*. Julian, dizzy on his feet, caught up with the two girls, following their rounds. He looked for Gjallimé.

At one of the makeshift cots, he saw R'qanar.

"J'liánh! Come sit with me." The nymph curio shop owner's weary smile lucid on his wrinkled face.

Oh my god! R'qanar's arm has been chopped off. Ah, there the wince of pain replaces his brief smile. Julian sat at R'qanar's right side; the other side soaked in blood. He grasped the nymph's hand with both of his, squeezing tight. "You will be all right."

"No, this wound rushes me toward death's abyss." His words like gasps, left Julian distraught. "I heard you took on Zhokul one-on-one and saved the day. What was the monster like?"

"Horrible. And I did not save the day. I just barely survived. I was losing when the moon-set of Z'th ended the onslaught." Julian could not look into R'qanar's eyes.

R'qanar shook his head, dismissing Julian's assessment. He gritted his teeth. "The dagger, Ilzjur, did not possess me when I took it into battle. Perhaps the evil curse is lifted." R'qanar's body tightened. His eyes grew foggy. "Here. Take Ilzjur. A last gift…"

And so, holding his friend's hand, Julian accepted Ilzjur and watched R'qanar die.

As winners of Enhendendor, Nova'h could tend to its wounded and dead on the surface of Naspia Dor, while Yetzer-Xie carried their wounded and fallen away.

Odd. The two forces do not engage, though they pass by each other. They all follow the crazy rules. "Weird." Julian whispered to himself, still reeling from R'qanar's death.

The Nova'h dead were grouped into four large burial mounds. Eswar raised his arms and spoke. A booming but solemn tone. "The dead are our brothers and sisters, our mothers and fathers, our children, our friends. We honor them. And we remember their selfless sacrifice which brought us victory. So shall our children be told and remember. And our grandchildren. And all who come after." Surviving Nova'h warriors bent their heads and muttered the tribute.

Julian lowered his head and wept for the dead. *There, but for luck, lay I.*

+++

"Gjallimé!" Julian shouted. His blue friend's weary steps sprung to life as they closed their distance. "Gjallimé! The Seal of Nova'h! Its inner pattern. The Seal pattern, it's the same as the bronze Avatar I use as my commander in Gattica! It's in my room on E'rth!"

Gjallimé's eyes bulged. "The missing piece of The-Key-that-is-Lost!"

Julian said. "We must tell Eswar."

"You must go back and retrieve it."

"I hope the scholars at W'lkyndh have succeeded so I can open the portal."

Eswar reacted thoughtfully to the news. "Add **Hero** to what the Adaa predicted. And perhaps **Taming Great Power**."

I like the sound of that.

142

The King's eyes squinted. "I wonder how **Youthful Folly** and **Wanderer** will manifest themselves. And how did the missing part of The Key end up on E'rth?"

The teenagers shrugged.

Gjallimé practically bounced. "We are ready to ride to W'lkyndh to retrieve the missing part."

"Yes. Of course. But stay for tonight's celebration."

+++

Iniqui sought Julian among the four large campfires forming orange-blue diamonds in the flattened Kem-nesh that had been the Nova'h pre-battle gathering site, a somber place the night before. A multitude of torches created an outer ring around the campfires, adding to the light of the ever-present sun.

Ah. The sun is higher in the sky than at the Khalil Hold, Zhon Jeul. We must be farther east. Julian walked aimlessly through the throng of boisterous Nova'h individuals, most of whom stopped as he passed, clapping his back, or embracing him. *I'm a hero.* It warmed his soul.

Xrarreth: the green, blue, white, and silver moons of Nova'h charged the atmosphere with good fortune. Plenty of mead flowed as the party commenced. Enhendendor had not occurred in seven generations, so the significance of the triumph could not be overstated.

Banging shield and sword together, Eswar got the rabble to subside. "Lift your mugs. All hail Jr'esh. He is now Champion and can wear lavender." Eswar did not mention the possibility of regaining The-Key-that-is-Lost.

Julian downed his mead. *The color of the power of Ava'cynh. To tap into what is in your heart. Magnified and mighty when used with The Key.*

Eswar let the roars, "Shyro! Shyro!", wane. "But that is not all. J'liánh, who faced the Overlord of Darkness alone, also deserves the mantle of Champion!" Uproar within the ranks resumed with fervor. Julian and Jr'esh were lifted above the crowd.

My head is spinning. Is it the mead or the attention?

Sounds of laughter and music rang sweet victory to his ears. He was lowered by the throng and wandered by a square-jawed Khalil arm wrestling a K'narikh youth with muscles taut in his neck. Two elves kissed along the edge of the torch circle, oblivious to the party. Drinking games he did not fully understand occupied many. But most omnipresent was the serious, yet cheerful regaling of battle encounters with Yetzer-Xie. The Earth teenager shared drink and retold tales of battle with many that eve.

Iniqui overheard his boasts. *You are drunk with yourself.* And chose not to be one of the enthusiasts.

+++

The roof of the tent twirled as Julian lay on his back on the bedding. Despite his dizziness, he fought off sleep, thoroughly enjoying the lingering buzz of the celebration.

She appeared out of thin air inside the tent's entryway. Teal and scarlet colors played paisley games across her sheer dress, which she slid off her shoulders and let drop to the floor. Julian lifted his head and chest, leaning back on his elbows, though he poised forward toward the ravishing naked body not two feet from the end of the bed. S'rrinha's face shone in the soft filtered light of the moons and sun, smiling broadly; but all he could see was the lovely fullness of her curvy form, the beckoning shadow of her nether region. It was his first view of what he now knew was the splendor of the live female form, this one hunter-green and delicate with aquamarine gossamer wings that beat strong and slow. *What happens now?* His loins responded.

With a sultry sway of her hips, and a single stride, she was on her hands and knees at his feet. His face was still frozen, his being in awe, his eyes locked on the heart-stopping shape of her hanging bosom. The muffled din of the party's twilight masked his shallow, soon to be heavy, breathing as the only sound in the world. She crept forward and with a single elegant hand untied his

144

trousers. His heartbeat quickened. Everything about her, to the finest detail, was exquisite and dazzling.

"You look very sexy in purple," S'rrinha purred as she unbuttoned the lavender tunic Eswar had presented him. Firmly pushing him back upon the bed, she placed her hands on his shoulders, straightened her arms, and deftly straddled him. Julian gasped as she lowered herself, her smile laced with subtle hints of pleasure and purpose, his with wonder. He shuddered with anticipation. She rocked, slowly at first – then with increased pace. He could do nothing but let her have her way with him. And he loved it.

S'rrinha dabbed the sheen of sweat on his brow with the cool inside of her wrist and the smell of honeysuckle bloomed ever stronger. Julian remained mesmerized by her exotic beauty, her velvet touch, and most of all, their joining. Her thin yet supple lips caressed his chest such that her soft bosom brushed wantonly against his taut stomach. Julian instinctively arched his back and threw his arms outward.

Smiling once again, challenge in her lime-green eyes, she moved anew against him. This time they locked in rhythm, feasting like hungry animals. He panted and dared to reach out and take her smooth buttocks in his hands. Time stopped. Their rocking continued.

Tilting back her head, S'rrinha's fine wings beating ever faster. His eyes closed as he felt sensation build. Their muscles tightened in the moment.

She fell upon his heaving chest and he wrapped his arms around her, the feathery touch of her wings tickling him. Julian lightly brushed her cheek with the back of his fingers, then ran them through her hair. They remained in quiet embrace for some time.

The nymph queen rolled off and over, curling up on the bed, her back facing Julian. He cuddled her, soft wings pressed against his chest, his hand finding a natural warm resting place. They fell asleep. Julian dreamt of slaying a magnificent, colorful dragon. S'rrinha's sleeping mind conjured paddling a canoe downstream, heading perilously toward a mighty waterfall.

Julian awoke and reached out. He was alone. A wily smile crossed his face as remembrance stirred heat in his chest. The entranceway flew open.

"Hey. Get up!" The blue teenager noticed Julian's bare upper body protruding from the sheet. "Get dressed. We ride to W'lkyndh to get the missing piece of The Key."

"What's your hurry?" *What time is it?*

But Gjallimé had already stepped outside the tent.

Julian tied his belt as he strode outdoors. "It feels like midday."

"No. Later than that. I've been waiting for you. Does it take you that long to recover from some mead?"

As they walked toward the horses, Gjallimé did not miss the glint in Julian's eyes, the bounce in his step. "What have you been up to?" A grin splashed upon his blue face.

"Dor'ossoss!" Julian grabbed the nightsteed by the muzzle. "Was your celebration as grand?" They mounted their steeds. As they abandoned camp, Julian finally addressed his tattooed friend. "Have I got a story for you."

+++

"You are kidding me."

"You've said that a hundred times."

They had ridden northwest until the sun was half-way lower toward the horizon, prompting the clean air to turn nippy, almost to the point of breathing mist. Their steeds flew quickly over the landscape, such that W'lkyndh was but hours away.

"S'rrinha?…I would have thought Iniqui if anyone."

"I was incapable of declining. Nevertheless, I am now the same as you…" He chuckled. "In that regard."

Gjallimé twitched. "Why all the details?"

Julian smirked.

146

"Okay. Okay. I loved the full description. I admit it. What now?"

"No idea. Except we get the missing piece of The-Key-that-is-Lost on E'rth."

+++

The Halili scholar, Amarhee, met them once again in the Cavern of Souls. "Ah. We have translated the critical portion of the book to the language at the time of Tamiel." She handed a parchment to Julian.

"I need the book, too." His words echoed in the capacious room as he faced a blank wall and read the parchment. The picture of his room appeared as before. He shot a glance at Gjallimé, gulped and with a dry mouth reached out to the 'painting' hanging in mid-air. Unlike last time, his fingers pierced the portal, and gasps escaped all those in the cavern. Julian swiveled his head briefly to give everyone a quick look, then walked into his bedroom. The picture disappeared. *I'm home.*

He sat on the end of his bed, taking short and shallow breaths. His bed felt so soft. "Man, I could use a good, hot shower." He said to no one. "I don't *have* to go back."

That's stupid. Crap. I must return. Besides I'm a hero. The clock is ticking. Twenty times faster in Edrym. Gathering himself he strode over to his desk. On the right rear corner rested his Gattica commander. Hopefully, the inner part of The-Key-that-is-Lost. *The-Key-that-is-no-longer-Lost.* He took the bronze game piece. And stood perfectly still.

The silence of the house enveloped him. *My parents will be back in less than two days. They'll never believe this, not even mom. Hell, no one will believe me.*

With the thought of his parents, he made a call to their hotel. They should not be there at the moment. He was correct, and he left a message that excused his lack of communication.

He took a long deep breath, puffed out his chest. Held it. And let it out with an audible whoosh.

Gjallimé waits. His shoulders relaxed as he scanned the walls. His gaze paused on the poster of Megadeth.

Oh! Has the book changed back to English? It had.

He read the words aloud. The 'painting' reappeared. A portal to the Cavern of Souls. He stepped through, holding his Gattica commander out for all to see.

Gjallimé strode forward to get a good look. From the consternation on everyone's face, Julian could tell something worried them.

"Have I been away too long? Is this not the piece?"

Gjallimé straightened. "No. And it is the piece."

The Earth teenager waited.

"During the time you were gone, The Chart of the Moons was updated. In twelve days, there will come a time when only the black moon, Ihl, is in the sky."

Amarhee noticed Julian's blank stare. "It signals Weynonovar Ha. One Champion from each side will duel on the sacred plateau, Naspia Dor. Unlike Enhendendor the contest will not expire from some configuration of the moons. It is to the death." The scholar's sing-song voice belied the gravity of the matter.

Weynonovar Ha. I remember a strange word followed by Ha on those different pages in the book on Earth. The time of Weynonovar Ha is near. Or something like that. That puts the individual who wrote those pages here, at this time. How did the tome get to the bookstore, Dylan Shrugged, a couple of Earth days ago? "What do you mean by Champion?"

"For Nova'h, one who wears the purple tunic." *That's me or Jr'esh.* "For Yetzer-Xie it can only mean the Overlord of Darkness himself."

"One-on-one… To the death." Said Julian softly.

"Yes."

Gjallimé's eyes beamed. "And you with The Key around your neck."

"What if it doesn't work because I am not from Edrym?"

Reaching forward, Gjallimé took the piece from Earth. He inserted it onto the bronze circular disc. The Key became whole with a click. Gjallimé placed the metal chain holding The Key over Julian's still befuddled head. "Well, what does it feel—"

Julian felt a jolt throughout his body and a rush through his veins. He held his face and became bug eyed. Both hands now slipped down to his throat. Grabbing. He dropped to his knees, making choking sounds.

Gjallimé rushed in, but before he could try to remove the key, Julian stopped choking, turned his head, snickered and said, "Gotcha!"

"You asswipe!" Gjallimé exclaimed, shoving Julian in the shoulder and knocking him over.

"You have to admit…I had you going. Really, it was funny." Julian suppressed his inclination to laugh.

Amarhee was still shocked.

Gjallimé couldn't resist a grin. "Not funny!" And they both took a moment to catch their breath as the Earth teenager stood.

"Okay. Seriously…A jolt hit me. I am imbued with energy. And now I am buzzing" *I won't tell them the buzz put a bitter taste in my mouth, the taste of fear.*

"So, it *does* work on you! The Key is special. It does *not* lose power when the wearer is in motion, unlike other talismans."

His blue-skinned friend and the Halili lowered their heads. "Blossfrist Or'lonoth Wh'nle."

Waiting for them to straighten, a daze enveloped Julian's mind. "I must go consult with King Eswar. And Jr'esh. Maybe even the soothsayer, N'ttala-Toor." He turned to Amarhee. "Please hold the tome for me."

+++

The Overlord of Darkness rapidly shifted his feet, flashed his training sword, and defeated his second practice partner. Staring at his subjects, he bellowed. "The battle to the death under the black moon approaches. I have seen it! Bring true steel! Now I train with actual weapons!"

His subjects cringed at the outburst. Injury or death awaited the next pair of training partners, but they were too afraid to argue. Two wraiths, their yellow eyes wide, their faces twisted into grotesque masks of fear, took their positions as Zhokul's large two-handed claymore was retrieved and bucklers were attached to his forearms.

Pausing, the Overlord's sinister eyes scanned his minions. As he drew himself to his full height he barked. "I shall be training with a variety of weapons. And I shall face all weapon types. Organize the combinations!" In the middle of this command, he leapt forward with surprise, skewered one of the wraith's gut, spilling melon-colored blood upon the land.

+++

Gjallimé and Julian rode their steeds at half speed northeast toward the Khalil hold, Zeon Jeul. Eswar should arrive about the same time, probably Jr'esh as well.

Zhokul would have beaten me at Enhendendor. The setting purple moon saved me. And Ihl, the black moon, the moon of the Overlord of Darkness, the moon of death, had already left the sky, weakening him. "The Overlord is almost two feet taller than me. I think Jr'esh will be the best choice."

"We will see..." Gjallimé squinted. Undefined, in the distance, a group rode toward them. "Whoa." He pulled his domo to a stop, and Julian guided Dor'ossoss to do the same. Through his spyglass Gjallimé observed a nymph leading ten soldiers from different races. "It is S'rrinha."

"Huh?"

"Nymphs and K'narikh, and some of my brethren accompany her."

Julian's eyebrows furrowed. "Let's go find out what's going on." He kicked Dor'ossoss lightly, and swung the nightsteed

150

east. Gjallimé squelched his *"wait!"*, and followed. Not long after, they met up with S'rrinha.

While stopped, S'rrinha's unicorn danced back and forth at her command. "Come. Join us."

Her ample cleavage distracted Julian, so Gjallimé responded. "Join what?"

"We go to intercept the draugrs heading home. We shall stalk them and wait until only our moons and Z'th honor the sky, which the Chart of the Moons puts at tomorrow, late in the day."

Julian looked up into her inviting, lime-green eyes. "Xrarreth, plus the lavender moon."

"Yes. You have become a soul of Edrym. We will be at our strongest, and they will be weak. We may only have numbers to engage the rear of their procession, but yes, we take the fight to Yetzer–"

To act as Yetzer-Xie is to become as Yetzer-Xie.

Gjallimé's stern voice interrupted. "Weynonovar Ha will lay upon the land some eleven days from now! We must not become the same as Yetzer-Xie, which will be marked by this attack. We must go into Weynonovar Ha remaining pure. J'liánh wears The Key. He will become marred by such a move."

S'rrinha, quick to react to the news, countered smartly. "Then J'liánh should face Zhokul with the moons stacked in his favor."

"That is absurd. The Law requires a contest on Naspia Dor." Gjallimé's domo rose, and its forward hooves clawed the air.

S'rrinha dug in her heels, yanked the reins such that her unicorn duplicated the angry move. "The Law will be obeyed. A duel will commence in eleven days. But it would be best if the Yetzer-Xie Champion is not Zhokul."

A confused Julian spoke. "I don't see how confronting the Overlord of Darkness on my own terms is wrong."

With this, S'rrinha's unicorn stood still, while her face radiated invitation.

As Gjallimé settled his domo, despair crossed his face. "If you do not know your destination, any path will do."

I will sleep in S'rrinha's tent tonight. Is that my true choice? He tasted desire. "When the Law stands on a different side than Honorable Opportunity, how do you decide?"

"It appears that desire shapes your priorities, and your priorities shape your choice. I ride on to carry the news of Weynonovar Ha." And with a huff, Gjallimé turned his domo toward Zhon Jeul and galloped off.

+++

The small squad followed, twenty paces behind S'rrinha and Julian, as they rode to intercept draugrs returning to their Hold, Frir'sk. The lovers exchanged glances but not words. S'rrinha gloated. With the addition of J'liánh she would become a hero, a now frantic quest. Within minutes they were stalking the draugr force. She continued their slow pursuit into the evening, waiting for the moons to align. Tomorrow.

The onset of evening did nothing to calm Dor'ossoss. The nightsteed pulsed, his mohawk mane of purple fire dancing in the wind. Without warning the stallion pivoted and galloped in the opposite direction. *What?* Julian nearly fell with the sudden movement. *This is as fast as he has ever run.* Shortly Julian realized, that far ahead a curtain rose from the land, reaching for the sky. It glistened. *Oh. No. This must be a shimmer storm I was warned about. Steed's dislike shimmer storms. Why is Dor'ossoss rushing toward one?* Julian pulled at the reins to no avail.

152

Chapter 15
Shimmer Storm

Without hesitation, the nightsteed plunged into the twinkling shimmer storm. A powder-blue fog with vertical slivers of sparkling silver surrounded them. *Like icicles on a Christmas tree. Shit! I cannot see the ground. I hope Dor'ossoss knows what he is doing.* Julian felt dizzy, mesmerized by the silver slivers and the smell of jasmine. Touching them was as frosty, thin, string. But they did no harm. The flickering threads randomly hung in the powder-blue fog, some long, some short. Some high, some low. *This is beautiful.* He didn't notice the sensations from wearing The Key had ceased.

Dor'ossoss proceeded slowly. Time slipped away. Julian awoke as if from a dream. *How long have we been here? They said most never come out.* His confidence in his nightsteed waning, he tried to keep Dor'ossoss walking in a straight line. *That should get us out. Eventually.* Little did he know that inside a shimmer storm, moving straight translated into going in a circle.

Distress kept him fully awake. The only sign of time passing, the growing grumble in his belly. Agitation and alarm drove him to take his nightsteed to a trot. *It's too cold.*

Getting nowhere, he turned Dor'ossoss hard left and cantered. The speed only stoked the fire of his panic. After quite some time he halted, bowed his head, and put the spread fingers of both hands on his forehead, thumbs resting on his cheeks. *Crap! What's happening? Can't think!*

In this condition, the Snow Jarl, seemingly made of cut ice under his dark coat, found him. "J'liánh! J'liánh! Look up."

Julian's eyes watered when he saw the legend. Nevertheless, he quickly took hold of himself. "Do you know the way out?" His voice broke.

"Indeed. I came to retrieve you. I have been searching for a day."

"A day?" *Really?* "Thank you. Thank you. Do you have any water?" As they gave the nightsteed something to drink, the teenager asked, "What's the secret?"

"In a shimmer storm, only traveling at one specific arc translates to a straight line. Come. Follow me. I know the arc to take. It is the only way out, unless the storm spits you out."

Weird. "What are the sparkling slivers?" Julian asked between gulps from the waterskin. "What direction are we heading?"

"The slivers may be the source of its power. No one knows for sure. As for direction, when you leave the storm, it could be any place or time. Even I do not understand."

"Are you the one they call the Wanderer?"

"My name is Khan-apal-apli. Your nightsteed took you into the shimmer storm. He is The Guardian. What do you make of that?"

The priest said The Guardian would keep me on the one true path. Dor'ossoss prevented me from going with S'rrinha's attacking party. "S'rrinha was the wrong choice."

Wisdom shone from the Wanderer's face. "Remember the Adaa prediction of **Youthful Folly**?"

Julian nodded, acutely aware of his mistake. He then changed the subject, "You provided the Yetzer-Xie formation?"

"Yes."

The legend in the flesh. The teenager experienced vertigo for a moment. "So, you are Nova'h."

"No. I am a Snow Jarl." The glinting slivers continued to brush against them both, like tentacles in a field of jellyfish. Julian carefully followed the Wanderer's steed.

"What is a Snow Jarl?" *And why Wanderer? More importantly, why did he rescue me?*

154

Hot air replaced powder-blue fog as they exited onto a barren sea of white sand. The sun hung higher in the sky. They emerged far to Edrym's east, their breath came dry and torrid.

Khan-apal-apli growled. "It is too hot. We must ride west, with speed, lest I collapse and melt." He kicked his steed and galloped at full velocity. The teenager followed and soon caught up with the Snow Jarl, who slumped forward, clinging to his mount. Terrible purpose showed upon his face.

Julian peered forward along their path, but only desert stretched before them. After a while, the Wanderer sagged even further. His breath came ragged.

The purple moon beamed from high in the sky and the nightsteed pulsed, ready to explode ever faster. The young Champion blazoned gratitude and strength.

"Hey. Come ride with me. Dor'ossoss can run faster, even with the extra weight. Your steed should keep up with us without your load."

When Khan-apal-apli mounted the nightsteed, Julian let Dor'ossoss run full out. Both riders clung on tight as a bone-white patch of sand flew beneath them. The dry heat followed them indifferently. A few scraggly plants appeared as the surface turned to sienna-brown, and breathing came easier. The Snow Jarl released his tight grip on Julian, sat up, and signaled the Earth teenager to stop.

He remounted his steed, and they proceeded at a fast but reasonable pace. "Your nightsteed is indeed a wonder. I thank thee."

"Consider it repayment for finding me in the shimmer storm. Besides I only did what anyone would do."

"There are those who are too self-centered to think of thanks. It is a giving thing - say it often, and say it true." A wash of honor flowed through Julian. "I believe you were asking about my title as Snow Jarl." The young Champion nodded.

"There was a time. A time before the Kings, a time before Tamiel, a time so long ago it is hard to reckon. Nova'h and Yetzer-Xie did not exist, as the beings and creatures of Edrym bowed to the Jarls, who watched over them: The Terra Jarl, the Moon Jarl, the Fire Jarl and myself. We were practically immortal, with powers that were used to sustain and improve prosperity. Edrym rotated, and the sun moved across the sky.

"Then came a time of great upheaval. Edrym's place in the heavens became as you see now. A thin band of habitability with desert and heat to the east, tundra and cold to the west. The sun stands steady in the sky, higher as one moves east, and lower as one moves west. The animosity that developed into Nova'h and Yetzer-Xie began. The Jarls lost command and most of their powers.

"Without purpose and appreciation, the other three Jarls spread themselves thin across the wind. Thinner and thinner, until only the wind remained. I can only guess that my purpose kept me from doing the same." Khan-apal-apli held up his ice-like hand to prevent Julian from interrupting. "My agenda serves to maintain *balance* upon Edrym. My power is to read a rock, a tree, the motions of the river, and gain insight to the state of affairs. I wander and thus my nickname. Remember, not all who wander are lost." He cleared his throat. "I aided Nova'h for Enhendendor because alone, the Overlord of Darkness and his forces would have reached the Seal. And yes, I sensed Zhokul's presence when he arrived from the cold pole, as well as your arrival on the path at Naspia Dor."

"So, if Nova'h was poised to crush and destroy Yetzer-Xie, you would have come to *their* aid?"

The ground grew darker and more plants sprung up. The heat became little more than a nuisance. "Yes. Indeed. You are most perceptive."

"But in helping me now, you are helping Nova'h. Yetzer-Xie must still pose an imminent threat."

"Weynonovar Ha. The battle between Champions called by the black moon, Ihl, alone in the sky."

"And you think I should be the Champion to face the Overlord."

The Wanderer did not answer, responding only with a knowing stare.

Uncertainty and respect flowed in Julian's core. "My fight with the Yetzer-Xie leader on Naspia Dor revealed the outcome of such an encounter. My strength and speed were no match for him."

"Heroes are made by the paths they choose, not by the powers that grace them."

"But he is two feet taller than me, with greater reach." Julian's nightsteed stopped to paw the air.

"No one really knows why they are alive until they know what they would die for."

Dor'ossoss continued to prance and rear. Julian patted his neck, trying to soothe him. *Why does he behave this way?* "I would die for Nova'h. I proved that at Enhendendor. I do not fear death, only a meaningless one."

"And yet here we are. Trapped in the amber of the moment."

"What does that mean? It doesn't change the fact that Zhokul is nearly as strong as I. And heavier."

They now galloped through short, light-green grass. The Snow Jarl looked at the grasses, felt the breeze. "We are due east of Zhon Jeul. It is three days after you bolted into the shimmer storm. It seems we have lost some days." The teenager's eyes widened. "I must ride south. Continue on west to the Khalil Hold. Take extra caution, you may ride close to the liche Hold, Pl'lliq. The Ja'tasarr, and wraith Holds are also nearby. Council with Jr'esh and Eswar. You may not have gone where you intended to go, but I believe you have ended up where you need to be." Khan-apal-apli swiveled to go.

"But—"

"Of all sad things of tongue or pen, the saddest are these: *It might have been.*" And he streaked southward.

Chapter 16
Coronation

Confusion endured in Julian's mind as he continued toward Zhon Jeul. *Should I be the one?* He was careful to skirt Pl'lliq. After two days riding, he arrived, mind still in a fog. As he entered the Hold and rode the avenue, he noticed many Khalil on the streets. "Where go you all?"

"To the coronation," said one Khalil, walking beside.

"What coronation?"

"Queen Iniqui."

She must assume the mantel of Queen and of Eptizar until Eswar takes another mate. Why don't they leave the position vacant? Must be an Edrym thing. "When?"

"Two hours from now."

Julian steered Dor'ossoss toward the stables. "I will join the celebration after tending to my steed."

"We welcome you, Champion J'liánh."

He left his shield with the stable hand, but kept Hellsbane.

During his walk back toward the castle, the white moon hung directly over a turret. Julian caught sight of a faint, small dot adjacent to the glowing orb. *Must be another planet. Oh crap!* The memory of that morning in the skate-park, the visibility of a planet in the daytime sky rushed into his mind. A planet visible next to the full moon over a steeple. Along with the significance. He now remembered, the same occurred the day of President Lincoln's second inaugural. Many took this as a sign of his assassination.

Holy shit! This could be an omen for the coronation. His leisurely walk turned into a full out run. *Iniqui!*

Racing over the cobblestone streets he tried not to panic. *I must get there before the ceremony. I must.* He arrived, breathing heavily, as the throng gathered beneath the balcony. "Please! Let me through!"

The crowd parted for the Champion. He stormed through the front gate and found himself sprinting down a hallway. The clatter of Hellsbane hanging on his side, and the pounding of his boots, echoed loud within the castle. *Perhaps this noise will delay the coronation.* He took the stairs two at a time.

Julian arrived in a long chamber. He continued running toward the light of the balcony, slower now, but as fast as he could. *I must. I must.* His heart beat so strong and rapid he feared it would burst. The incantations of the priest wafted into his ears. *Oh no!* Reaching the guards at the curtained entrance to the balcony he was delayed at most ten seconds until they let him through. He was prepared to cut them down if the delay had been any longer.

Iniqui and other Khalil on the balcony, including Eswar and the priest, jumped, as a gasping Julian erupted through the curtain. The crowd below exclaimed a unified surprise. Eswar turned to Julian. "What is this?"

"Sire, Iniqui is in danger." Julian stooped, putting his hands on his knees to regain his breath.

"What?"

"I ask that you allow me to stand at your daughter's side to protect her." Recovered, he rose up, and went to Iniqui's side before Eswar could protest. She wore pearl earrings and matching necklace. A majestic cerulean cape trimmed in silver draped over a gown of snow-white. She was breathtaking. Iniqui's plum-colored eyes stared at him with an I'll-talk-to-you-later purpose. Then she turned to the crowd and signaled the priest to continue. Eswar deferred to her wishes.

+++

S'rrinha had called out to Julian when he had galloped toward the shimmer storm. *If not for that stupid steed! It was not*

J'liánh's idea, rather his nightsteed, to bolt and run into the shimmer storm. It's a big loss. Colossal. I had him seduced. But I will still return a conquering hero. With the aid of our moons, we will slay scores of draugrs. All will know that I am a fearless fighter. Willing to do whatever is necessary for the good of Nova'h. The people will rise up around me.

The rogue group took S'rrinha's lead and waited patiently for the moons to align. The tail end of the draugr procession remained in the sight of her spyglass. *I must avenge my mother's death.* They would swoop in and kill as many draugrs as possible before the Overlord of Darkness could arrive from the front of the procession with his most capable lieutenants. On spotting Zhokul they would disengage and flee. Each rode a steed, which was unusual, but arranged by S'rrinha.

The first few draugrs fell easily, surprise and isolation against them. S'rrinha barked commands and invoked *Heal*. Each warrior's abilities were amplified by their moon. The Hassjidar's swiftness under the blue moon and the K'narikh's strength under the green moon, made them more formidable.

S'rrinha shouted. "Do not let them flank you! Hassjidar to the edges!"

After the first ten or so minutes, S'rrinha became alarmed. *My troop is not fighting as a cohesive group. They cannot hear my commands. We are being overwhelmed by numbers even before setting sight on the Yetzer-Xie leader.*

Indeed, the draugrs folded themselves over the small attack force. For every three draugrs sent to their graves, so went one from S'rrinha's small platoon. Myriad emotions tugged at her. Ambition now dashed, courage now fear. Turning her back to the fight, S'rrinha fled. The lone survivor. Her previous confidence twisted into disgrace and vengeance.

News of her misguided attack on the draugrs, her abject failure, had not yet reached the Khalil Hold. During her dash toward Zhon Jeul, S'rrinha's mind snapped like a rubber band breaking from being stretched too far. She hatched a self-serving plan. She was about to be ostracized anyway. If she could not be the hero queen, then neither would Iniqui. *I don't like her relationship with Julian*. Her last act of rebellion, fueled by a system of laws that led to her mother's death on the day that Julian arrived, would elevate her legacy. She would never be forgotten.

+++

Julian scanned the crowd. *The assassination attempt could happen here*. The air was still and heavy. Out of the corner of his eye he saw the weapon streak directly toward Iniqui. The Key's power surged through him, enhancing even his advanced abilities. His arm was a blur as he reached out and caught the arrow in mid-air. Thwang! The shaft of the arrow sang as Julian held steady. The tip, two inches from Iniqui's throat. To her credit, she hardly flinched. She had no time to understand what had just happened until she stared, mouth agape, at Julian. And at the arrow in his hand. The throng's exclamation was also on a small delay. Everyone on the scene froze in the instant. Except Julian who calmly pulled back the arrow and snapped it in two with one hand.

He asked, "Are you all right?"

Iniqui righted herself, watching as a section of the crowd became a small, writhing mass of people holding down and obscuring the attacker. "Yes. Yes, I am all right." She glanced over to her father; they shared an "Oh H'rol" moment. Then she pivoted to face Julian. "How did you do that?"

"I don't know." Their eyes locked.

They were interrupted by a scream from the on-lookers. "It is S'rrinha!" Matted was her hair and her eyes glowed madness as she looked at Iniqui and the crown on the cushion.

Feeling an unexpected pang in his chest, Julian remembered her in his bed. *She is lost to us now*.

+++

Eswar summoned Jr'esh and Julian to his chambers. The curtains were drawn as if to fend off a chill. As Julian arrived, the

162

Khalil King came up to him, placing his hand on Julian's shoulder. "My thanks are a never-ending Dz'ntra of moonlight."

Julian bowed. "Forever in service, my King."

"I do not believe I am your King; however, I accept your courtesy and commitment."

Jr'esh entered in full battle gear, settled to one knee and lowered his head. "At your command."

"Rise. At ease. Weynonovar Ha is in six days." Eswar came out from behind his desk. He motioned for the Champions to sit. Standing with feet apart, his arms across his chest. "What are we to do?"

Jr'esh responded. "I–"

Hushing him, the King continued. "We have but a few days until we must begin our trek back to Naspia Dor. The fate of Nova'h rests in one of you. Zhokul is sure to be their Champion."

"I volunteer gladly." Jr'esh finally had his say.

Eswar did not let Julian speak. "Sometimes honesty is the greater part of honor. J'liánh, you have faced the Overlord of Darkness. What say you?"

"Sire, it did not go well. He is nearly two feet taller than I, with a longer reach. And his strength is nearly as great as my own. Despite that, I shall confront him if that is your decision." Cowardice did not flow from The Key, rather humbleness.

"You have your speed."

"Yes."

"Jr'esh?"

"I have taught J'liánh much, but there are many techniques I have not had time to teach. This knowledge is not just a tool against Zhokul, it gives me lower reaction time. The best move and countermove come without thought. I stand a foot taller and I am heavier. Also, The Key will amplify my skills, counter the pentacle of death, and make me stronger. As my true nature, gladiator."

"Have you sparred with each other?"

"Yes." From both of them.

"And…?"

"We are evenly matched."

"That was without The Key. I believe it is J'liánh's destiny to wear it, that it will be more powerful around his neck. However, I sense too many shades of doubt."

Julian spoke up. "Destiny or not, I am willing to oppose him." *I only fear that I will let down the people of Nova'h. That is a pressure I would rather not have.*

"No. It is not enough. Your confidence is also compromised. Give the Key to Jr'esh."

As he took off The Key, Julian physically weakened, as if he had less blood running through his veins. Immediately after handing The Key to Jr'esh, Julian took his leave. He shuffled through the castle, head down. *Am I a coward?*

Chapter 17
Trapped in Amber

Thoughts flew in and out and through Julian's mind, but he couldn't grasp any of them. Dor'ossoss cantered westward and upward, away from the Khalil Hold on the mountain pass. An increasing chill sank into Julian's heart, seemingly making it freeze.

I'm ashamed.

Gjallimé galloped his Domo, drawing even with the nightsteed. "Hey, my friend. Do not go riding off alone."

"I feel alone."

"You are not. Eswar made his selection for a reason."

"Yeah. But not the right reason."

"What do you mean?"

Julian still had not looked up at Gjallimé. "He did not make his choice based on fighting ability…" Gjallimé waited for his friend during the awkward silence. "He does not believe my heart is in it." And his shoulders slumped even more.

"I still do not understand."

"Eswar believes I am fated to wear the Key. That it can empower me the most. But obviously not if strength, focus, and honor are brittle on my soul."

"This is not the J'liánh I know. You are Champion."

"It is not titles that honor warriors, but rather warriors that honor titles." With misty eyes, he looked at Gjallimé for the first time.

"Of all in Edrym, I know you best. I believe you will rise to the occasion. Eight minutes after the black moon, Ihl, is alone in the sky the lavender moon begins to rise. Your power with The Key will grow during the contest." Gjallimé wondered what he could do to revive his friend's confidence, his swagger, his commitment.

"I'm not afraid for myself. I'm afraid I will let down the races of Nova'h. Why did they not tell me about the rise of the lavender moon?"

"All of your actions since your arrival in Edrym have shown that you have a love of Nova'h."

Julian sat straight, wiped his cheeks of tears. "You are my best friend. In either world."

The Domo reared and Dor'ossoss shook. The teenagers studied each other. "What the hell?" they said in unison and looked around. A tall wall of blue, with silver streaks glided in from their left. Moving fast.

"A shimmer storm!" Gjallimé pointed, trying to settle his Domo.

"We must release our steeds! They will find a way back to Zhon Jeul." *Why is Dor'ossoss uneasy this time?* They dismounted. Immediately the Domo and nightsteed bolted away.

Gjallimé asked. "What about us?"

"I know the arc to take to escape the storm. Follow me. Hold onto my shoulder lest we drift apart."

As the flickering, shimmer storm approached, they watched in awe and fear. The powder-blue fog and silver slivers engulfed them and they were on level ground, the mountain pass gone.

Even as Julian's mind started to drift away, he said. "We must resist and keep our thoughts clear." The hairs rose on the back of his neck as he felt something sentient around him. *I didn't notice this before. Perhaps I was too caught in its spell.*

"This is beautiful."

"But deadly just the same. Come follow me step for step." *Is the storm alive?*

The slivers brushed against them as they walked. In short order they emerged into a stinging cold and a soft, flaky snow. The orange sun was lower to the horizon. Cthomechdul and Calixto cast a purple haze to the land, while the white moon peeked over the horizon. They skirted the edge of a mountain range running east-west.

Julian asked. "Do you recognize anything?" The pearl-white snow stuck on everything. It tasted like spring water with evergreen.

"Not exactly." Gjallimé swiveled and peered through the falling snow. "The draugr Hold and the banshee Hold are believed to be this far west. The Xoldre mountains protect the banshee Hold to its north."

"Are these the Xoldre mountains?"

"I'm not sure. Maybe." They both shivered in the eerie silence. "We should head toward the sun." Taking exaggerated high steps, they walked through eight inches of snow.

"So, the banshee Hold could be on the other side of these mountains."

"Yes. The blue moon, Calixto, glows at the apex of the sky. I will have full access to my innate speed for six more hours." They leaned forward, picking up the pace. "The shimmer storm was a powerful force on my mind. I am brushing the cobwebs away."

Julian said. "Myself as well."

"Has your mind cleared enough to reconsider facing the Yetzer-Xie leader?"

Julian replied with a far-off look in his eyes. "I'm not sure."

"And when are you going to tell Iniqui?"

"Tell what?"

Gjallimé's cobalt eyes twinkled. "That you want her in the worst and best way."

Julian responded with a shove, but there was a grin on his face. "That's crazy."

"Come on. It's written all over you when you two are together. She knows. And yet she is all smiles for you."

"Really?"

Gjallimé screamed "Yoowww!" The cry pierced the cold air, coupled with a loud metallic clatter.

"My leg!" Gjallimé fell to the snow, grasping his right leg, twisting in intense pain.

Julian knelt and saw the blue teenager's leg impaled by an animal trap with serrated iron teeth. Red colored the snow. "What is it?"

"A snare for Jekaulis. My calf is shattered."

"Hold on." Julian couldn't find a mechanism to disengage the spring, however his strength allowed him to pry the two sides with metal teeth apart enough for Gjallimé to pull his leg out of the trap with his hands. Blood flowed from the wound. Julian released the trap, which closed with an empty, loud clank.

"Do not touch it!" Gjallimé's face contorted into a grimace. "How bad is it?" He sat up with legs sprawled, still holding the injured leg with both hands above the knee.

Julian tore a seam along Gjallimé's trousers and pulled it up away from the bloodiest area. "Your bone is sticking out."

"Aaargh!"

"You are losing too much blood and need a tourniquet." Ripping cloth from the trousers, Julian made and applied the tourniquet. "We must find a doctor." He didn't add *soon*. "Where is the nearest Nova'h Hold?"

"I do not know where we are. If we are near W'lkyndh, it is at least a three-day walk toward the sun and then north. Most likely four or five. Or perhaps Methedriel. If so, add a half day, due east. That assumes these are the Xoldre mountains." And he clenched his teeth with a scowl.

Julian scooped up his friend and ran. "Hold on. I'll release the tourniquet from time to time to keep blood in your leg."

His blue friend winced. "With each jostle it feels like my leg will fall off."

"Shut up."

Gjallimé failed to retort because he had passed out. Julian ran as if the devil was on his heels.

+++

After eight hours or so, Julian moved out of the thick fallen snow, now traveling on tundra melt. He gently lowered his blue friend to the ground, propping him to a sitting position, his back against a boulder in the foothills. Julian fell to his hands and knees. Sweat clung to his clothes as he took labored breaths. He had not been able to keep up his initial frenzied pace for long, so he ran for about a half hour then walked for maybe fifteen minutes, repeatedly. *Where am I going? I need Gjallimé to navigate.*

The blue teenager stirred. "Where are we?"

Julian's mouth shaped a soft smile. "I was hoping *you* would tell *me*."

The look on Gjallimé's face was calm, his voice measured. "I am going to untie the tourniquet. For good." He was not asking. "I want you to give me an ice boot." His deadpan voice punctuated the eerie silence. Not even a breeze presented itself.

"But—"

His friend's stony stare stopped him. They looked hard at each other until Gjallimé broke into a simple smile.

The Earth teenager could only smile back. "I will gather enough snow." It took several trips up the base of the mountain to accumulate what was needed. The ice boot, high enough to cover the wound, was gently applied, packed, and smoothed. Gjallimé cringed. Exhausted from the run, Julian sat beside his friend.

Gjallimé crossed his arms, fighting back shivers. "Have I ever told you about my sister?"

Sister? "No. I never knew you had one."

"When I was ten and A'jelh was eleven we lost our father to the horrors of Ravoq-Ma. It was a very hard time. We leaned on each other to make it to the next day." Gjallimé took a large breath, raising his shoulders, while Julian remained silent. "As time went on, we mended. Though each of us carried a hole in our hearts. I wished to become a skilled, vengeful warrior but was tagged to be a Rider five years later.

"A'jelh was known to have the largest heart in all of Methedriel. She sought out troubled children to comfort, tutor, and support. Many of them lost a parent as well. For me, there were times our mother left us with many chores, and sometimes A'jelh would let me sleep, tired from my long night out. On other occasions she would lie for me." Gjallimé paused briefly to grab the ice boot and shudder.

"When I was eleven and A'jelh twelve, my favorite game was Endsvar. My friends and I played in the back alleys. Occasionally we let A'jelh join us. The others let her play, probably because she was cute. Her green hair done up in sixteen, shoulder-length cornrows. Slanted, sparkling hazel eyes and slightly upturned nose. She tried mightily to keep up, usually succeeding through her dauntless effort. For a girl so sweet she could show unexpected ferocity.

"One day we snuck out of the Hold in order to play in the forest. This was strictly forbidden. A'jelh tugged my sleeve, begging to come. I looked at my sister, a recent tattoo on her forearm. Her first. She had a loving, I'll-be-good, sincerity splashed across her face. I gave in though I shouldn't have. She jumped up and down, squealing in delight.

"By twenty minutes into the game we had strayed far from the Hold. We separated, as usual during Endsvar. Crashing footfalls and snapping tree limbs startled us. The intense silence of the woods should have been a warning.

"A lava giant!" Several of us cried in unison. "Run!"

"I looked for A'jelh. She was fifty yards away, frozen, staring at the monster, standing directly in its path. I screamed at her to come. And again, with no response. I ran to her and she finally moved. She turned her face to me, pointed away, and shouted "Go!" Her face was hard, with furrowed brow and cold steel in her eyes. I started toward her but she yelled, "Brother, go now!"

"Come! Hurry!" I hollered as I stopped, then started toward the Hold. The crashing in the forest grew louder. She had turned to face the creature, but still pointed at me to go. I was afraid and ran away. I failed to go to her. I looked back over my shoulder and saw a massive rust-colored hand holding her in mid-air. Only her head and feet stuck out from the giant's fist. I ran faster. I failed her."

Gjallimé had presented stoic as he told his tale, but now tears flowed down his face. His shoulders hitched and his voice cracked. "I have nightmares. Horrible nightmares." His chest heaved. "I see the monstrosity raise his fist toward its mouth. I see its lips furl back revealing yellowed, craggy teeth. I see it bite off my sister's head. I wake sweaty and screaming.

"Why did she do it? Did she think it was too late to run? Did she think she could slow the fiend down and save us? Oh H'rol, why did she do it? And why didn't I try to save her? I am a coward."

Gjallimé's chin slumped to his chest. His weeping eyes closed.

Julian tried to think of something to say. Each idea that floated through his mind sounded inadequate, so he took Gjallimé's hand in both of his, holding firmly. A weak squeeze answered back. Julian almost whispered 'goodnight' and 'I love you' but didn't.

+++

Slobber landing on his face jolted Julian awake. He reached out aimlessly and opened his eyes. His arms embraced the steed's head and he sunk his face into Dor'ossoss's muzzle. "Am I glad to see you! How did you find us?" The words echoed in the cold silence. His nightsteed could take Gjallimé and himself to safety. Dor'ossoss carried him and the Wanderer once before.

Julian reached out his hand toward his blue friend, but froze in mid-air as his gaze settled on Gjallimé. His friend's body, face and head were covered by a thin glistening frost. Only a centimeter thick. But even his nose and closed mouth, lips bluer than usual, lay under the veil. His chest did not move.

Brushing the frost off Gjallimé's face, Julian grew composed and somber. "You saved my life... I failed to do *my* part."

Julian's arms fell heavy into his lap as he stared. His hands clenched into fists and he pounded his own thighs. Dor'ossoss

171

stepped back and watched his rider madly swing his head from side to side, slam his fists, and shake his legs, all while sitting in the frost.

Guttural whimpering exploded into screaming. "Noooooo!" *He was my best friend. My only ever best friend. Why did I stop running?*

After a time, Julian's pounding fists and gyrations slowed and then ceased. Scarcely had he risen when a shudder went through his body. Dor'ossoss carried his shield, which he used to dig a deep grave. After gently settling Gjallimé's body within, Julian placed the special shield atop the blue teenager's chest. Anguish kept thoughts away as he topped off Gjallimé's resting place with a cairn of large rocks.

He stood at the base of the mound, head down. After a time, he said. "From your remains shall flowers grow. And you shall be in them. Their color shall be blue to mark your presence. And that is eternity." He turned, with a river of grief flowing down his face, and mounted his stallion.

+++

East, toward the sun, he rode. First slowly then at breakneck speed. An impassioned intent, welling up from deep in his soul drove him onward. His terrible purpose. It must come to pass; he just couldn't be late. Within a day he caught up with five Khalil, also riding east.

Julian slowed. "Where am I?"

The lead ivory skinned man with two braids of silver down his back ignored the demand in Julian's tone. "At your service Champion J'liánh. With your pace, Methedriel is less than one day ahead, through the Ad-nykal forest."

Methedriel, Gjallimé's people. I do not know how to face them. Besides, I must council with Eswar. He remembered that the shimmer storm may have carried him through time, forward or back. It must not be forward. "How long until the black moon is alone in the sky?"

172

"Eight days till Weynonovar Ha."

Good. The shimmer storm has thrown me back in time. Are there two of me? It matters not. I must ride to Zhon Jeul. The other, earlier me, will council with Eswar and Jr'esh. I need to alter the outcome. "Which way to Zhon Jeul?"

"Proceed back west to the crossroad. Head north to the Khalil Hold."

"How long?"

"Dor'ossoss's speed rivals a Domo. You can arrive in under two days."

That's cutting it close. The Khalil army, with Eswar and Jr'esh at the lead, may already be heading to Naspia Dor. I must arrive before they leave or intercept them. How do I convince them that I should wear the Key into battle with Zhokul? Shit! The earlier me and Gjallimé will be in the shimmer storm. Gjallimé will die. Again. Would that I could warn him. A large breath escaped his lungs. "Many thanks."

"At your service."

+++

Julian arrived at the gates of Zhon Jeul in just under two days. *I have not passed Eswar and Jr'esh on the road. They should be inside.*

He found King Eswar dressed in silver and black, hands behind his back, staring out the window in his chambers. "My King," he began.

Eswar turned, his face burdened with the fate of Nova'h. "J'liánh, what is on your mind?"

"Gjallimé is dead." His voice broke, a period of silence ensued. Emotions unchecked; he told the whole story. At the end, his manner became serious and his voice was strong and true. "I want to fight for Nova'h at Weynonovar Ha. I am ready for the Key; I am ready for Zhokul. I am the best option."

"Your newfound commitment is obvious. However, Jr'esh has the Key and is also ready."

173

Julian straightened his shoulders. "I fight for more than just Gjallimé. I fight for right. I fight for all of Nova'h."

The King eyed him carefully. "I will call for N'ttala-Toor to resolve this quandary."

Jr'esh was summoned as well. The two arrived with haste.

"Jr'esh. J'liánh wishes to carry the Key into battle. I believe he no longer has doubts." He turned to the nymph soothsayer, N'ttala-Toor. "I ask that you shed light on this matter."

"Of course, My Lord." N'ttala-Toor reached into his cloak, emerging with a slew of small rods and stones that Julian remembered tossing back in Sayll. Without hesitation he threw them on the rock floor, between Jr'esh and Julian. The rods and stones scattered, except for one group of six, an Adaa used for prediction. Rod-rod-rod-stone-stone-rod. "My King. The Adaa speaks to **Innocence**."

"Julian pumped his fist into the air. "That's me!"

"Not so fast," said N'ttala-Toor. "**Innocence** in this context also means purity of heart."

Jr'esh made his case. "My intent is unshakeable. My heart is filled with the honor of serving Nova'h."

Julian took a breath to speak, but Eswar cut him off with a question. "J'liánh, has Gjallimé's death brought a darkness to your heart?"

"At first, rage consumed me…so yes there was darkness. But on the second day of riding, the purple moon rose. When atop the sky, the electricity in Dor'ossoss flowed into me. I could feel the anger go, to be replaced with loyalty and purpose. Purpose to face the Overlord of Darkness and help all of Nova'h."

King Eswar glanced at the soothsayer who nodded, then to Jr'esh, with a hard set to his jaw. He too gave his assent. "It seems you may have found your destiny on the very path you took to avoid it."

174

Chapter 18
To the Death

The Hassjidar's Hold, Methedriel welcomed Julian, sharing sadness over Gjallimé's passing, with charity to support Julian's travails going through the loss of his friend. Genuine admiration was given in support of his upcoming battle with the Overlord. King Eswar, N'ttala-Toor, and half the population of Zhon Jeul traveled to witness the fight to the death to be contested four days hence on the sacred plateau, Naspia Dor.

Jr'esh and Eswar accompanied Julian to Hjerim's weapon shop, for Julian indicated he desired special requests concerning his armament.

Strolling through Methedriel, Julian asked the King. "What is the outcome for the winners and losers?"

"One generation of peace ensues. However, the loser will not condition, train, make weapons, or undertake any other battle-related activity, neither tactical nor strategic." Eswar turned his head to look directly at Julian. "Also, the winner can take as indentured servants, up to fifteen percent of each race to assist the victors at their Holds. The winners shall not harm, maim, kill nor take any similar action against any loser."

Peace. In Edrym? "That doesn't sound totally horrible."

"Aye. It is. For without training and new weapons the impact on the loser's capability to engage in battle is severe."

"And how long is one generation?"

"The beginning of the period commences with the first birth on either side. Then, the first eighteen-year-old born during the period to give birth herself, signals the end. The servants return home. There are four months of peace and adjustment before hostilities recommence.”

“How are these rules enforced? Why must the war continue?”

“It is Law and cannot be broken.”

Julian grimaced. *Like everything else in this land.*

“Hjerim! Hellsbane has been all you foretold and more, however I have an idea for a new shield.” Julian bowed his head. His voice quieted. “I am sorry for what befell Gjallimé, especially my failure to save him.”

“Death is a constant voice among us. Your friendship with Gjallimé was heartily rejoiced by the souls of Nova’h. You are not to blame. Spill the blood of Zhokul to allay the loss.”

Julian nodded slowly; head still hung in silence.

“Come now. I have a special suit of chainmail for you.” Hjerim proceeded to the back of his shop and produced a magnificent outfit that would cover Julian’s torso, arms, lower body and head. “We start with defense.”

Julian’s face hardened. “No. I want a small, open vest and no headgear. I want to flaunt my courage, announce my bravado. And most of all, I want the Overlord to see The Key. To know I wield the greatest power on Edrym. And to know it will destroy him.”

Eswar, who had accompanied Julian to the smith shop, beamed with pride as if Julian were his own son. “I agree wholeheartedly. The confidence you show now will follow you to the duel.”

Hjerim dipped his head. “As you desire.”

“I also want a unique shield. I want a circle, with eight extended tips, each honed to an attacking point, similar to the bottom of the shield I buried with Gjallimé.” Julian sketched his concept on parchment. “With this design I can swing the shield from any angle, forehand or backhand, and Zhokul will feel its sting.”

Eswar assessed this design. "The small loss in protective area is well worth the additional offense. I like it."

Julian pulled back his shoulders, chin up. "I will call it Deathstar. I would also like you to make me special boots. Inside each, under the toe, I want a wide, straight dagger that is originally hidden. If I tap a mechanism inside the boot, the dagger will slide forward. On Earth it would be compared to a switchblade. I saw it in a spy…" There was no word for movie in the Edrym language.

Eswar and Hjerim looked at him quizzically, but with further explanation and detail, agreed. Eswar smiled. "You are shorter with a significant speed advantage. This weapon could surprise the Overlord of Darkness, the first time you use it."

+++

How did it get so late, so quick? Julian worried while at camp near the base of Naspia Dor. The evening prior to the day of the duel brought a quickening to his pulse as he met with Jr'esh, Eswar, Ib-Amel, and Iniqui.

"You will have the advantage in speed, strength, and agility." Voiced Jr'esh.

Eswar said, "Zhokul will have the advantage in size, reach, weight, and to be honest, skill."

Julian countered. "I am well trained."

"Nevertheless, he has a substantial advantage in experience. Do not underestimate his prowess."

Iniqui chimed in. "Nor his viciousness and trickery."

"I will match those qualities and more." The Key amplified Julian's swagger and excitement. He was eager, confident. "He is a bully, and that will be a weakness."

"Avoid close quarters. And try not to get into a weapon's-locked shoving match, his weight will counter your strength."

"I will dance like a butterfly and sting like a bee." He had heard this from his grandfather.

Eswar took Julian by the shoulders and stared into his eyes. "Stay keenly aware of the expressions of The Key. It may well change focus during the match. Welcome and harness its power. This will be your greatest advantage.”

Julian nodded, looked around, and acknowledged the rank and expertise of his counselors.

The soothsayer appeared at the tent opening. “You are a beacon of pride and hope. We trust you.” Then addressing the others, “Now, let J’liánh focus on his thoughts.”

All left, save Iniqui.

They sank to the ground and faced each other cross-legged. Iniqui reached out and took his hands. Her grip was firm, her hands hardened like a warrior’s, as he lost himself in her plum-colored eyes. “I can feel your eager confidence, it flows into me. The purple moon must consort with the sky. I did not know the Key could emanate such power. Be wary. Eagerness plus confidence can equal cockiness.”

“I am cocky. I will be as cocky as I want. But I will not allow it to persuade my thinking, my strategy nor tactics. I am focused.” He withdrew his hands and stood. “I will come to you after I am victorious.”

She rose, bowed her head slightly, backing out of the tent with her gaze upon him. “If you do not sleep, make sure you relax. Your jaw, your shoulders and down to your toes. Practice the meditation the soothsayer has taught you.”

+++

The black, blue and white moons embraced the sky when Julian emerged from his tent. *If only the green moon was in the sky, instead of the black. That would be all the good moons.* But Julian knew the black moon, Ihl, still rose, while the others set.

He found his way to Dor’ossoss while uneasy quiet marked the camp. Clinging to the thick neck, face buried, his arms encircled the purple mane. The lavender moon, Z’th, did not grace the sky, however Julian could feel love, as well as loyalty and strength, pour from the nightsteed’s heart. “Thank you…Thank you.”

178

Khan-apal-apli stood at the base of the path up to Naspia Dor when Julian arrived, ready for battle.

"Tell the others I await above."

The Snow Jarl placed his hand on Julian's shoulder. "Go with honor. You do the right thing."

And so, several hours prior to battle, Julian assumed the lotus position at the center of the sacred plateau and calmed his pounding heart.

+++

A slowly rising rumble rang in Julian's ears. He stood, and for the first time noticed the surface of Naspia Dor was not sand. As if old man wind opened his mouth over the plateau and blew with a force that scattered the sand. Revealing a maroon and beige, baked clay skin, cracked and hard. He scuffed and kicked his boot across the ground, testing its resistance under the sky's dark cobalt canopy. The blue and white moons already halved by the horizon. Ihl neared the ominous sky's apex.

Where is he? Yetzer-Xie creatures crowded the west end of Naspia Dor, but no sign of Zhokul. *Is he waiting to make an entrance? The time for Weynonovar Ha is nigh.* Julian checked his waist. Hidden in the belt, he felt the bejeweled dagger, Ilzjur.

The opposite side of the field of battle bustled with Nova'h souls. Nearly half the population of his adopted brethren had arrived to witness the combat. Julian scanned the crowd. There, a cluster of his friends stood talking, probably about tactics and strategy. Iniqui, her visage radiant, and other familiar faces.

He turned once again to survey the enemy. The crowd parted and the skinless monstrosity sauntered forward. Crimson eyes glowed over a fearless smile as Zhokul emerged from the cheering throng. Behind Julian, Nova'h hissed.

The Overlord of Darkness' sword looked long and menacing. But that did not command his attention. A bronze mace with a long chain hung from the grip of the Overlord's right hand.

A mace! I haven't trained much against that weapon. He regained composure. *Don't let that be a problem.*

Zhokul stopped when he closed the distance to four paces. He hissed. "I knew it would be you." He held his blade at ready, and rotated the mace in a circle through the warm air.

"Your scribes will mark this the day you died." As Julian delivered the last few words, he darted forward with a hard jab step to his left, sword side. The surprise attack caught Zhokul flat-footed. Julian's superior eye-hand co-ordination, conditioned from skateboarding and videogames, allowed him to hit the spiked ball of the mace square with the flat of Hellsbane, causing it to wrap around his enemy's arm. The Yetzer-Xie leader leaned toward this action. The spikes entered the Overlord's forearm and stuck. But produced no reaction from the monster.

The move was a feint. Julian sprinted to the right knocking Zhokul's sword outward with Deathstar. He streaked by the Overlord, who began to turn. Julian ducked. He used the spiked shield to follow up with a downward slash, gashing the Overlord's forearm. *Yesss!*

Zhokul roared and sliced downward, his blade carving only air. He completed his hundred and eighty degree turn to face Julian. Both had weapons ready. They circled each other clockwise. *Should I try it now?*

Julian sneered. "I draw first blood!"

The Nova'h mob, now behind Zhokul shouted "Shyro!"

Julian continued circling, keeping out of range. Both, half jabbed their weapons at the other, playing it safe. Julian hoped to delay engagement until the purple moon appeared. He knew of the precarious situation for Hellsbane. The Overlord of Darkness would surely try to wrap the chain of the mace around the sword. Perhaps yanking it out of his hand.

Zhokul suddenly jumped into the En Guarde position for classic fencing, lunging forward with his heavy sword. He was strong enough to wield his weapon this way, using the mace for balance.

Julian faced his foe, using his shield to block while shuffling backward. This gave up any practical offense. He refused to turn sideways and engage Zhokul in fencing, because he knew the Overlord enjoyed greater skill. And most importantly, he did not want to present his back to the mace. In a fencing duel, his multi-purpose shield would be practically useless behind him. *That mace! If only I were right-handed. Deathstar would be opposite the mace.*

The purple moon peeked over the horizon. The Key thrummed. Julian felt fury and pride in his heart rush into his body. He still circled clockwise then leapt to the right blocking the inevitable blow of the mace with Deathstar. Simultaneously he attacked Zhokul's mace hand with Hellsbane. The hard clay enhanced his ability to move and push off.

The ghoul's skill prevented the blade from hacking him. However, Hellsbane's guard, though not sharp, slammed into the Yetzer-Xie leader's hand. With a crunching sound the mace flew forward onto the cracked clay. Julian used Deathstar to sweep the weapon behind him. His speed advantage had rewarded him.

These movements left Julian in a vulnerable position, Deathstar touching the ground, Hellsbane caught in the follow through of the assault. Zhokul's sword dashed downward, attacking Julian's exposed shoulder. Julian stepped and leaned back as quickly as he could. It was not enough. The villain's weapon connected a glancing blow that scraped across Julian's chainmail armor protecting his shoulder. But the sword also swept down Julian's unprotected upper arm, drawing a line of blood.

"Yowwww!" The wound was shallow but extremely painful.

The Overlord ignored the loss of his mace, ignored the damage to his hand. He bellowed. "You are cut!"

The Yetzer-Xie crowd screamed "Krai! Krai!"

Julian resumed a normal fighting stance, opening the distance lost in dislodging the mace. They resumed their cautious dance. *Now?* Julian managed to back-kick the mace farther behind their engagement. He no longer circled, for that would give the evil leader access to the mace. With two weapons, he was able to block Zhokul's sword, and counterattack, pushing forward. *Not yet.*

Although shallow, the wound to his sword arm throbbed. He knew that with time his grip on Hellsbane, and his effectiveness wielding the blade, would diminish. Magenta blood still dripped from the gash Deathstar had caused to Zhokul's sword forearm. *He seems able to take punishment without loss of ability. I must press the fight.*

He focused the fury the Key empowered, launching a series of forceful attacks against the Overlord's sword, shoving it right. Julian rushed to the left. Zhokul turned. Julian closed distance enough to throw a snap side-kick. While in motion he activated the switchblade in his boot, impaling Zhokul's thigh. The Overlord's crimson eyes opened wide. Julian hurled himself into a flying forward roll, hopped up and twisted in time to face the fiend, out of range. Julian had practiced this difficult move prior to the duel. Now that Z'th was higher, the Key glowed purple.

The mace now lay behind Zhokul. "Get your weapon." Julian goaded. He wanted the Overlord to turn his back and stoop. Instead, the Yetzer-Xie leader backed up until the mace lay before him.

Gladiator replaced the pride inside Julian, fueling a vehement onslaught on the Overlord of Darkness himself. *I shall not let up for a second lest he recover the mace.* He swung Hellsbane, and the clang of the two swords clashing rang loud across Naspia Dor. A follow-up sweeping attack at Zhokul's midsection with Deathstar forced the Overlord to jump backward to avoid the shield's sharp points. Unlike at Enhendendor, Julian gained ground. *Now I have a strategy. Now I have the Key.* He bent his knees, dropped Hellsbane, and flung the mace far behind.

Zhokul's counterattack punished the Earth teenager's shield. But Julian retrieved Hellsbane. He flung himself in a laid-out backward flip, landing upright in time to parry his opponent's blade. Jr'esh hooted, impressed by Julian's agility. The sour smell of his own sweat accompanied the ensuing stalemate of blows. Julian begrudgingly gave up a few paces. Pins and needles signaled numbness coming to his wounded arm. He shook off concern.

They hacked and slashed at each other. His shield and speed offset Zhokul's reach, and Hellsbane cleaved a chunk of muscle out of the monster's hip. *He does not slow down.* The Overlord spat at the Earth teenager. Julian spat back.

Now! Julian initiated a premeditated move. He jumped high into the air, spinning three hundred and sixty degrees. With his back toward Zhokul, he flung Hellsbane skyward, spinning end-over-end, catching sunlight and sparkling. Zhokul's eyes followed the sword as Julian knew they would. Surreptitiously, he produced the dagger from the hidden sheath at his waist. As he finished his turn, Julian threw Ilzjur with all his strength, toward the Overlord's neck. The dagger raced through the air as fast as an arrow from a bow. But its flight as it approached the fiend bent outward.

Ilzjur flew directly to the Overlord of Darkness' hand, who snickered. "At last my friend. You return to your rightful owner." Zhokul tucked Ilzjur into a small scabbard on the inside of his wrist.

Oh shit. Julian deftly reached out, plucking Hellsbane from mid-air during its descent.

The Overlord sneered.

Taking advantage of this momentary lapse by the Yetzer-Xie leader, Julian smacked Zhokul's sword aside using Deathstar. At the same time, he dashed forward, bent to his knees, slid on his shins, and thrust Hellsbane below Zhokul's right ribs, penetrating five inches. A foul smell assailed Julian's nose as a flow of sticky magenta-colored blood gushed forth. *His heart! Finally. He will succumb.* Julian paused for half a beat.

"You fool! I have two hearts." The Overlord laughed as if reading Julian's mind. Zhokul's sword connected with Deathstar over Julian's head. But unchecked was the Overlord's right fist, which, damaged as it may be, caught Julian square on the side of his head. The blow knocked him over causing Julian's head to ring, his eyesight to blur. It was enough. Zhokul stripped Julian of his weapons. Ilzjur appeared in his hand like a switchblade and pierced Julian under his right collarbone. Blood spilled around the protruding blade. Zhokul grabbed Julian's torso in his enormous hand and lifted the bleeding teenager over his head. The Yetzer-Xie mob roared.

Julian regained his senses, staring down at a triumphant Zhokul, ribs nearly crushed by the tight grip. *I am done.*

The Yetzer-Xie leader spun to face his brethren and then the souls of Nova'h. "Krai!" He continued to circle, pumping his hand with limp Julian. Howling like a beast, the Overlord raised his sword with his other hand.

Despair washed over Julian as he looked down on the ugly monstrosity. *What am I doing here? I'm so stupid. I should be home.*

Zhokul's fathomless, crimson eyes blazed like burning coals. The lavender moon climbed ever higher.

As the Overlord turned, time froze for Julian. *Even as Aemiluria died, she was knitting me into the fabric of Nova'h. I miss Gjallime's jesting banter, his profound friendship.* Iniqui in white pearls, Iniqui quipping at him, her indominable spirit. *Oh no! She mustn't become a slave.* Then realizing because of her station, she would. *Nova'h... I am so sorry.*

Three quarters of the shamrock-green moon joined the black and lavender moons. They glowed fiercely into Julian's brain. *This place is special.*

The Julian on Earth would not have risked himself for others. Then again, that Julian would not have found friendship and comradery. Inclusion. He decided the later was worth anything. Even his life. His own predicament forgotten, he glanced down at the beast. *He has no friends.*

Pity took hold of Julian. Zhokul stopped, his jaw dropped. A hush descended upon the crowd.

He has no friends.

A bolt of compassion in Julian's heart flowed through the glowing Key, directly into Zhokul's soul. The Overlord gagged. He dropped his sword, clawing at his throat. Pity and compassion broke the fiend. They could not coexist with the depth of evil within him.

The Overlord of Darkness dropped Julian and stumbled. He crumpled to the ground. With horror plastered on his face, Zhokul crawled backward, crablike. Toward the stunned Yetzer-Xie masses. Julian hit the hard clay and blacked out.

Chapter 19
Last Rites

A cool wet cloth across his forehead brought Julian out of the darkness. The concerned smile and plum-colored eyes of Iniqui greeted him.

"Wha–"

Iniqui gleamed. "Shhh. Regain your strength. You have brought us victory!"

"Victory?"

"The soothsayer could feel Zhokul's soul break. You won."

"I was dying…How?" Julian felt pressure on his chest. A nymph held the *Healing* ankh of bone over the wound the dagger caused.

The young nymph smiled. "Looking for this?" And he held Ilzjur by the blade, its bejeweled hilt glistening.

Iniqui spoke with reverence. "The Key…what did you do?"

"I felt compassion. It poured into Zhokul, overwhelming him"

"Compassion? That is what defeated the Overlord of Darkness?" Iniqui paused using the wet cloth as she glanced at the Key. "**Taming Great Power…**"

"Yes. He has no friends."

The young nymph interjected. "You will have only a small scar under your collarbone and none on your arm. I began healing just minutes after you fell. And most of the green moon paints the sky. All of Nova'h call you brother and friend."

Iniqui winked. "Some, closer friends than others."

Gjallimé, Jr'esh, Aemiluria, Khan-apal-apli, R'qanar, Hjerim, Iniqui. That last, Julian could imagine taking beyond friendship. A loud snort caused Julian to lift his head, look toward the noise, and see Dor'ossoss. *Dor'ossoss! On Naspia Dor?*

Iniqui recognized the shock on Julian's face. "We were as surprised as you. It is the first time hooves have set foot on the sacred plateau. Then again, he *is* special."

Feeling much better, the nymph now gone, Julian stood. Dor'ossoss nudged the Earth teenager with his muzzle and pawed the ground.

With a bright smile, Iniqui said, "He must have been worried about you."

Julian could sense Dor'ossoss's purpose for coming to the surface of Naspia Dor. He looked, the Yetzer-Xie had gone. King Eswar, N'ttala-Toor, Jr'esh, and Khan-apal-apli gathered several paces away. Julian could hear the clamor of their conversation. His voice came out friendly but firm. "May I ask that you wait for me at camp? I will talk to each of you."

Turning, Iniqui led the others down the spiral path. The very path where Julian first entered Edrym.

When the plateau was clear, Julian put his arms around the nightsteed's great neck, locking fingers inside the cool purple fire that was his mane. He whispered in the stallion's ear. "Dor'ossoss." The steed whinnied. Julian continued. "Let's ride."

They cantered around the battlefield, Julian leaning forward, Dor'ossoss and teenager blissful. They moved as one. Julian closed his eyes, serene and contented. When the nightsteed came to a halt they were at the top of the Nova'h path.

Julian dismounted and buried his face in Dor'ossoss's shoulder, sobbing. After a time, the spate of tears subsided. "You must go back from where you came. I know."

Dor'ossoss moved so that his head faced Julian, who took it, hands on either side. Each pair of steely-blue eyes staring into the other's. The depth of feelings unsaid.

With a great nod of his head, Dor'ossoss backed away. He turned and dashed across Naspia Dor toward the purple moon. This time he galloped and ran. *There goes another friend. A true friend.*

The black and glowing purple nightsteed receded in the distance. When Dor'ossoss reached the far side, he leapt and soared through the sky, eventually disappearing in the cobalt. Julian stood and reverently watched. *Godspeed... Godspeed my friend. A piece of me goes with you.*

Julian waited, sighed, and descended to bid the others farewell.

+++

After handing the Key and Ilzjur to the King, Julian, on a deep-auburn borrowed stallion, and Iniqui, on Idrazel, cantered away from Naspia Dor until they moved out of sight. Whereupon she eased them to a more casual pace. Mild weather like the first day of spring on Earth carried nary a hint of breeze.

Iniqui offered, "At this speed it will take three days to reach the high elves' Hold, W'lkyndh. Do you want to arrive sooner?"

He winked. "Hell no." And a cagy smile marked his face.

Iniqui's plum-colored eyes sparkled. She wore mahogany trousers, conspicuously without her sword. A flowing, pleated, cerulean blouse contrasted with her ivory skin. Five small, silver gems spread from the inside of one eyebrow to the next. They were flat, oval shaped, and curved slightly down toward the bridge of her nose. The dazzling effect, subtle and elegant, rendered her beauty breathtaking. Perfect for royalty.

"So, tell me of your home world."

"E'rth. It is called E'rth." Julian said as he stared up at the vibrant moons.

"What is it like?"

Julian found himself rambling, including facets that flashed through his memory but probably meant little to Iniqui. Games. School. The internet. Sure enough, she asked for explanations. His own detailed descriptions brought a memory of home that warmed him.

189

"What about Nova'h and Yetzer-Zie, or as you call it, good and evil?"

"It is not one or the other on Earth, most people have some of each. And evil, in particular, is often hidden."

"Only one to three percent of your people train for battle?" She asked, brows raised.

"Remember, there is very little hand-to-hand. The powerful and complicated weapons and vehicles allow less manpower to inflict massive destruction."

"Here, everyone trains."

Julian changed the subject to phones, then other technologies.

Though skeptical, and lacking a foundation to understand, Iniqui listened intently. At times she chuckled at his remarks. He became used to her benevolent sarcasm. And she was fascinated with all the telling.

When they stopped mid-day to eat from their provisions and let their mounts drink at a small pond, it was his turn to ask about Edrym. Present and history. Particularly, the omnipresent Law. She was eager, at ease talking about her world, just as he had been.

The first evening came upon them quickly. As they built the fire and ate, they recalled the kidnap and rescue of her unicorn during that first trek to Zhon Jeul.

Iniqui downed some wine from a flask. "You kept stalling before our attack on the draugrs. So many questions. Was that to delay the action I laid out?"

"I didn't think so at the time, but looking back, it may have been. Hey, it all worked out."

"Except when you threw the dagger that bounced off. That was pathetic." She grinned. "Gjallimé had to finish the monster."

He pursed his lips, his eyes danced. "Like I said. It all worked out."

"I remember calling you 'the frod under my sandals' and you retorted with 'asswipe'. That seems a bit extreme."

He chortled. "The word 'frod' did not translate in my language, but I got the idea. There is much worse than 'asswipe' on my world."

"You need not spare me." Her face feigned coyness. "I am Queen."

Their eyes met, they paused, and bent over in laughter. Wheezing.

They talked leisurely for another hour. He remembered when she kissed him on the cheek. She reminded him she did the same to Gjallimé. Although more than at ease with each other, they pitched separate tents. Neither thought that arrangement would last long. Surprisingly, they both fell asleep in a quick.

+++

Their conversation significantly changed during the second day's ride. Now they wanted to know about each other's lives: day to day, when they were younger, fears and dreams. They gave voice to the promise of the future, especially what would happen in the immediate days after Julian's return.

Iniqui asked. "Will others know of your lost time?"

"No, I don't think so." Julian had a difficult time imagining his life on Earth. "Hey, what will you do upon returning to Zhon Jeul?"

"I shall recharge the scepter of *Enhancement*."

This comprised the only awkward moment between them. Neither wanted to elaborate on the near future. For that would mark their separation. After a short while spent staring off in the

191

distance, she wanted to know more about videogames. The quiet affability between them returned.

+++

She pulled her mount to a stop. "*You* were shy?"

"Well, a better way to put it is that I was introverted and a loner." He bit his upper lip and rode forward. She caught up, changing the subject.

"Well at least we know *why* you came here."

"But not *how* I found the book, or who was behind it all."

They had some fun speculating. Did one of the Halili of the high elves place the book in the *Dylan Shrugged* bookstore? But when he involuntarily took the book, where did that spell come from? They explored a slew of unexplainable theories, chuckling with many crazy ideas.

Alongside the evening fire they shared personal, even intimate elements of their lives.

Julian confessed. "Teens begin things so much earlier here."

Each heart opened to the other. An affinity they had never before experienced, connected them.

They spoke of Iniqui's mother, Aemiluria, with reverence, respect and admiration. Iniqui drew quiet and Julian put his arm around her. After a while she rose and pitched her tent. Julian helped. With unspoken agreement, he followed her inside.

Julian awoke, feeling her pressed against him. Soft, silver hair spilled around him while her unique scent, lilies and the sea, washed over him. Their nakedness bespoke of wonderful circumstance. He watched her sleep, provoking warmth to blossom in his chest. A wide smile crossed his face, his eyes closed, and he lay very still.

192

The times she had thrown back her head, arched her back and whispered "J'liánh…J'liánh" burned bright in his recollection. His surrender of body, ego, and soul persisted still. She stirred.

Her gaze shone a balmy, sweet radiance upon his face. "Good morning." She spoke in a musical tone.

His eyes smiled. "Hello there." Her transformation from the formal Iniqui continued to endear him.

Blushing rose-pink beneath her high cheekbones, she planted tender kisses on his chest, pausing on his scar, then sliding down to his navel. Her tongue drew eager circles across his abs and ventured farther. He felt like closing his eyes, but kept them open to watch.

As her silver moon rose, they exited the tent and began breaking it down, talking only when the task required. Stolen, furtive glances brought small giggles to her, and impish grins from Julian. He surprised her, lifting her up on Idrazel before they continued the ride to W'lkyndh. Although she harrumphed because she embraced her independence, she also beamed a happy smile.

"Where were we?" Julian asked rhetorically as he mounted his stallion.

"You know I can manage myself."

Julian urged his steed into a trot. "I know. I know." But he could not conceal his affection as she settled in beside him.

Iniqui asked, "Would Dor'ossoss have approved of this path?"

"Yes." And Julian's eyes had a far-away look. "I am sure. I sensed something, maybe excitement, maybe delight, when you were near. That is, *when* we were getting along.".

Treading cautiously, Iniqui offered, "I miss him."

Julian put his fist to his mouth, coughing. "That terribly understates things. I would never have survived without him. He gallops now beyond the purple moon. The Guardian made me feel safe. He was truly a phenomenon."

Several minutes later, he turned his face away from her, eyes cast downward. His limp shoulders screamed guilt. "There is something you should know."

"If it concerns S'rrinha, I already know."

He tilted his head, wide-eyed, as he looked at her. "How—"

"She spread the story of her conquest. You were not to blame, and so I ask no questions. Surely you knew it was not *my* first time."

"I guess we both held back that detail of our pasts... No secrets from now on."

She curled her lips inside her mouth in self-reproach. "Yes. No secrets." She nodded. "No more secrets."

"Good." And he smiled in a way that lifted the temporary cloud of tension. "Let's ride." He leaned forward, took the reins in both hands, each on one side of the stallion's neck, and barked, "Hee Yay!"

Iniqui let Idrazel go and the trot turned into a canter. The rush of the canter transitioned into an all-out gallop, flying over the land like a hawk.

Julian pulled adjacent. They galloped together like the wind. Their frenetic ride fed their spirits with elation. Rolling plains of Kem'nesh stretched before them. Iniqui's silver hair flowed freely behind her.

Their hearts and stomachs fluttered with weightlessness, and faces glowed with freedom. Euphoria enveloped them. They raced and raced, shook with laughter, and raced some more. Surely they would reach the sea.

Leaping over a creek, Iniqui ceased pumping her hands. "Whoa."

Julian followed her lead. They eased their mounts to a halt then headed back to the creek.

While sitting side-by-side on the ground, leaning into one another, they chewed dried berries from her saddlebags. Their horses drank and rested.

Iniqui's eyes peered into his. "We are not far from where we will pitch camp on the outskirts of W'lkyndh." Her body shook with anticipation.

He finished the berries in his mouth and reached for her. "Why wait?"

Their lips and tongues found one another.

Afterwards they lay naked on their sides, facing each other. Julian softly stroked her cheek then neck then on down to her belly button. "When I look upon you, it is like walking out on a cloudy day only to find the sun suddenly shining bright." He was trying very hard.

She blushed. "When I look at you...I see a skinny boy." Giggles escaped as she spoke.

Julian pounced atop her with grin. They rolled around laughing and tickling and wrestling in the soft Kem'nesh until she begged him to stop. Lying on their backs, they gasped for breath. Their eyes beheld the shamrock-green moon, Weeqq, at the apex of the sky, while with arms outstretched, they held hands.

After a time, she teased him. "If you want more it will have to wait till we make camp." And she bounced up to her feet to fetch her clothes. He turned sideways, rested his head on his hand and watched.

She steals my breath.

As she laced up her boots and climbed onto Idrazel, he rose, dressed, and mounted his horse. She waited patiently for him with a gleam in her eyes and they headed toward W'lkyndh at a lazy trot.

The chattering, easy-natured tone of their conversation, sometimes personal and ofttimes not, furthered their closeness. Chortles, offhand verbal jabs, and smiles marked the joviality, while Julian could not stop thinking about the night to come. They arrived at another creek; an area surrounded by open plains. Only a couple hours walk from the Z'ngil-Toth mountains that marked the entrance to the high elves' Hold. A quiet fell over them as they made camp and ate a simple meal.

Julian retrieved the blanket from the tent, spreading it over the delicate grass. He walked toward her. Her hands were on her hips, a peaceful smile shining on her face. Without warning he took her over his shoulder, slapped her on the buttocks, and lay her on her back on the blanket.

"You dare you slap a Queen!" she smirked.

She was startled, but not upset, as she watched sublime purpose play across his face. His eyes fell on the points protruding from her blouse. Was it the nip in the air, or did a rush of heat arouse her? He cared not which.

As they came together under four colorful moons, he was gentle but firm. He took and he gave, he commanded and he obeyed. *We become one spirit within two frames.* Only three moons saw them slip back into the tent.

Julian awoke to find Iniqui, in full military dress, straddling the tent opening, as if on guard. Her plum-colored eyes fixated on the mountains in the distance, as sunlight flitted across her chainmail. *Iniqui. Warrior. Queen.* He arose and dressed in quiet. Nevertheless, she heard him, glancing his way with a warm, happy smile. He strode toward her and she took a step outside the tent.

Without a word he took her in his arms. Their mouths hunted each other's. A long passionate kiss sent fire coursing through their veins.

How can I leave her? Will I come back? Would that she could come with me.

She teetered; the world spun. *This is Bl'nell Toz. He* **must** *go. He must. Perhaps he will come to Edrym again. At least once.* Iniqui gathered herself. She stepped back and grabbed his shoulders, looking directly at his lips. "I have only the tent to pack."

"Will you accompany me to W'lkyndh Hold?"

"No…I'll take your horse back to Zhon Jeul. Do the high elves have your E'rth clothes?" Her eyes rose to stare into his.

He nodded; despite the fact they had gone over all this on the road.

"And will you make it back before your parents return?"

"More than one full day."

"Will your girlfriend accept you as you are now?" She grinned.

Julian tilted his head, flashing a wry smile. She knew he had none.

"You will take the book with you?"

"Of course."

"Take your Champion tunic—"

"Purple is my new favorite color."

Iniqui gave his shoulders a single, firm shake before releasing him. "Good." Her eyes misted, reflecting the ever-present sun.

Julian was trying to memorize her face when she suddenly reached for her belt, producing a small, hidden blade. Before he could react, she grabbed his right arm and cut his wrist, drawing a line of blood. She then tossed the glistening steel to her left hand and drew a line of blood from her own right wrist. She grabbed his forearm, resulting in a forearm-to-forearm grip that caused the two lines of blood to touch.

They looked up and their eyes locked as if a powerful magnet held them.

Iniqui spoke strong and slow and clear. "Godspeed, my J'liánh…Blood of my blood…Bone of my bone…Heart of my heart."

He reached out. They fell into each other, arms still fixed firmly, pressed by their bodies. Their free arm wrapped round each other in desperate embrace. He buried his head in her silky, silver hair. She sweetly and lightly kissed his neck.

Neither could measure time.

Eventually, she stepped back.

Julian's head seemed to spin as he voiced in a low, hushed tone that cracked. "Blood of my blood… Bone of my bone…Heart of my heart." His face turned a whiter shade of pale, a single tear fell from the middle of each eye, and he could not move.

She eased away, but he kept his arm still, spellbound by the smeared blood. Iniqui turned swiftly and walked into the tent.

His arm fell, his chin lowered to his chest. He turned slowly toward W'lkyndh, striding to the high elves' Hold without thought. Breath came as mist as he climbed the foothills. Halfway to W'lkynd he raised his head high. *I am **not** the cat that walks by himself.*

Chapter 20
The Painting

Walking into his bedroom, Julian stopped and mindfully examined his belongings on the walls, desk, and shelves. The portal closed behind him. The book felt slick in his hand. He had held his breath coming through, and forgot to breathe as he acknowledged his room. Air in his lungs was exhaled with a long, low whistling sound, as he relaxed his muscles. His eyes closed and he saw Iniqui's face, like a mirage in the desert. *Eighteen years of peace with Iniqui. That's what I gave up in Edrym.* He took in a large breath, held it, and sighed.

He fired up his computer. Sunday, 1:43 PM. Still 1999. About twenty-six hours since he left. *More than three weeks in Edrym.*

But now I'm back. Tomorrow my parents will be home. Spring break will give me seven days to get comfortable again with my world. Where can I hide the book? I want the chance, the choice, to go back. Even for just a short visit.

He decided to hide the tome in plain sight. In the middle of his floor-to-ceiling bookshelf, the least likely place for his parents to accidentally stumble upon. *Maybe I can sneak out for a couple hours. A couple days in Edrym.* The spiral musical instrument given by R'qanar was hidden under a pile of junk in the back corner of his closet. Julian belly flopped onto his bed. *Ahhhh!*

He kept his eyes open while mental exhaustion seeped down through his body into the mattress. Thoughts of returning ran through his head. His loins burned. *That wouldn't be fair to Iniqui.*

Staying on his bed for the foreseeable future eventually butted heads with the need to get going. A long, hot shower beckoned, and held him for more than a half hour.   His mind remained blank as an empty canvas.

As he toweled himself dry, he recognized the change in his body. He remained lean, however now his muscles were toned and taut. *I'll have to hide this with baggy clothes.* His finger ran over his scar. *It was all real.* Ruminating, he stared at the scar in the mirror.

It was the realest part of my whole life.

The relative weakness of the Edrym sun, and its low position on the horizon precluded a tan. Nevertheless, another problem presented itself. Julian's buzz cut hair on his right side, had grown substantially. The long, left side unruly. *I'll get a haircut tomorrow morning. Maybe start going to the gym next week.*

Oh crap! Folks will be home tomorrow. Need to get my shit together. He dressed quickly and proceeded to go through each room in his house to make it look like he had been home the entire weekend. In order to make three nights sleep abundantly obvious, he mussed the bed even more than normal. A couple videogames were scattered near the gaming console. He left some clothes in the hamper. He ordered another pizza, extra-large, planning to leave leftovers on the coffee table. A day's meal from the fridge was trashed. *A meal I would have eaten.* Monday, some pizza would be added to the garbage and he would take the bag out to the bin. He stood in the kitchen trying to think of anything else. *The mail.*

The bright sun floated an hour above sunset causing a broad smile to break upon his face. Oddly, the position of his sun in the azure sky matched that of Edrym. Nevertheless, he welcomed its warmth, and the Earth sky, with joy. As he walked slowly to the mailbox, he searched. The moon was not visible. And no other moons either.

Man. I'd like to gallop Dor'ossoss.

With Saturday's mail in hand he turned, walking back toward his door. Julian heard a crash, metal smacking and scraping on concrete, followed by a loud cry. Turning, he saw a bike on the sidewalk across the street, with a boy of about ten sprawled next to it.

Last Friday, before his experiences in Edrym, he would have continued to his house. Now, he stashed the mail back in the box and sprinted across the street.

"You all right?" He asked the boy who was getting up.

"Think so."

Julian noticed skinned knees and hands. "Anything broken?" He stood the bike upright, straddled the front wheel, and straightened the handlebars. The boy checked himself, but before he could answer, two sneering high school bullies strolled around the corner. Julian recognized them.

Un-straddling the wheel, Julian stood firm and glared at the bullies. "Can I help you?" Gravel in his voice.

The bullies stopped. They recognized the confidence in Julian's eyes, the steady set of his facial features, and the come-and-get-it poise of the way he carried himself. One bully, never taking his eyes off Julian, pulled at the t-shirt of the other. He whispered something, and the bullies turned, walking back around the corner from where they came.

The boy looked up at Julian wide-eyed, in an awe-exuding manner. "Thanks. Nothin' broken. I live down the street."

Julian retrieved the mail and sauntered into his house. *Cool. Very cool.*

+++

The next day his parents arrived home in the afternoon to find Julian playing a videogame in the living room.

"What happened to your hair?" They both exclaimed as they set down their luggage.

"I decided to get a regular cut." He answered, not turning his attention away from the game. *Time to make friends. May they be even half as good as Gjallimé.*

His mom continued. "We had a very nice trip. Thanks for asking."

Julian lost his last life, stood up, and gave them each a soft hug. "Oh. That's great." He fought hard to quash any trembling. *Can they tell?*

His dad squinted. "Something happen while we were gone?"

"Naw."

"You seem different. And not just the hair."

His mother came to the rescue. "He seems older, more mature." She moved forward, almost in-between her husband and her son. "It's normal. Whenever we don't see him for a while, he looks older."

Her husband stared for a couple seconds, cocked his head, and looked at his wife. "If you say so," he said, grabbing the luggage.

His mother wandered off to her studio.

A short while later, Julian heard his mother call him. He walked into her sanctuary, stopped dead in his tracks, and shook his head in disbelief. She had unwrapped a painting and placed it on an easel. The painting that was delivered last Friday. The painting he took from the delivery man and placed in the studio. He had noticed a rip in the packaging, exposing a purple iris. It wasn't just any shade of purple. It was plum. He gawked in wonder at an exquisite portrait of Iniqui, rendered in his mother's unique style.

"Why…how…did you paint that?"
His mother's eyes twinkled.

The End

Edrym Glossary

<u>A Clustering</u>: Adaa (I Ching) prediction of a clustering

<u>Adaa</u>: group of six stones and rods (same as I Ching) interpreted by soothsayer N'ttala-Toor, a possible prediction (each Adaa is always **bold** in the text).

<u>Aemiluria</u>: Khalil Queen and Eptizar

<u>A'jelh</u>: Gjallimé's younger sister

<u>Ak'yrk</u>: lava giant Hold (Yetzer-Xie)

<u>Alok</u>: manticore Hold (Nova'h)

<u>Al'uah</u>: steely-blue of J'liánh's and Dor'ossoss's eyes

<u>Amarhee</u>: Halili scholar of the high elves

<u>Ava'cynh</u>: power of Z'th (lavender moon) to express one's true heart

<u>Ayse'a river</u>: origin in the Kholsnikh-Yal mountains, it runs west to the sea

<u>banshee</u>: Yetzer-Xie creature bespoken by the black and pale-yellow moons (Hold: Yngol Ednj)

<u>Barzakh</u>: manticore general

<u>B'jnh forest</u>: home to the nymph Hold Sayll

<u>*Blind*</u>: Nova'h enchantment causing blindness (white moon)

<u>Bl'nell Toz</u>: Edrym term akin to "bullshit"

205

Blossfrist Or'lonoth Wh'nle: a blessing to The Key

Borgakh: Yetzer-xie humans bespoken to the black moon (wiped out, now the draugrs)

Boshnjaku: Hassjidar power of speed enhanced by the cornflower-blue moon

Brygul forest: forest of hardwood trees (found in the west near Frir'sk) for strong bows and arrows

Calixto: cornflower-blue moon (Nova'h)

Conflict: Adaa (I Ching) prediction of conflict

Corwin: Prince of the Hassjidar

Cyrodilh forest: forest between Zhon Jeul and W'lkyndh, the pass between Cyrodilh and the Leywyn-Pah river is a choke point

d'rrn: An Edrym unique metal of a golden hue

Cthomechdul: blood-red moon (Yetzer-Xie)

Danger: Adaa (I Ching) prediction of danger

Death: Yetzer-Xie enchantment of death (black moon)

Dhov'nh: high elves Eptizar

Domo: a Rider's special steed, bred for speed and endurance

Dor'ossoss: J'liánh's nightsteed (a nightmare with purple flames), origin beyond the lavender moon

draugr: Yetzer-Xie dead human bespoken by the black moon (Hold: Frir'sk)

Dzejai: K'narikh Hold (Nova'h)

Dz'ntra: Edrym term akin to "shine"

Edrym: paisley shaped continent of the fantasy world, positioned between the world's dark-side and light-side and thus habitable

efreet: Nova'h creatures bespoken by the quicksilver and cornflower-blue moons (Hold: Sneprttai)

Elite: superior K'narikh warriors

enchantment: a talisman of power, wielded by an Eptizar, greatly increased when the partner moon is in the sky

Endsvar: outdoor game played by Hassjidar youth, including Gjallimé and A'jelh

Enhendendor: time of all eclipses signaling battle of all Edrym races on Naspia Dor

Eptizar: sorcerer/sorceress

E'rth: Earth in the language of Edrym

Eswar: the Khalil King (also leader of Nova'h)

Fear: Yetzer-Xie enchantment causing fear (pale-yellow moon)

Fenianh: Julian's nymph captain in game of Nevinrynh

Fjolti: Nova'h warrior lost in the battle Waykenim

Frir'sk: draugr Hold (Yetzer-Xie)

frod: Edrym term akin to "muck"

Gemstazah: Ja'tasarr Hold (Yetzer-Xie)

Gjallimé: Hassjidar Rider who becomes friend to J'liánh

Gobanh': pale-yellow moon (Yetzer-Xie)

Gotlibaaj sea: sea surrounding Edrym

Greatness: Adaa (I Ching) prediction of greatness

Halili: scholars among the high elves

Harridan: manticore of the Dzejai Hold (Nova'h)

Hassjidar: Nova'h humans bespoken to the corn-flower blue moon (Nova'h)

Hattrad: a Hoosforanh warrior fighting with Champion Vr'Vachal during Enhendendor

Heal: Nova'h enchantment of heal (shamrock-green moon)

Hero: Adaa (I Ching) prediction of hero

high elves: Nova'h creatures bespoken by the white and shamrock green moons (Hold: W'lkyndh)

Hjerim: Hassjidar blacksmith

Hold: a fortified city, home to a single rase of Edrym

Hoosforanh: unrivaled Hassjidar warriors who follow Vr'Vachal

H'rol: Edrym God of Creation (similar to J'liánh's middle name Harold as explained by N'ttala-Toor)

Ib-Amel: general of the K'narikh

Idrazel: Iniqui's unicorn

Ihl: black moon (Yetzer-Xie)

Ilzjur: legendary, bejeweled, cursed dagger

Infect: Yetzer-Xie enchantment causing Pox (black moon)

Iniqui: Khalil Princess (later becomes Eptizar and Queen)

I'rnh Alon: quicksilver moon (neutral, but Nova'h currently wields the scepter of *Enhance*)

Irulahna: nymphs bespoken by the shamrock-green and cornflower-blue moons (Nova'h)

Is'mbard forest: far north forest, wraith Hold Nelipi directly east. Liche Hold, Pl'lliq, to the south

Isvitsyny: manticore Eptizar

Ja'tasarr: Yetzer-Xie humans bespoken by the pale-yellow moon

Jekaulis: Edrym wild animal living in the tundra of the west

J'liánh: Julian in the language of Edrym

J'nnir desert: northeast desert

Jr'esh: Khalil general and weapon master, best trainer in Edrym

Julian: protagonist: Earth teenager: egocentric, loner, mean-spirited

Kem'nesh: tall golden grasses of central Edrym

Ken Noru: Hassjidar Eptizar

Khalil: Nova'h humans bespoken by the quicksilver moon (Hold: Zhon Jeul)

Khan-apal-apli: The legendary and ancient Snow Jarl from before the time of Tamiel, also known as the Wanderer (neutral), the last of his kind

Kholsnikh-Yal mountains: northmost mountain range, the Khalil Hold is in the east foothills

Kjobaaj: The-Key-that-is-Lost

Klaiwohaya: white moon (Nova'h)

K'narikh: Nova'h humans bespoken by the shamrock-green moon (Hold: Dzejai)

Kolinia river: origin in the Melhador mountains, it runs east to the sea

K'rai: Yetzer-Xie battle cry

lava giant: eight-foot tall Yetzer-Xie human bespoken by Cthomechdul (Hold: Ak'yrk)

Leywyn-Pah river: origin in the Kholsnikh-Yal mountains, it runs underground in spots collecting heat on its way west to the sea

liche: Yetzer-Xie creature bespoken by the blood-red and pale-yellow moons (Hold: Pl'lliq)

Llaholleri: Nova'h high elves bespoken by the shamrock-green and cornflower-blue moons (Hold: Sayll)

Mass Gathering: Adaa (I Ching) prediction of a mass gathering

Mb'ntth: Julian's Khalil lieutenant in the first game of Nevinrynh

Melhador mountains: mountain range south of Naspia Dor

Methedriel: Hassjidar Hold (Nova'h)

Mind Shield: Nova'h enchantment of mind shield (good against *Fear* and some use against *Death*) (white moon)

Mitha: talisman of *Speed*

Mneri: female nymph who attacks Julian

Naspia Dor: the sacred plateau

Nchaud-Zel: the book (*Beyond the Known Universe* on earth) from the time of Tamiel

Neko-Te desert: southeast desert

Nelipi: wraith Hold (Yetzer-Xie)

Nevinrynh: capture the flag game, played on Edrym with three teams

Nova'h: Good

Ns'rullah: Gjallimé's Domo

N'ttala-Toor: nymph soothsayer

Par'mth: efreet Champion

Pl'lliq: liche Hold (Yetzer-Xie)

power: each race has an intrinsic power (like death for the draugrs, and speed for the Hassjidar) that is increased when their moon is in the sky

Pris: Gjallimé's girlfriend

Qeobl plateau: large plateau in the west Ad-nykal forest

Quash: Nova'h enchantment to counter (or partially counter) a Yetzer-Xie power (cornflower-blue moon)

Rafnh: Khalil snob

Ra'jhan: Nova'h warrior lost in the battle of Waykenim

Ravoq-Ma: time of the bad moons (blood-red, black, pale-yellow)

Rider: select Hassjidar who ride the fast Domo, used for communication

ROTC: Reserve Officer Training Core

Sayll: nymph Hold (Nova'h)

Shock: Yetzer-Xie enchantment causing powerful shocks (blood-red moon)

Sh'rrikh: S'rrinha's unicorn

Shyryo: Nova'h battle cry

s'lennh: Yetzer-Xie expletive akin to the F-bomb

Sneprttai: efreet Hold (Nova'h)

Snow Jarl: Khan-apal-apli, neutral being from before the time Tamiel, last of his kind

spearmen: high elf spear throwing warriors

Speed: Nova'h enchantment providing the power of speed

S'rratha: nymph general

Stenvar: Hassjidar general

St'lggar: first to sleep with the dagger Ilzjur

Strength: Nova'h enchantment providing the power strength (shamrock-green moon)

Taa're: K'narikh Eptizar

Talen-Jei: nymph priest

Tamiel: Time when Nchaud-Zel was written

Taming Great Power: Adaa (I Ching) prediction of great power (with The-Key-that-is-Lost)

Thania: potion causing lethargy and confusion in animals

The Wanderer: Adaa (I Ching) prediction of The Wanderer (perhaps a nomad, or referring to the Snow Jarl, Khan-apal-apli)

Trample: Yetzer-Xie enchantment that augments running over the enemy (blood-red moon)

V'nnath: a Hoosforanh warrior fighting with Champion Vr'Vachal during Enhendendor

Vr'dan: liche Eptizar

Vr'Vachal: the Hassjidar Champion, leader of the Hoosforanh

Wanderer: the Snow Jarl, Khan-apal-apli, neutral

Waykenim: blue-yellow eclipse and silver-lavender eclipse, first battle on Naspia Dor after which Julian arrives

Weakness: Yetzer-Xie enchantment causing weakness (pale-yellow moon)

Weeqq: shamrock-green moon

<u>Weynonovar Ha</u>: Champions battle to the death on Naspia Dor, under the black moon

<u>W'lkyndh</u>: high elves Hold (Nova'h)

<u>wraith</u>: Yetzer-Xie creature bespoken to the blood-red and black moons (Hold: Nelipi)

<u>Xoldre mountains</u>: white mountains in the far west: banshee Hold, Yngol Ednj, is to the south

<u>Xorn</u>: Khalil priest

<u>Xrarreth</u>: time of the good moons (cornflower-blue, white, shamrock-green) plus the quicksilver moon

<u>Yetzer-Xie</u>: Evil

<u>Yngol Ednj</u>: banshee Hold (Yetzer-Xie)

<u>Youthful Folly</u>: Adaa (I Ching) prediction of youthful folly

<u>Zhokul</u>: The Overlord of Darkness, leader of Yetzer-Xie, freak draugr (almost seven feet tall with power to sense the upcoming configuration of the moons)

<u>Zhon Jeul</u>: Khalil Hold (Nova'h)

<u>Zhuaidh</u>: a Hoosforanh warrior fighting with Champion Vr'Vachal during Enhendendor

<u>Z'ngil-Toth mountains</u>: western mountain range: high elves Hold, W'lkyndh, is on eastern slopes

<u>Z'th</u>: lavender moon, also referred to as purple: (neutral), confers the power of Ava'cynh

The Moons

Cthomechdul: blood-red moon: *Shock, Trample*: Yetzer-Xie

Ihl: black moon: *Death, Infect*: Yetzer-Xie

Gobanh': pale-yellow: *Fear, Weakness*: Yetzer-Xie

I'rnh Alon: quicksilver: *Enhance*: Neutral

Z'th: lavender: the power that is in one's true heart: Neutral

Weeqq: shamrock-green: *Heal, Strength*: Nova'h

Calixto: cornflower-blue: *Speed, Quash*: Nova'h

Klaiwohaya: white: *Blind, Mind Shield*: Nova'h

Quotes

John Wooden: "Failure to prepare is preparing to fail."

Buddha: "Three things cannot be long hidden: the sun, the moon, and the truth."

Edvard Munch: "From my rotting body, flowers shall grow, and I am in them, and that is Eternity."

Trisha Yearwood: "What's meant to be will always find a way."

Rudyard Kipling (Just So Stories): "I am the cat that walks by himself, and all places are alike to me."

Craig D. Lounsbrough: "Sacrifice should be a noun in your vocabulary and a verb in your life."

Harry S. Truman: "Actions are the seed of fate; deeds grow into destiny."

Jean de La Fontaine: "A person often finds his fate on the road he took to avoid it."

Martin Luther King: "No one really knows why they are alive until they know what they would die for."

George Harrison: "If you don't know where you are going, any road will take you there."

Douglas Adams: "I may not have gone where I intended to go, but I think I have ended up where I needed to be."

John Whittier: "Of all sad things words of tongue or pen, the saddest are these: It might have been."

Dr. Seuss: "How did it get so late so soon?"

217

<u>Kurt Vonnegut</u>: "Here we are, trapped in the amber of the moment. There is no why."

<u>Machiavelli</u>: "It is not titles that honor warriors, but warriors that honor titles."

<u>Anne Bishop</u>: "When honor and the Law no longer stand on the same side, how do we choose?"

<u>Huey P. Newton</u>: "My fear was not of death, but a death without meaning."

<u>Rachel Vincent</u>: "Sometimes compassion is the greater part of honor."

<u>Brodi Ashton</u>: "Heroes are made by the paths they choose, not the powers they are graced with."

<u>Dallin H. Oaks</u>: "Desires dictate our priorities, priorities shape our choices, and choices determine our actions."

Acknowledgements

Many thanks to:

My beta readers: Callie Johnson, Sharlene Lim, Amber Meyer, Sheila Klein, Erik Ferguson

My critique groups: A Novel Idea, Henderson Writers Group, OLLI at UNLV, Sin City Writers Group

Sheryl Rhoades for the totally awesome artwork, covers and inside

Robyn Yavorsky for the proofread

Bio

Richard Stephen Kram loves white pizza, table-top games, the movie Blade Runner (Casablanca is a close second), and walks around barefoot. He worries about extinction from a random gamma ray burst, the decline of classic rock and roll, and invading minions. Most skies (especially stormy ones) and monster waves are among things he considers most beautiful. He lives in Las Vegas with far too many nostalgic knick-knacks, where he gave up playing poker to write science fiction, fantasy, and poetry.

Website:

richardstephenkram.com

e-mail:

kramrs311@yahoo.com

Facebook:

facebook.com/richardstephen.kram.5

Tumbler:

aiyannatimewitch.tumblr.com/tumbler

Book Preview (available now)

Aiyanna, Time Witch

In 1980, graduate student Jack finds enigmatic, seductive Aiyanna on a deserted Florida key. She has no memory of who she is or where she came from. Their only clues, a strange artifact and a poem of prophecy from a deceased friend.

In 2046, the asteroid, Jupiter's Hammer, has a cataclysmic impact with Earth.

In 2167, *after* the calamity, a secret government agency rushes to discover time travel in order to stop the collision. If they are successful, they, and their timeline will disappear.

Jack and the mysterious Aiyanna stumble onto time travel using the artifact and one of Aiyanna's Psy abilities. They learn of the asteroid's collision and decide to try and save the Earth. They are pursued by the mafia in 1980 Las Vegas, street gangs in 2014 San Diego, Homeland Security in 2040 New York, and time travelers from 2167.

A growing Interaction develops between the efforts in 2167 and Jack and Aiyanna's multiple jumps through time as they try to stop the catastrophe.

Who is Aiyanna? Why is she here? What are the meanings of the magical tattoos appearing, morphing, and moving across her body? Where did the artifact come from?

Despite their growing love, they must exploit the benefits of time travel and avoid its perils, to uncover the roles of Fate and Free Will in the outcome of Jupiter's Hammer.

Excerpts

1)

It's crazy, we've just met, and yet somehow, someway, we casually share the tent, ignoring the fact that she is the opposite sex. We lay on our sides, facing away from each other. I feel this is the polite thing to do, although in my gut, I want to watch her sleep.

She falls asleep immediately. I on the other hand, have anything but sleep on my mind. A girl. An incredibly ravishing girl. Alone on a desolate Florida Key. With no memory.

And then there is the cryptic poem from my best friend, Rick. It screams *riddle* with each and every verse. An unnerving phrase from his poem keeps bouncing around in my head: *...zero the tangent, billions expire...* Is Rick being literal here? Most of the poem is certainly metaphor. Maybe this is too. Or is the whole poem simply the ramblings of an injured brain?

Bizarre is not too strong a word to describe this otherwise, lovely, night.

She shifts in her sleep and I turn to see her long, lustrous, ink-black hair, spilling outside the sleeping bag.

My body is flushed and practically tingling. How did I get here?

I replay the day in my head....

2)

"Not in the least. I've already explained that our brains are wired to believe in free will, *the illusion rings true.* It's natural to feel that way."

"But you believe the poem's ending, *these words were not written by me.* All of our actions, fated, predetermined. Writing your poem, our effort to find my time, are all just the universe following the rules?"

223

I think she is about to add her incomplete premonition to the list, but she skips over it.

"Yes, that is what I believe. But I don't claim to know the truth. And I make my choices as *if* they are mine to make. Day to day, my belief in determinism doesn't impact anything. Unless we are talking philosophy. Don't worry about it. It doesn't change the fact that you are beautiful…"

I freeze, my fork with egg stopping in mid-air. I can't believe what I just said. I'm afraid to look up from my food, then slowly I raise my head.

Buoyant, whimsical, flirtatious, even mischievous could all describe Ayianna's smile.

"I'm flattered. When were you going to tell me?"

We are separated by the table, I'm sitting with my fork in the air, my face must be white. I'm not ready to follow up that confession. "Well…you are." And before this intimate moment can linger, I squash it. "I'm flattered you like my poem." As if that statement was the same thing as my faux-pas.

"No. You don't get away that easily. Why did you say that?"

"Because it's true."

"And?"

"And…and…and wherever we go, people stare at you. They're going to remember you…We have to be careful."

Aiyanna glares at me. Hard. She turns, throwing back her hair. "I'm going to the little girl's room," and she walks away down the hall.

There, I tied that up neatly. Why should I be happy about that? I'm not.

3)

"But what about your previous self?" I peek at Devon. His face is blank, his eyes stare out the windshield into nowhere, saying nothing.

"She never saw me. She should proceed down the timeline as I did, as we previously discussed."

"But, does that mean there are two of you? One here, and one on the way to bank? And another Devon as well?"

"I'm not sure. It's confusing. Maybe there *is* an Aiyanna number two, twenty-five minutes behind me." Aiyanna's face turns white. "Oh no. It's much worse than that! Aiyanna number two will jump back in time creating Aiyanna number three who would be twenty-five minutes behind Aiyanna number two. On and on to infinity."

"I'm not sure about the infinity bit." I stare, trying to think clearly.

Aiyanna shakes me. "But if I'm right, Aiyanna number two will catch up to us if we linger here."

Website:
richardstephenkram.com

My Heart is Full

(gladly)

blues and greens in the ocean.
blues and reds in the sky.
what canvas do i paint you on?
and how do i make you fly?

the ocean, she is mighty.
the sky, so easy to adore.
shall i write a verse to make your heart stop?
and how do i make you soar?

to find the person who cannot live without me.
to find the person i cannot live without.
to surrender (gladly) to one's feelings.
to find passion (madly) without a shadow of a doubt.

indigo and turquoise in the ocean.
cerulean and fuchsia in the sky.
what melody do i sing to you?
all i want.
     is to try.

and i wait
with breath (so) still
your fancy

while fairies dance
unhurried
on the Lilly in the wood

                              velvet darkness

falling through the velvet darkness
screaming loudly, no one hears
arms are flailing
wet, so wet
in this river of rain

no, not rain, salt water
as i plummet through this duct
of my eyes
(and i am a cavern of emptiness, covered in tears)

falling through the velvet darkness
laughing madly, nothing funny
mind is flailing
wet, so wet
in this river of rain

no, not rain, blood
as i plummet through this chamber
of my heart
(and i am a cavern of emptiness, covered in blood)

for you have torn me inside out
and outside in

left me in the ruin of confusion
left me in the fracture of hope
left me in the center of my nightmare

left me.

let me stay in my velvet darkness

let me stay

Pick a Daisy

If I could live my life again,
I'd be a little lazy,
I'd stop this rushing to and fro
And stop to pick a daisy.

Through all the lovely summer months,
Though days be clear or hazy,
No more to fret of tasks undone,
I'd stop to pick a daisy.

Not so important what I did,
This fact time now discloses,
While running through life's garden green,
I'd stop to smell the roses,

If I could hold my little ones,
The children in my care,
I'd scold them less and love them more
with so much joy to share.

If I should pass this way again,
Though folks might think I'm crazy,
I'd work, and worry less.
And stop to pick a daisy.

Website:

richardstephenkram.com